LION'S HEAD REVISITED

DAN SHARP MYSTERIES
Listed in suggested reading order

Lake on the Mountain
Pumpkin Eater
The Jade Butterfly
Shadow Puppet
After the Horses
Lion's Head Revisited
The God Game

JEFFREY
ROUND

LION'S HEAD REVISITED

A DAN SHARP MYSTERY

Copyright © Jeffrey Round, 2020

All rights reserved. No part of this publication may be reproduced, stored in a retrieval system, or transmitted in any form or by any means, electronic, mechanical, photocopying, recording, or otherwise (except for brief passages for purpose of review) without the prior permission of Dundurn Press. Permission to photocopy should be requested from Access Copyright.

All characters in this work are fictitious. Any resemblance to real persons, living or dead, is purely coincidental.

Publisher: Scott Fraser | Editor: Jess Shulman
Cover designer: Laura Boyle
Cover image: istock.com/Dorin_S
Printer: Webcom, a division of Marquis Book Printing Inc.

Library and Archives Canada Cataloguing in Publication

Title: Lion's Head revisited / Jeffrey Round
Names: Round, Jeffrey, author.
Description: Series statement: A Dan Sharp mystery
Identifiers: Canadiana (print) 20190127341 | Canadiana (ebook) 2019012735X | ISBN 9781459741379 (softcover) | ISBN 9781459741386 (PDF) | ISBN 9781459741393 (EPUB)
Classification: LCC PS8585.O84929 L56 2020 | DDC C813/.54—dc23

We acknowledge the support of the Canada Council for the Arts and the Ontario Arts Council for our publishing program. We also acknowledge the financial support of the Government of Ontario, through the Ontario Book Publishing Tax Credit and Ontario Creates, and the Government of Canada.

Care has been taken to trace the ownership of copyright material used in this book. The author and the publisher welcome any information enabling them to rectify any references or credits in subsequent editions.

The publisher is not responsible for websites or their content unless they are owned by the publisher.

Printed and bound in Canada.

VISIT US AT

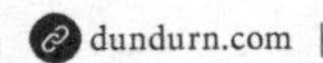 dundurn.com | 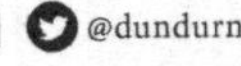 @dundurnpress | dundurnpress | 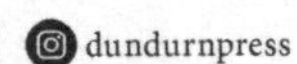 dundurnpress

Dundurn
3 Church Street, Suite 500
Toronto, Ontario, Canada
M5E 1M2

For Gail and Ted Bowen, Don Oravec and
Jim Harper, David Tronetti and Giuseppe Gioia,
Geordie Johnson, and Minola Nistor

And in memory of Shirley Lecuyer (1935–2018),
a.k.a. Aunt Marge

I got my mind on eternity
Some kind of ecstasy got a hold on me
And I'm wondering where the lions are

— "Wondering Where the Lions Are,"
Bruce Cockburn

The wicked flee when no one is pursuing,
But the righteous are bold as a lion.

— Proverbs 28:1

AUTHOR'S NOTE

As with the previous volume, *Shadow Puppet*, *Lion's Head Revisited* was written out of sequence from the rest of the series. Chronologically, it comes sixth, following *After the Horses* and preceding *The God Game*.

PROLOGUE

Georgian Bay, 2012
Promontory

SHE KNEW SHE WAS GOING TO DIE. The feeling persisted, like something pushing out from inside her until it took on a kind of force. The climb had been a mad, nerve-wracking scramble, up from the campground over moss-covered rock and low-lying brush to the top of the escarpment. She'd fought panic all the way. It was only on reaching the top that she paused for breath, her sides heaving. The drizzle had finally stopped. On any other day this would have been a dazzling view. The town of Lion's Head lay in the distance across the bay. A ghostly finger of light slipped through the clouds and slid over the water. Far below, seagulls wheeled over treetops and the broken boulders lying scattered along the shoreline like pieces of an unfinished puzzle. If she fell, she'd be smashed to bits.

"Ashley!"

The breeze gusted the words away.

She checked her cellphone. No signal yet. The logging road was still another twenty minutes up ahead. They should have stayed together.

The promontory gave way to bare rock. A white blaze on a twisted cedar showed where the trail picked up again before disappearing in the woods on the far side. She followed where it led down. Stray branches whipped her cheeks; stones cut her fingers as she grabbed them, passing from handhold to handhold to steady herself, all the while fighting panic.

A sharp turn near the bottom confused her. The blazes seemed to switch back on themselves. Had she come the wrong way?

Here the rocks were treacherous, greasy with moss and damp. She was nearly at the bottom when her foot gave way. Instinctively, she reached out and caught a branch. It held for a heart-stopping moment then slid through her grasp as she fought to right herself.

Too late.

Her back slammed hard, knocking the wind out of her. For a second she lay there, too stunned to move.

She tried to cry out, but her lungs refused to draw breath. The merest whimper was beyond her capability. An ache clutched her chest. Where it had first been cold and numbing, now it was an excruciating burn, a hot knife jabbed between her muscles.

Panic overwhelmed her as she gasped for the breath that failed to come. She struggled to rise, but an invisible hand held her firmly down. Forest stretched in all directions, a dim twilight world. By nightfall the blazes would vanish entirely then the fear would set in for real. She had to get to the car.

She pictured the blue-and-yellow child's tent, a tiny bubble set beside the larger khaki-coloured one. Jeremy's favourite bear — a one-eyed, fur-shedding monstrosity that he clung to through thick and thin — had lain just inside the entrance when they had woken. She'd cried to see it.

"Ashley!"

Her voice sounded barely above a whisper.

A gnarled root protruded from the dirt. She wrapped her fingers around it, gripping until her knuckles turned pink-white. As a child she'd visited a farm and watched a chick break out of an egg, first one small feathered wing then the other, everything in the world focused on that struggle. Just so, she raised herself now, gripping and pulling, the ache so intense she thought she might black out.

Then, somehow, she was sitting upright. A small miracle. For the moment, it was all she could do.

Slowly releasing her grip, she slid to the bottom of the incline and squatted, trying to get her lungs to breathe. Just breathe.

Ten minutes went by. At last, when the pain had retreated a little, she fought to get to her feet then headed haltingly for the parking lot.

Five minutes in she had to stop again. The effort was making her light-headed. She leaned against a smooth-skinned tree and lowered herself to the ground, legs stretched out in front. Her chest pounded. She was having a heart attack. She was going to die up here alone. They would find her like this, broken, wretched.

Somehow the thought calmed her. It wouldn't be the worst way to go. The Head had always been a sanctuary, a place of peace and respite. But, no — there was Jeremy to think of.

Where the hell was Ashley?

Anger shot through her. *Get it together, you stupid bitch!* If nothing else, she would simply lie here, fighting mosquitoes and black flies till Ashley rallied help. Unless there were marauding bears. Then she wouldn't stand a chance. The best she could hope for was that they would smell her pain and give her a wide berth. Wolves might not be so cautious. They'd heard them howling the past two nights, coming closer and circling the tents, hating the fire and the smell of people.

She struggled to stand then —

When she came to, her nostrils caught an acrid scent. Wood smoke. It took her a moment to remember where she was. She'd fallen and blacked out. The ache was far worse now, every breath a knife thrust.

Gently, she pulled on her collar and looked down. A purple stain spread across her chest under her left breast. A fresh wave of panic backed up in her throat, making her retch. She'd broken a rib … punctured a lung … that was why she couldn't breathe. The premonition had been real. She was going to die.

A dragonfly buzzed overhead. Its wings shimmered, green and purple iridescence, as sunlight broke through the leaves, lifting the gloom. She sniffed at the air. Unless the woods were on fire, in which case she was clearly doomed, then someone had to be nearby. She pushed against the tree until she stood upright, her head woozy. The pain wasn't getting any better. She needed to hurry.

The smoke came from up ahead. She simply followed it. Within minutes she reached a wire fence and limped alongside it for a while, but the bush grew thicker again. She retreated and headed back until she discovered the open field.

She pushed down on the wire and hauled herself over one leg at a time, collapsing in a heap on the other side. She fought to stand again then staggered toward the smell.

The farmhouse looked like something out of a fairy tale. Smoke issued from a chimney. The day was warm, so it wasn't for heat. Someone was cooking.

She dragged herself forward, bent over, gasping with each step.

An old, grey wagon wheel had been planted in a bed of yellow nasturtiums. A wide porch seemed to invite visitors, despite the secluded surroundings.

"Help!" she cried, her voice faint.

She headed for the house, one arm clutching her chest, the other striving to keep her balance as she stumbled along. Somewhere a dog yelped.

"Please! Is anybody there?"

A door opened. A grizzled man in jeans and red-checkered shirt peered out. He had a long, white beard like a biblical prophet. His expression was stern, as though he disapproved of her. Whether that was because she was trespassing or for the sorry state she was in, she couldn't tell.

"I'm lost," she called out, as though it might not be apparent.

She couldn't make out his reply. He flapped his hands in the direction of the fence, as though telling her to leave.

Like hell am I leaving, she thought. Not that she could have even if she'd wanted to.

Sweat fell from her brow and clouded her eyesight. Something rustled in the bushes off to the right.

The man disappeared back inside the house. A moment later he returned bearing what looked like a tea towel, waving it furiously. He came toward her with a jarring motion, as though he had to make an effort to swing his hips to get his legs to work, first right then left, like rusty hinges long out of use. He was ominous, a figure in a dream.

She opened her mouth to cry out, to say she needed help, but the words wouldn't come. Sparkles formed at the edge of her vision, waves of tiny lights followed by black clouds. As she fell forward, she wondered if she was about to find herself in far more trouble than she was already in.

ONE

Blood Money

PI Dan Sharp sat with his back to the window. Behind him, the Don River murmured quietly after the previous night's storm. His office on the top floor of a warehouse import-export business had long been a sanctuary for him. Currently, however, it was feeling a bit crowded.

The three people facing him looked to be in their late twenties. The blond had multiple piercings and tattoos on her arms. The young man, slender and bearded, was agitated. The third, a quietly attractive woman, watched him with gentle eyes. They were waiting for his answer.

"You have no choice," Dan said. "You have to report it."

"But we want to keep it private. At least for now," the man insisted.

His face was ravaged with red eruptions, like a perpetual adolescent. While his concern was evident, it wasn't anything Dan could agree to.

"It can't be private, Eli. This is a police matter. Kidnapping is a criminal offence."

"It might be a hoax," the pixie-haired blond, Janice, argued. "We don't know for sure if a crime has been committed."

"Do you want to take that chance?" Dan asked. No one answered. "Why do you think it might be a hoax?"

Janice frowned. "Because when they called, they never mentioned Jeremy. They just said they were raising money for missing children. When I asked how much, they said a million dollars."

"They were probably playing it safe in case someone was listening in," Dan said. "Your son has now been missing for three days. The police found no trace of him on the trails up on the mountain or anywhere near the shore where you were camping. You've already had one phone call and soon you'll get another. The only choice you have to make is whether you're going to pay the ransom or not."

Eli shook his head. "But what if it's someone who heard Jeremy was missing on the news and is trying to extort money from us? We need to buy ourselves time."

"Time is a luxury you may not have, but whether the kidnapping is real or fake, you need to let the police know." Dan hoped he sounded sympathetic.

"But so far they haven't found anything useful," Eli persisted. "We don't have faith they can help us, to be honest."

"Look — even if you think the police aren't doing their job, the best I can do is run a parallel investigation. I can't interfere with what they're doing. If you know something, you have to tell them."

"But we don't know anything!" Eli exclaimed.

Janice put a hand on his arm. "No, Dan's right. We do know something — we know that we were asked for money."

Eli threw his hands up in the air. "And where do we get this blood money from? Is there some government fund for kidnap victims that we can apply for? Or maybe I should just ask my boss for a raise of, oh, I don't know — a million dollars?"

He wrapped his arms around his chest and slumped into his chair. Dan had had enough of his petulance.

"Eli, I appreciate that this is difficult for you, but what you do now could make all the difference in getting Jeremy back safely." He turned to Janice. "Did they say anything else?"

"Yes. They said not to mention the call to anyone."

"That's to be expected. How's your back, by the way? I understand you had quite a fall coming down the escarpment."

"She nearly got gored by a bull, but a crazy man came out waving a tea towel and chased it away," Eli interjected.

"That was *after* I fell." Janice gave Dan a rueful smile. "The doctor said I'll live. Though I'm not sure I want to right at this moment."

"Janice!" The rejoinder came from the other woman. "Please! Let's have none of that."

Her speech was clipped, almost a bark.

"Oh, go to hell, Ashley!" Janice snapped, then she turned suddenly contrite. "I'm sorry. I have no right to act like this."

Ashley nodded. "It's all right. You've been through a lot."

The name suited her, Dan thought. Lithe and willowy, with hair the colour of ash wood.

She turned her eyes to him. "We don't know what to do. We need you to advise us."

"Thank you. The first thing you need to do is report the call to the police. That's what I advise."

"Then what?" Eli asked, still sulking.

"Then we start looking. For now, tell me everything that's happened." Dan picked up a pencil. "Start with anything irregular or noteworthy you recall in the days before Jeremy disappeared."

Janice nodded. "There *was* something odd. I saw an older woman outside the house twice right before the camping trip. She seemed to be waiting for something. I went out to see what she wanted, but then Jeremy came out with Ashley and she walked away."

"Did she say anything at all?"

"She called me Kathy."

Dan glanced up from his notepad. "Kathy?"

"Katharine is my first name, but no one ever calls me that. I go by my middle name, so I don't know how she'd know that."

"Can you describe her?" Dan asked.

"She was plain. Mousy looking. The sort of woman you barely notice even if she's right beside you."

Dan looked at the pert blond with triple ear piercings. There was no chance of not noticing her.

"Was she short? Tall? Slender? Overweight?"

"Average height. Dumpy, but not huge. A little bulky. She had brown hair going grey."

"Was there anything memorable about her face?"

"Her eyes were sad. That was my first thought."

"Good. Anything else?"

Janice shook her head. "No, I don't think so."

"Okay. That's a start," Dan said. He turned to the others. "Did either of you see her?"

Eli shook his head. "No."

"I did. Briefly," Ashley replied. "She looked exactly as Janice described."

"Any idea who she was?"

"None. But what sort of monster kidnaps a child?"

Janice caught her breath and turned aside. Her shoulders shook.

"Give us a moment," Ashley said, putting an arm around her.

"I'm fine," Janice said, regaining her composure.

"You were asking what sort of person would kidnap a child," Dan continued. "That's the most important question we need to answer right now. Why would someone target you?"

"Definitely not for the money." Janice rubbed away a tear. "I mean, do we look rich? I work in an art gallery on commission. Eli's a designer. Ashley isn't working at the moment. We barely scrape by."

"Apart from the money. Is there anyone who would be likely to do such a thing? Someone who might bear a grudge against any one of you?"

"What about Sarah?" Ashley prompted.

"Jeremy's a surrogate child," Janice said. "Sarah was his birth mother."

"And you suspect the birth mother? Why?"

Eli snorted. "She was bad news from the beginning."

"We couldn't know that," Janice said, her voice icy.

"It was obvious," Eli said. "I warned you right at the start."

"All right, let's not go down that road again." She turned to Dan. "Sarah and Ashley went to school together as kids. That's why we chose her. She was from a good family, but she was a bit wild. She lied to the agency that arranged things for us. They terminated her contract after we ran into problems with her."

"What sort of problems?"

"Not diseases or infertility. She passed all those tests. She'd done a surrogacy once before. We chose her because we knew she was capable of carrying a pregnancy to term. Her problem was drugs, though not while she was carrying Jeremy, thank god." Here, she looked at Eli. "But later — after Jeremy was born — she showed up at our door asking for money. She said Jeremy's birth was so difficult she'd turned to painkillers and got addicted. She said she lost her contract with the agency because of us. None of it was true, as it turned out. She was on meth. I gave her fifty bucks to go away. It was a mistake."

"She still comes by every few months to ask for a handout," Eli said. "Like we're made of money."

"Okay," Dan said. "An angry surrogate with a drug problem would be a big red flag in this case. Who else might hold a grudge, for any reason, however small?"

"We let a nanny go," Ashley said. "Marietta Valverde."

"When was this?"

"April. Her boyfriend was trouble."

"We thought we were doing her a favour by letting him stay on weekends," Janice added. "But then we discovered money missing on two occasions and some of my jewellery another time. I told Marietta if her boyfriend confessed to what he'd done we wouldn't press charges, but he kept denying it. I had the feeling she knew it was true, but she was loyal to him."

"Did you mention it to the police?"

"Yes. They talked to them, but nothing came of it. It was impossible to prove, so we took what was for us a very drastic step and let her go. It was hard. I hated doing it, but I couldn't feel safe with a thief in the house."

"Is there a current nanny?" Dan asked.

"No," Janice said. "We advertised for one and we interviewed a few people, but we didn't find anyone suitable. Ashley looks after Jeremy when Eli and I are at work. She's been a positive saint." She smiled and took Ashley's hand.

"Okay," Dan said. "So that's at least three people with a potential grudge. What about locks? Did you change them after she left?"

"Yes. Immediately."

"Smart. Who else is there?"

Janice looked to Eli. "Do you want to tell him about Elroy?"

Eli looked embarrassed. "I lost on an investment. My former business partner, Elroy, is after me for the money. A lot of money."

"How much?" Dan asked.

"A couple hundred thousand."

Janice turned to Dan. "Elroy made death threats to Eli."

"Any witnesses?"

Eli shook his head. "No. He threatened me one day when we were alone. That was a few months ago."

Dan eyed him. "Did you believe he would try to harm you?"

Eli hesitated. "Not really. But you never know, do you?"

"You don't, so don't discount it," Dan said. "Okay, so there's a surrogate mother with a drug habit, an unknown woman seen outside your place twice, an ex-nanny who was fired because of her boyfriend, and an ex–business partner with a financial grudge. Anyone else?"

The three people watching him were silent.

"Chances are something else will come to mind. It could be someone you saw hanging around the post office every time you went there or a person at the daycare centre who seemed a little too curious about Jeremy. For now, let's deal with what we've got." He looked at Janice. "I want to know immediately if this strange woman you mentioned shows up again. I'll also need names and addresses for everyone we just discussed. Is there anything else you can think of that might be relevant?"

"I suppose we should tell you about our complicated history," Janice said, looking to both Eli and Ashley. "Jeremy's parentage, I mean."

Dan nodded. "That might help."

"I used to be married to a guy named Dennis Braithwaite. Dennis and I were trying to have a child, but no luck. We spent a lot of money on a fertility clinic's recommendation and, lo and behold, I got pregnant." She smiled ruefully. "But after eight weeks, I miscarried. On further testing, the clinic told us I was unlikely ever to carry a pregnancy to full term, so I decided to hire a surrogate."

"And that was when you hired Sarah?" Dan suggested.

"No." Her expression changed. "That was when I met Ashley. When I mentioned I was looking for a surrogate, she suggested Sarah. As we got closer, it became clear to me that I'd been hiding from myself. I knew I wanted to be with a woman, not a man."

She searched Dan's face for judgment and, finding none, went on.

"What happened inside me was instantaneous, but changing my outer life took a bit longer. By then Sarah had been successfully implanted with an embryo. Nine months later, Jeremy was born. That's when I left Dennis."

"How did Dennis take it?"

"Not well at first, but later he seemed to accept it. He said we weren't suited for each other."

"Did he resent all the money you'd spent on the fertility clinic?"

"I thought so at first, but when I offered to pay him back his share of it he refused. He's rich. He's an investment banker."

"How much did you spend in total?"

"Loads. Nearly a quarter of a million overall."

"That's a lot of money," Dan said. "I think we should add Dennis to the list of people with grudges against you. Is he in your life now?"

"We stay in touch, but I keep him at arm's length. He feels uncomfortable with Ashley around."

"He treats Janice badly. He hit her once," Ashley said. "I won't stand for it. That's why he's uncomfortable."

"Understandably," Dan said. "What about Jeremy? Do they have any connection?"

"No — none." Janice shook her head. "Jeremy is autistic. Non-verbal. It's quite severe. Since Dennis and I are still legally married, I asked him to insure Jeremy through his company policy when we got the diagnosis. But he turned me down."

"He refused to put his own son on his insurance?" Dan asked.

Janice shook her head. "No —"

"I'm Jeremy's father," Eli interjected.

Dan nodded as the final piece of the puzzle clicked into place.

Janice leaned forward. "I knew Dennis and I weren't going to be staying together, so I asked Eli to be a donor. He agreed on the condition that he could take an active part in Jeremy's life."

"Janice and I have known each other since we were kids," Eli added. "When she asked, I jumped at the chance. I'd always wanted to be a father."

"How does Jeremy deal with his 'complicated history,' as you call it? Is he aware of it?" Dan thought of his own son's easy acceptance of both biological parents, despite the fact they'd never been married. As far as Kedrick was concerned — at least while growing up — it had always been a case of the more the merrier.

"Jeremy seems to take it all in stride," Janice said. "He's a happy boy for the most part, so we don't really worry about whether he fully understands the situation or not."

"All right," Dan said. "I'm beginning to see the complications. Nevertheless, I'll do everything I can to help." He waited a beat. "Tell me again about the phone call. Was it a man or a woman?"

"I couldn't tell. The voice sounded a little weird."

"They would have used a voice modulator. When did they call?"

"This morning around ten. The number was blocked. At first I thought it was a telemarketer. They said they wanted me to donate a million dollars. Then I knew. I said I didn't have that much money and that I'd need time. They said they'd call back and hung up."

"Is there some reason a kidnapper might think you have money? You said Dennis is rich. Could it be someone who thinks he will pay?"

Janice shook her head. "I doubt it. Even if they did think it, they'd be wasting their time. In the meantime, I'm going to talk to the bank about a second mortgage."

"And if that doesn't come through?"

She winced. "There is a chance we might be able to raise the money. Through my mother. But it's slim. So far she hasn't even accepted Jeremy as her own grandchild. Because of the circumstances of his birth. She doesn't approve."

"She's a tight-fisted witch," Eli broke in. "Can you believe she won't accept Jeremy as her own flesh and blood?"

Dan paused, thinking what to tell them. In fact, he could easily believe it. Family feuds were his area of expertise. Walls built instead of bridges, tough talk instead of healing words. Until the moment of truth turned everything around.

"You might be surprised how people react when a crisis arises. Something like this can bring out the true feelings of a parent or even a grandparent."

"That's certainly what we're hoping," Janice said. "But I'm not holding my breath."

Dan looked at the faces watching him. "I take it you haven't asked her yet?"

"Not yet," Eli said. "We've only just heard from this supposed kidnapper. You're the first person we've shared this with. To be honest, we haven't really had time to digest it, let alone discuss it properly, but Janice's mother seemed the obvious choice. None of us has that kind of money. She does."

"My mother owns Clarice Magna. It's a cosmetics company," Janice said.

Dan nodded. The name sounded familiar. "And you think you can talk her into paying the ransom?"

"My mother is a rich woman. More importantly, the money is mine. My father left his estate in her trust until she dies. Then it reverts to me. For now, she's got it all tied up in her company."

"She could help if she wanted to." It was Ashley who spoke. "She wants Janice to suffer."

Janice nodded. "Screw her. She could release the estate early. I'm hoping I can convince her to do that. Because really, it's mine."

Dan's mental image of Janice shifted suddenly. From a tough-talking young woman with a rebellious attitude, she had just become an entitled rich kid.

"Okay, that makes sense. I urge you to discuss it thoroughly and fast, before the kidnapper calls again." He stopped to think. "Is it possible the kidnapper is someone with a grudge against your mother, since she's an obvious source of money?"

"It's possible," Janice said, nodding. "I don't know much about my mother's business affairs, but she's not an easy woman to like."

"Just one last question. How did you hear about me?" Dan asked.

"I don't think anyone in particular recommended you, but you've got a good reputation in the community," Eli said. "We'd all heard your name."

"That's good to know."

Dan saw them to the door.

Eli paused in the hallway. He waited till the women were headed down the stairs then turned to Dan.

"In case you're wondering, I love my son very much," he said. "We all raise him together."

"I don't doubt that for a moment," Dan said. "The fact that you came to me before going to the police tells me a lot."

"Good. I'm glad you see that." He hesitated then said, "My son is everything to me. I would do anything for Jeremy. Anything. Please remember that."

Dan nodded. "I will."

TWO

Serious

DAN WAS LATE and that bothered him. Because it was never good to keep a cop waiting. Even when you had what sounded like a reasonable excuse, such as lack of parking. Everyone knew good valet service was hard to come by. But then again, Sergeant Nick Trposki wasn't just any cop. That fact was very much on Dan's mind as he scouted for available curb space.

They'd been dating for just over a year. Lately it seemed it might be good to make a decision one way or another. Otherwise, further time invested without a commitment was time wasted. He'd recently assessed the situation and realized to his surprise that he was happy with the relationship. And he was pretty certain Nick felt the same. He didn't know how his son, Ked, felt about Nick, however. On the other hand, his best friend Donny had dismissed him with a curt, "Let me know if he's still around by Christmas." As far as Donny was concerned, Dan was dating the enemy. Private investigators did not date cops.

Only Ked's mother, Kendra, had taken whole-heartedly to Nick. That, at least, was as good as saying she trusted Nick to be a trustworthy companion to the father of her only child.

"He's nice. He's respectful. And he's got such beautiful eyes," she'd confided. "Those lashes are wasted on a man. It's like free mascara!"

Dan pulled up in front of the restaurant. For once, luck was with him. He snagged a spot right out front then dashed inside only to find the place half empty.

He and Nick liked Café Frederic because it was quiet on weeknights. Soft music, low lights, red-and-white-checked tablecloths, with a handful of regulars always sitting at the bar talking to Ted, the beautiful bartender who should have been at one of the high-power downtown restaurants where the tips would have put him in a top-tier tax bracket. In fact, he would have been there but for a drug habit that tended to go a little haywire whenever he had cash to burn, as he confided one evening on learning both Dan and Nick watched their alcohol intake for much the same reason.

As Dan entered, Ted paused mid-conversation, nodding him to his regular table one down from the window where he could see the street without easily being seen. Something in Dan's nature always made him want to step back into the shadows. Or so he would have said if anyone asked, though no one ever did.

A minute later, Ted was on his way over with a glass of San Pellegrino, a crisp wedge of lime snapped onto the side. He set it on the table and looked at the empty chair.

"Where's that sexy boyfriend of yours?" he asked.

"I'm not sure," Dan replied. "I thought I was the late one."

It always floored Dan when young men like Ted — for all intents and purposes straight — joked casually about his relationship with another man. When had the world got turned on its head?

"Tell him he better not keep you waiting around. I've seen more than a few heads turn when you enter this place."

"You mean they actually stop looking at you for a few seconds?"

"I do my best to fade into the woodwork and let my customers shine." Ted smiled. "Let me know if you need anything."

"Will do."

A few minutes later the door opened and an unsmiling Nick entered. He spotted Dan and came right over.

"Sorry I'm late," he said.

"Late is fine, but no smile is never a good thing with you. What's up?"

"You know me too well." Nick crossed his arms over his chest as he sat. "I think I'm getting a new boss."

"Is that like getting a cold?"

"Kind of."

"Bad news?"

"Don't know yet, but rumours are Lydia's being replaced by an out-of-town guy named Bruce McDormand. An old-school homophobe, from what I've heard."

"Time to think of looking for a new job?"

"Yeah — as if. I'm a career cop. Don't forget that."

"Then keep your head down and pray for the best."

"I was getting a little too comfortable with Lydia, that's for sure. She was the only boss who ever joked about my sexuality. *With* me, that is, as opposed to behind my back."

The door opened and four boisterous men entered, heading for the far side of the room. A miniature storm of rowdy good cheer. A moment later, Ted showed up and eyed Nick.

"Hey, buddy. You better not leave that boyfriend of yours alone for too long. I can't be held responsible if he goes missing on you."

Nick reached across the table and grabbed Dan's arm. "I'm not worried. I've got a handle on this one."

"This a non-drinking night?" Ted asked.

Nick's eyes flitted over to Dan. Dan shrugged.

"I'll have a Mad Tom," Nick said. "I'm losing my boss and I need some consolation."

"Atta boy! One Mad Tom coming up," Ted said and headed back to the bar.

"Does he still remind you of your son?" Dan asked.

Nick made a defensive gesture with his hands. "Weird, isn't it? He'd be a little younger, but that's what I always thought Jakob would look like when he got older."

Ted returned with Nick's beer and set it down in front of him.

"I'm doing double-duty tonight," he told them. "Elaine's off. I'll be back in a few minutes to take your order."

"No rush," Dan said as Ted turned away.

Nick lifted his glass. "Cheers!"

They clinked.

"Your regulation drink," Dan said.

"That's all it will ever be so long as I've got you."

"Is that a promise?"

"Absolutely. Any doubts about that?"

"No doubts."

Nick eyed him. "But?"

"No buts, just …" Dan shook his head. "I sometimes wonder what the future holds."

"Whatever you want it to hold. I told you, I'm the commitment type. I don't scare easily."

"I know that," Dan said softly.

"You don't sound certain. What do you want to know? I'm an open book."

"No — it's nothing. I just don't know the ropes here. I didn't get issued a relationship manual when I grew up."

"You're doing fine. In fact, *we're* doing fine. I was thinking about having this discussion too, so maybe now's as good a time as any. It seems to me we get along pretty well. It might be time to kick it up a notch."

"Meaning?"

Nick held his gaze. "Move in together."

Dan felt himself stiffen. Worse, he saw that Nick saw.

"Oops!" Nick said. "Too abrupt there, Nicky. Change of tactics. How 'bout those Blue Jays?"

Dan fingered his water glass. "Sorry," he told the glass absurdly.

Nick laughed. "You're not ready to discuss it."

"It's just … big. And Ked back for the summer and everything."

"I know — you're not sure about him. And then there's your bestie who doesn't seem to want to warm up to me."

"Donny?" Dan looked up. "He'll be fine. He's just not used to men sticking around for long when I meet them. He says I'm too intense. Like it's a bad thing."

"Yeah, that. At least I can see through your seriousness."

Dan smiled. "That's what I like about you."

"Is that all?"

"There are a few other things."

"Sure. It's just breaking through your icy reserve that's so much work." He winked. "Okay, subject's been broached. We'll take it up again later. Deal?"

"Deal."

They looked up as Ted returned.

"What's new with you, Tedster?" Nick asked. "Any gorgeous ladies in your life these days?"

Ted shrugged and looked suddenly bashful. "You know me. I'm just staying clean and trying to get back on an even keel."

"Good. That's really good to hear."

"I have to say, you guys are an inspiration. I see what you have together and I know what it took to get there, and I think to myself, I can do that too. And I am doing it."

"You can do it so long as you want to," Dan said.

Ted looked crestfallen for a moment. "I do, for sure." He smiled again. "All right, enough serious talk. What are you having to eat?"

Music played softly, a generic beat lulling diners into a state of reverie and encouraging them to prolong their stay. Dan relaxed, watching the candle flame flicker.

"You haven't told me how your day went yet," Nick said.

Dan looked up. "The usual."

Nick studied his face. "What exactly is 'the usual' for you, o man of mystery? I mean, my day consists mostly of looking like a tough guy and scaring stupid kids into behaving when I think they might do something they'll regret for years to come. But you? I still don't know what it is you actually do."

"I try to scare stupid kids into behaving too. Only some of them are grown-ups. And once in a while I even do some good and locate a person who may or may not want to be found." He paused. "Today I had to talk sense into three millennials who weren't going to report a ransom call on their missing kid."

Nick's expression turned serious. "You mean they didn't want to report a crime? That's a code 22."

"That's what I told them."

Nick nodded slowly. "Is this the four-year-old who went missing in the Bruce Peninsula? Autistic kid?"

"You know the case. Maybe I shouldn't be talking about it."

Nick shrugged. "The file is already on Lydia's desk. She's the Toronto liaison for the cops up north."

"No way!" Dan looked to see if Nick was joking, but his expression was serious.

"Way."

"Then you probably know as much as I do. The call came this morning. I told them they had to report it."

"Why didn't they want to?"

"They were warned to keep quiet about it."

"Wait. You said three people?"

"Two mothers, one biological and the other adoptive, plus a biological father."

"Oh, right — the modern family."

"They want me to run a parallel investigation because they're afraid the police might not be totally on board with it."

Nick made a face. "Because we're all so incompetent, no doubt."

Dan shrugged. "Compounding things is the fact that they don't actually have the money. They're thinking of asking the mother of one of the women. Apparently she's rich, but won't acknowledge the boy because of the facts of his birth."

"I thought blood was supposed to be thicker than water."

"In this case, I think it's a matter of whether money trumps blood."

Nick cocked his head. "So if these three kids have no money, then someone must know that the grandmother does."

"That's what I think," Dan said. "I'll look into it, but so far there's enough motive to go around for the original three, including an abusive husband who got dumped when his wife left him for the woman she now lives with."

Nick whistled. "Sounds like a movie plot."

"It does, doesn't it? Maybe I'll have to phone Donny to find out which one. He's usually good at that."

"Sure, but don't tell him I said so."

Dan studied Nick's face. "It bothers you, doesn't it?"

Nick leaned forward. "What bothers me?"

"The fact that Donny won't warm up to you."

Nick was silent for a moment. "He's your best friend and he's known you a lot longer than I have. It worries me, yes. I need to be able to get along with the people in your life. As you do mine, though that's a bit easier, since the few people who matter to me are far away, except for my boss, who already likes you."

"And now it sounds like she's leaving too."

Nick's face took on a gloomy cast. "Don't remind me."

"Tell you what," Dan said. "I'll see if Donny and Prabin are free for dinner. You can dazzle them with your cooking. How does Saturday sound?"

"I'll make it work."

THREE

Faith

The dismissed nanny wasn't hard to locate. Dan found a listing for Marietta Valverde online. He called the number, explaining why he wanted to see her. There was a slight hesitation when he mentioned Jeremy, but she agreed to meet him.

She lived in Etobicoke in a plain neighbourhood a lot of other immigrants called home. It was a throughway for city workers from the outlying suburbs who didn't want to stop in this no-man's land of quickly erected high-rises; street gangs were becoming more prevalent with the influx of competing nationalities, making it difficult for any kid living there to just stay a kid as long as possible. Marietta's building was one of several with dilapidated balconies and overcrowded parking lots that threw back the sun's glare from every windshield and shiny chrome trim.

When she opened the door, she wore the look of a cornered animal. Her round face was pretty, but her eyes were wary. Dan's appearance probably did nothing to relieve her. He towered over her. His rangy muscles and the scar on his temple gave him the aura of a prizefighter. Nevertheless, he saw she could hold her own if she needed to. He'd seen that same look in beaten dogs and street kids outrun by cops. They puffed themselves up with defiance before everything suddenly deflated, all fight and resistance gone.

Marietta Valverde held out till the last moment then let go as Dan introduced himself, quietly explaining how Jeremy had disappeared while on a camping trip to the Bruce Peninsula with his mother and her partner.

"I know. I saw it on the news. It's terrible!" she wailed. "That little boy, he's so sweet." Her appeal seemed to suggest she hoped he would do everything he could to solve the problem.

"We'd all like to see him brought home," Dan assured her. "I just wondered if you would answer a few questions."

"Why does everyone ask me these things? The police came and scared us both," she said, at last acknowledging the other presence in the room, a well-groomed young man in dress pants and white shirt. "That's Ramón."

"Hello, sir." Ramón nodded to Dan, his deference close to servility.

"Hello, Ramón."

Dan looked around. The room was drab. Brown furniture, everything worn or second-hand. A lovebird twittered in a cage over in the corner, its colourful plumage in stark contrast to the rest of the room. The door to a bedroom lay wide open. He glanced inside. No chance they were hiding a small boy in there.

"The reason I'm here," Dan began, "is because I'd like to get a full picture of Jeremy's life. There might be some detail you can recall that his parents overlooked. Maybe a person you remember who seemed a little too interested in Jeremy or possibly someone who held a grudge against his parents."

"No, there's no one," Marietta said. "I told the police I can't think of anyone."

"When did you leave the Bentham residence?" Dan asked.

Marietta sighed and shook her head. "April."

"That's four months ago."

She nodded. "They told me I had to get out. Just like that." Her expression hardened. "It wasn't fair, even if they gave me a month's wages. My parents are coming to Canada. I had to get another job." She nodded to a framed photograph where two elder Filipinos gazed curiously out at the room. "They didn't even have a good reason to fire me, you know?"

"They seem to think Ramón stole from them." Dan glanced over at the young man, who dropped his gaze.

"But it's not true, Mr. Dan. Ramón never stole in his entire life." She turned to her boyfriend, who was becoming more fidgety by the second. "Ramón, tell him it's not true."

"Sir, I didn't steal the money." Ramón spread his empty hands before him as if offering proof of his sincerity. "I wouldn't steal. It's not right."

"He never stole anything," Marietta interjected. "That's not Ramón."

The boy looked sulky, but not aggressive. He seemed like a kid who had been kicked around one too many times and would put up resistance if cornered, but not start a fight he knew he would lose.

"What do you do, Ramón?" Dan said.

Ramón's eyes flitted to Marietta then back to Dan. "I don't have a job, sir. I used to work at a tile factory, but I got fired. Now I'm on welfare."

So when the money went missing they automatically suspected you, Dan thought.

"I don't have much education," Ramón continued. "I'm not dumb, but I didn't finish high school. I got caught selling drugs and I was expelled."

"But he's good now," Marietta pleaded, as though Dan were a higher court of appeal and this her last chance to convince anyone of his reformation. "He doesn't do things like that now."

"Can you recall anything unusual around Jeremy's home before you left? Maybe a stranger who passed by the house a lot? Anything like that?"

They stared at him blankly. It was tricky asking questions without seeming to be directing the answers; people were often too willing to tell him what they thought he wanted to hear.

"There was always someone around," Marietta said at last. "I don't know if they were strangers."

Ramón said something in Tagalog. Marietta nodded and spoke a few words in return.

"It could be for revenge," she said softly. "Because of those two together like that."

Dan's interest was piqued. "Which two?"

Marietta looked to her boyfriend for reassurance or confirmation they were on the same page.

"In our church, it is not okay for two women to raise a child together like man and wife." She looked to Dan, who nodded for her to go on. She put a hand on her heart. "We say 'love the sinner but not the sin.'"

"You think someone kidnapped Jeremy because his parents are two women?"

Marietta nodded. "What they are doing is wrong," she said, with the unquestioning conviction of the simple-minded.

"Yet you didn't mind working for them," Dan said.

"Because I needed the money," she replied, as though the need excused her hypocrisy.

"Can you tell me where you were when Jeremy disappeared? It was the twenty-ninth of July. This past Sunday."

Marietta brightened. "On Sundays we're always at church."

"It would have been some time between midnight and dawn," Dan added. "So, technically, we're talking about Saturday evening. Janice and Ashley stayed up late at the campsite then went to bed. Jeremy was missing when they woke in the morning."

"We were here!" she said. "I told the police. We don't even drive, like. So how can we get somewhere else if we don't even drive?"

"There are buses," Dan reminded her, though he doubted this couple capable of planning a daring kidnapping and making their way over rough terrain in the middle of the night to do it. "Or someone else could have driven you."

"I know — but it wasn't us!" she wailed, her voice rising. "You have to believe us, Mr. Dan. We were here all night.

We don't even have money to go to a movie. I work at Dollarama till four o'clock almost every day. Saturdays too. The pay is really bad. It was supposed to be better to come here in Toronto, but it's not for us. It's worse."

"Was there anyone else here? Someone who can vouch for you?"

Marietta shrugged. "No one else was here but us. We made dinner. I made fried chicken."

"Did you talk to a neighbour at all that evening? Take the garbage out or see anyone in the hall?"

She shrugged. "No one. I never went out once. Neither did Ramón. All we did was sit and watch television. And also I talked to my sister back home. That's it."

"You talked to her by phone?"

"Yes, that's it. I didn't see nobody."

"When did you talk to your sister?"

"One hour we talked. It's a good rate. We talk every Saturday night at ten o'clock. She is in Manila. It's already morning there."

"Did Ramón talk to her too?"

"Yes, a little. He was watching television and I had to tell him to turn it down. Ramón always puts it too loud. He said hi to her."

"And you went to church the next day?"

"Yes, for sure. In the morning for mass. It's my day off from Dollarama. We never miss church." She smiled at her boyfriend. "Sometimes Ramón is lazy, but that day for sure I made him get up and come with me to pray for my parents to come safely to Canada."

"Did you tell the police you made the call to your sister?"

"No, I forgot, I guess. They made me so nervous."

"Your phone records will show that you made a call," Dan said, getting up. "Make sure you let the police know this if they come back to talk to you."

Her face showed surprise. "My phone records?"

"Yes, they will show what number you called and for how long. And I'm sure the people at your church will remember if you were there."

She scratched her head, as though the simplicity of it had evaded her. "I didn't think of that," she said, smiling. She turned to her boyfriend. "You see, Ramón? I told you it's going to be okay. I prayed last night. And now everything is okay."

Dan wished it could be that simple for everyone.

"The ex-nanny said she spoke with her sister in Manila on the phone around ten o'clock. Apparently she does so every Saturday evening."

Dan had just left Marietta and Ramón's apartment and was on his way back downtown.

"Yes, I remember those calls," Janice said. "They were like clockwork when she lived with us."

"Still are, apparently. She says the boyfriend also spoke to her sister. I guess the police would have to get her to swear to that. According to Marietta, the next morning they both went to church. Just simple, good-hearted people apparently."

"Then obviously they couldn't have done it." She sounded almost pleased.

"Not necessarily," Dan said. "They could have driven up after the phone call. It's what, three hours?"

"About that. Maybe a little more."

"So it's possible they left here at eleven and arrived at your campsite by two, two-thirty in the morning. An all-night drive would put them back here in time for church."

Janice sighed. "I don't know how they could have known we were there. Though honestly, I don't know what to think anymore."

"They're sticking with the story of Ramón's innocence about the thefts. She's working at a Dollarama, but he's out of work right now. I gather they're very much in need. Did you know her parents are coming over?"

"Yes, she's sponsoring them. It's one of the reasons we found it hard to fire her. But Marietta's hard-working. We knew it wouldn't be difficult for her to get another job."

"Are you aware they think you and Ashley are sinning by being together?"

"Really? They told you that? It's the first I've heard of it, considering all the time she spent with us."

"She never discussed religious beliefs with you? She never said she disagreed with the fact that two women were parenting a child together?"

"If she did, I didn't pay attention to her. I don't bother with things like that. Do you?"

"I never ignore people who hate," Dan said. "It's too dangerous."

FOUR

Advice for the Lovelorn

DAN HEARD MUSIC PLAYING AS SOON as he opened the door. Some sort of ethno-funk. Kedrick was home. His son's tastes were surprisingly varied, whereas he, Dan, stayed largely within the bounds of the tried and true. Jazz and old-school rock. The real stuff. When Ked had moved out to attend university the previous fall, the house seemed empty. Gradually, Dan got used to it. Then suddenly his son was back and he found himself having to adjust to living with a teenager all over again.

Ked had left while still a boy in many ways, but he'd come back a refined young man, no doubt due in part to the influence of his new peers. To no one's surprise, he'd enrolled in an oceanographic studies program at the University of British Columbia, spouting theories of biodiversity and ecosystem management on his return. Although he'd changed in some respects, his taste in music was the same. As was his habit of dropping his dirty clothes on the floor behind his bedroom door. After all, he was still an eighteen-year-old.

Ralph, Ked's geriatric ginger retriever, had seemed especially relieved to have him back. It was as though he'd considered Dan at best a reasonable substitute for his true master, but only for the duration of Ked's absence. The household balance would change again if he invited Nick to live with him, Dan knew. He thought of their aborted conversation the previous evening. It suddenly struck him that Nick may have intended to suggest living in his waterfront condo, a pricey little pied-à-terre Dan felt entirely comfortable visiting, but knew he would find it too close-quarters to move in there.

His own house in a leafy enclave of Leslieville, on the other hand, had been built to accommodate a family. He looked around and tried to imagine it with a second adult in residence. Nearly a century old, it was located in what had only recently been proclaimed one of the city's chicest neighbourhoods. While the hipsters had headed to the city's west end the previous decade, a new generation had lately been crowding the sidewalks and snatching up residences in the east.

At some point, Dan had resignedly shrugged off his fellow Torontonians as a self-absorbed and uncharitable lot, but lately he'd had reason to reconsider. On reflection, he realized he'd kept his head down for so long that he hadn't noticed the transformation from the narcissistic yuppies who cared more about their property values than about their neighbours to a younger, more socially conscious set who preferred building bridges to erecting fences.

The city had grown up in a good way. Just so, Dan reflected, something inside him was changing as well.

Despite his rough upbringing, he no longer felt as cynical about life and what the future might hold as he used to. If there were problems, they didn't lie with Nick, whose affection was genuine. They had more to do with whether Dan could accept his good luck and not sabotage a budding relationship before it had a chance to succeed.

In part, that depended on Kedrick. As long as Ked was still in his charge, Dan intended to provide him with a home environment where he felt welcome. In the beginning, at least until he was sure of his feelings for Nick, he'd purposely kept the two of them apart. Growing surer, he had allowed them to come together on occasion. Then Ked left for school.

Nick, too, had once been a father. But his son had died, precipitating a decade of grief on Nick's part, which he drowned in alcohol. Dan was acutely aware of this, knowing Nick had only regained his equilibrium not long before they met, and he didn't want to tip the balance the wrong way. He'd watched carefully at Nick and Ked's first few meetings. But Nick had taken it in stride that his partner had a teenage son while he was missing one.

Ked, on the other hand, hadn't seemed overly responsive to Nick. Dan wondered if he worried that his father's affection might be divided. By the time Ked had left for Vancouver, Dan wasn't sure at all what the boy thought about his new partner.

On his return, when he wasn't working, Ked spent much of his free time with his girlfriend, Elizabeth, and his mother. He and Dan spent less time together, particularly when Nick was around. But summer was winding down and Ked would soon return to BC. As far as Dan was concerned, the verdict was still out.

Ked came down the stairs now with Ralph at his heels.

"Hey, Dad! Good day?"

His son was affecting a beach-bum look. Cut-off jeans and floppy hair, a black Nirvana tee — old rockers never really died. He'd always been a happy-go-lucky kid. Agreeable and open. All the things his father no longer was. If he ever had been.

"Good enough, thanks. How's yours? Enjoying your last few weeks of freedom?"

"Oh, yeah! Elizabeth and I took the ferry and spent the day at Centre Island."

"Centre Island," Dan mused. "I haven't taken you there since you were a kid."

"Yeah, I was ten." He shrugged. "It's pretty much the same."

"I guess it never occurred to me to take you back there again."

"Don't worry. You're still a great dad."

"And you're a great kid. I'm glad I had you. In case you were wondering."

"Never considered it." Ked grinned. "Once you had me, I guess it was too late to send me back."

In fact, Dan had had to convince Kendra not to abort on discovering their one-time fling had resulted in pregnancy. He'd never mentioned it to Ked before and he certainly wasn't about to do that now.

"I was always sure," he said. "Right from the start."

"Cool." Ked considered his father, seemed to conclude that the timing was right for something, then said, "So — you and Nick. Is it serious? I mean, he's still around after more than a year."

Dan smiled, remembering how Donny had said much the same.

"It's serious."

"How come you two haven't shacked up yet?"

"Shacked up?" Dan pretended to consider the phrase. "Do people still 'shack up'?"

"Well, whatever it's called. I mean, you're probably too conservative to think about actually getting married, so in that case —"

"Me? Conservative?"

Ked hesitated. "Hmm. Maybe the other *C* word. Cautious? Whatever it is, you're not really the marrying kind. Are you, Dad?"

Dan just looked at his son.

"I mean, I know you're the loyal-unto-the-death type, but marriage is probably a bit too restrictive for you. Am I right?"

Dan scratched his head. "Is that how I seem to you? Cautious and conservative?"

"Well, not in everything, but in personal matters, yeah. For sure. You wouldn't want to make another mistake. I know Trevor was a mistake —"

"Not at all," Dan interrupted. "Trevor was not a mistake. Trevor was afraid for me, and therefore for himself, if anything should happen to me because of my work."

They'd hardly spoken of it since the split, though Dan was aware that Trevor and Kedrick had bonded in their time together. He also knew the bond extended beyond that, as Trevor lived on Vancouver Island. Ked reported occasional visits, though Dan avoided asking for news lest he seem overly curious.

"Yeah, okay. That's one way of putting it. I just mean you wouldn't want to invest in a new relationship and have it fall apart on you again. Right?"

"That's true," Dan said. "I also wonder what it's going to mean if Nick and I do decide to … shack up. I mean, how it will affect family dynamics."

Ked reached down and scratched Ralph behind the ears. "There's just me and Ralph. If you want to know how we feel about it, just ask."

"There's not just you and Ralph. There's also your mom and Donny and Prabin to consider. But since you brought it up, how do you … and Ralph … feel about Nick? Specifically, how would you feel if we moved in together?"

Ked regarded his father. In that moment, Dan suddenly sensed that something had got turned around. His son was looking at him as though he were the father and Dan the son. Just how much had Ked changed? *They grow up,* he reasoned. *And you let them go. The rest is up to fate.*

"Well, now that you mention it," Ked said, "I have to say I would approve with certain provisions."

"And what might those be?" Dan asked, resisting an urge to laugh at his son's earnestness.

"Number one — you need to be as happy as or even happier than you already are if he moves in. Number two — you need to know he will love and respect you for as long as you are together. Number three — things change, so you need to ensure that if you move in together and it doesn't work out, say, after a year or maybe two, that there are provisions for you to safely separate without enduring any great emotional or financial loss." He looked at his father. "As much as that's possible to do, of course."

Dan shook his head. "Why do I get the feeling that whatever gains Oceanographic and Environmental Studies made by having you on their side will prove an enduring loss to the future of romance counselling?"

Ked bared his teeth in a grin. "The love industry will be okay with or without me."

Dan laughed. "Did you pull those things out of thin air just now or have you been saving up this lecture to try it out on me?"

Ked shrugged. "Elizabeth and I have been having the same sort of talks. You know it's been tough for us being so far apart while I was in BC. We decided if we're going to continue there have to be ground rules in place. Otherwise, we're heading for disaster."

"So, from your observations, do you think Nick and I have a chance?"

Ked nodded. "Better than average, in fact, as long as all eventualities are considered."

"Does your mother know you talk like this?"

"Sure. I had to give her the talk about what her future holds too. She's been single far too long and she's not getting any younger."

"And what did she say?"

"She said if she needed a counsellor she would definitely come to me."

FIVE

Crystal Lullaby

THE FOLLOWING MORNING, a curt-sounding secretary answered Dan's call to Elroy James, Eli Gestner's threat-making ex–business partner. Her tone said she was not impressed enough to put him through to her boss. Either that or she was genuinely telling the truth when she said she didn't know where he was, but that he would soon be on his way to Hong Kong for a business deal and unavailable to return Dan's call till he returned.

"What's it about?" she asked.

"Kidnapping and extortion."

"Hmmm. Sounds serious."

"It is."

"In that case, he might call you back."

"It would be in his best interest."

"I'll let him know."

He hung up wondering whether she would indeed let him know and what exactly Mr. Elroy James's business interests consisted of. In the meantime, he had other names to check off his list.

Sarah Nealon looked surprisingly well-put-together for a meth addict. Safely enrolled in a government-sponsored rehab program, she was one of the lucky ones who hadn't ended up on the streets or working as a hooker. Instead, she lived in a bright public-housing unit and was well dressed, with her hair done and fingernails painted. Dan sat watching her butterfly-like movements as she toyed with a tea set in a slow-motion parody of a homemaker's routine: put tea in the pot then smile at your guest; pour water from the kettle then smile at your guest; offer your guest his cup then smile again. Everything seemed designed to reassure him that all was well and she was fully in control of her situation, despite the unnatural sheen in her eyes.

A sun-catcher dangled over the table. She reached up with spidery fingers to spin it. The coppery faces reflected light haphazardly throughout the room, random acts of beauty in a harsh and unpredictable world. It tinkled softly, dispelling gloom while keeping the world and its demons at bay.

Dan was familiar with meth users. Most of them wanted a good time, not a self-destructive ride to hell. Unfortunately, the latter was more often what they got — a never-ending trip that ensnared everyone around them, the people who watched in disbelief as a wonderful friend/co-worker/brother/sister/son/daughter/spouse turned into an abusive monster/liar/thief who needed desperately to support a habit that had started out as just an escape from the humdrum routine of life. Why do nine-to-five when you could get five-to-ten instead? But Sarah Nealon was lucky, in a manner of speaking. Her addiction meant she could exist on a disability pension that would extend her life of purgatory and pay for her habit for as long as she wanted.

"Do you mind if I ask where you were over the weekend?" Dan said.

"When Jeremy disappeared?"

"Yes."

She smiled again, her movements light as a feather, as though she were trying to avoid making contact with anything more tangible than the air surrounding her.

"Oh, I was here," she said, brushing the hair from her forehead and cradling her tea. "I'm always here."

As with Marietta and Ramón, Dan doubted whether she would have been capable of plotting and pulling off an abduction on her own even if she'd wanted to. Then again, addicts were surprisingly tenacious.

"I'm not supposed to leave." She showed him her ankle monitor. "They always know where I am. It's part of my probation agreement."

"I understand you got off surprisingly easy."

"It's because of the pregnancy." Her face twitched at some memory reaching through the fog of her brain. She unconsciously patted her swollen abdomen. "When the judge heard I was pregnant, she took pity on me, I think."

"Three months is a very light sentence," Dan agreed.

"Oh, but there's still my probation," she said, as though he might be considering that the judge had been too lenient. "It's for another two years. After that, we'll see."

Dan wondered whether her probation would be rescinded if the judge learned she was using meth again. Then again, with the city's restricted budgets most felons were self-reporting under the new rules. And so the system failed them again.

"I'm also not allowed to have credit cards or enter a bank without supervision." She watched his every movement, her eyes focused on him as she sipped from her cup.

"It's probably for the best," he said.

"Oh! I wouldn't do it again. I know better now." She gave a light laugh. "I really believed I was on a mission to end world hunger and poverty. I was convinced God sent me to that bank to ask for funding." She smiled. "Isn't that crazy?"

"It's a nice thought," Dan said. "If all the banks around the world put their resources together they probably could do just that."

"I know — that's the crazy thing. My thinking wasn't that far off. It was just ..."

She reached up. The sun-catcher tinkled again. She smiled at it as if it were a friend calling her name.

"Your method of going about it?" Dan asked.

"Yes! I thought I was asking for a contribution to help end world hunger, but they thought I was robbing the bank." Her expression darkened. "Though I guess that's what I was doing, really, when you think about it."

"Sadly, yes," Dan said.

She turned back to him. "Why are you here again?"

"I came to ask you about Jeremy Bentham. He's been abducted."

"That's terrible. I didn't know." She paused. "Or did I? I don't remember. It seems to me I did know it, but then I forgot."

"Do you remember asking his mother, Janice, for money after Jeremy's birth?"

"I do remember that. She was very nice. She gave me money when I explained that giving birth to Jeremy made me turn to ..." She frowned and shook her head. "The fertility clinic fired me. After that I went away and promised not to ask her for more."

"And did you stop asking?"

"I ..." She looked away for a moment. "Janice was very nice to me. She promised to help." She smiled sadly. "I'm getting better."

"That's good." Dan considered. "Do you know of anyone who might want to harm Jeremy or take him from his mother?"

"No! Why would anyone harm a child? Did someone tell you I did?"

"No. No one told me that."

"Good, because I would never." Tears formed in her eyes. "There was an accident once, though. It was terrible."

"With Jeremy?"

"Oh, no. Not with him." She shook her head. "Something terrible happened to a boy I knew."

"One of the children you were carrying for someone else?"

"Oh, no." She looked relieved. "Another boy. It was very sad. But I don't really remember it now."

"How did you learn where Jeremy lived?"

"I wasn't supposed to know!" She suddenly looked mischievous, a child who had done something naughty but clever. "It was at the clinic. When they told me my services were no longer required, the doctor was distracted for a moment. I looked down at my file and saw the address. I still remember it!"

"And when you went to ask Janice and Ashley for money, did you think you were helping end world hunger again?"

She stared at him for a moment then stood.

"I'm afraid you'll have to excuse me. Marjorie is coming soon. She's my social worker. I have to get ready for her."

Dan stood. "Thank you for seeing me."

She saw him to the door.

"I hope they find Jeremy." She unconsciously reached down to feel her stomach. "I love children. I'd hate to see any of them hurt. I'm going to have my own soon. My mother is very happy she's going to have a grandchild of her own."

Dan nodded, wondering how long a drug addict and convicted felon would be allowed to keep a child. The door closed behind him. A young woman was coming along the sidewalk toward him. Her clothes were prim, her look officious. The social worker.

"Are you Marjorie?" he asked.

"Yes." She looked at him uncertainly. "Who are you?"

"My name is Dan Sharp. I'm a private investigator."

She gave him a shrewd look. "About the missing boy, Jeremy, I suppose?"

"That's right."

"I doubt I can tell you anything, but ask me whatever you like."

Dan shook his head. "No, I wasn't going to ask you anything. I've just had a visit with Sarah."

"The police were already here."

"Yes, I know." Dan hesitated.

"What is it?"

"I just wondered if you knew that Sarah is getting high while pregnant."

For a second, Dan thought he detected a smirk on Marjorie's face.

"She's not."

"She's definitely high," Dan said.

Her expression softened. "No, I meant she's not pregnant. She uses a pillow to make it look as though she is." She gave a rueful little smile. "But yes, she very likely is high. That's a given, sad to say."

She opened the door and disappeared inside.

He found himself near Beautique, the high-priced aesthetics shop on Avenue Road where Donny worked. After the usual tussle with traffic, cursing under his breath at drivers who passed on the right or didn't use their indicators, Dan found a parking spot then crossed the thoroughfare on foot, dodging SUVs and luxury vehicles.

He entered the wide glass doors, his eyes roaming over the shelves. Lotions and potions were the store's specialties. Top-of-the-line, non-invasive skin-tightening services that rejuvenated the faces and sex lives of bored housewives, overpaid CEOs, and on-camera newscasters. An alert young man looked up from the counter, his bright red hair standing painfully erect. On seeing Dan, his expression hovered between welcoming and wary. The store seldom catered to a rough-and-tumble crowd who looked more like construction workers than high-powered executives, but every now and then a movie star with an addled expression came in and demanded top-quality treatment.

"Hi, there. I'm Chad."

"Hi, Chad. I'm Dan. I'm here to see Donny," Dan said to relieve him of his worried look.

"Ah, yes! You're the *friend*," he said, adding the final word in an ominous undertone. "I've heard all about you."

"Not half, I'm sure."

Chad held up a pinky and picked up the phone. "One moment!"

A minute later, Donny came from behind a heavy door at the back of the shop.

"Good timing?" Dan asked.

"Depends what you're trying to time. I'm just on a quick break."

"Nothing in particular, just thought I'd make contact with planet Earth and see how the working stiffs are doing."

"Big meeting with clients this afternoon. Revolutionary new fragrances coming out that are going to shake the world order, bringing peace and enlightenment to all. The usual."

"Sounds daunting, but I applaud the effort. And how is the charming Prabin these days?"

"Good. We're both good. Working to the bone, though. Quite busy."

For a second, Dan wondered if Donny was trying to head him off at the pass, making excuses before he could even say what he'd come to ask.

"Not too busy, I hope."

Dan thought back to the carefree days when they were both single men with a penchant for listening to jazz late into the night, even after Dan won his battle to stop drinking, a win Donny had approved of when it occurred.

Donny's expression indicated his thoughts were otherwise. "You know. He's … busy."

"Okay, well. I was just wondering if the two of you would like to come over for dinner tomorrow. Nick's been trying out some new dishes. He makes a killer beef Provençal."

The pause was telling.

"I'll have to check with Prabin. He's usually exhausted come the weekend."

They stood there staring at one another before Dan broke the silence. "Why do I get the feeling you're avoiding me?"

At least Donny made an effort to look surprised. "I don't know."

"It seems a while since we saw you."

"We saw you two weeks ago at Larry's birthday party."

"Yeah, well, that was hardly quality time spent between the four of us. And come to think of it, you barely spoke. Prabin did all the talking."

"I wasn't feeling well that night."

It was the kind of evasive answer he was used to hearing from clients. Not the sort of thing Dan wanted to hear from a friend.

"What is it about Nick that you don't like?"

Donny pressed a hand to his chest, dignity asserting itself. "It's not that I don't like him —"

"No? What is it then?"

He shook his head, as though the answer were obvious to everyone but Dan. "It's just that I don't like cops in general. Hello. Racism? Carding? I don't trust them."

"You haven't given him a chance," Dan said. "He's not just any cop. He happens to be the cop I'm dating. And he's not like that. I've never known you to be so unreasonable about anything."

Donny tried a half smile. "Maybe I'm afraid I'll like him."

"Would it be so awful if you did?"

"It remains to be seen, doesn't it?"

"I'll take that as a no," Dan said. "Let me know if you change your mind."

He took care to smile at Chad as he left, not to add to the growing state of his reputation.

SIX

Tilt

DAN SAT IN HIS CAR, trying to calculate how much time he had before downtown traffic became totally unbearable. An hour at most, by the looks of it. While the city's driving stats might not be the worst on the planet, Dan was willing to bet they were damn close. He pulled out his cell and dialed the number.

"Dennis Braithwaite?"

"Yes, hello." The voice was friendly. Everybody's favourite investment banker.

"My name is Dan Sharp. I'm a private investigator. I've been hired by Janice Bentham to look into the disappearance of her son, Jeremy."

Caution crept in. "I see."

"Do you have time to talk to me, either now or sometime soon?"

"Well … I suppose." The voice was hesitant but not reluctant. "Does this really concern me? I mean, it's sad that he's missing, but I doubt I could tell you anything."

"Possibly not, but you might be able to throw some light on the situation that Jeremy's parents haven't been able to so far."

"Okay. I guess. Do you know where my office is?"

Half an hour later they were sitting across from one another in Dennis's office on the thirty-first floor of the Toronto Dominion Tower. The afternoon sun struck at precise angles, illuminating the gold-tinted windows of the Royal Bank Plaza across the way, sending flares in all directions. Dan was reminded of Sarah Nealon's sun-catcher.

In person, Dennis Braithwaite was corporate success personified. Hair coiffed, clothes immaculate, handshake perfected. His solid frame showed that he spent plenty of time at the gym. Dan tried to picture him with the petite Janice: his status quo crewcut and tan with her tattoos and piercing. They must have seemed an odd mix. But then it hadn't lasted.

On his desk, a photo showed him accepting a plaque for Employee of the Year. His smile told the viewer just how proud he was of the designation. It was flanked by photos of Dennis and Janice together. In one, he laughingly held up a rod with a dappled fish dangling from the end of the line as Janice looked on in amusement. In the other, the pair relaxed side by side in twin Muskoka chairs. They appeared happy, placing the shot prior to Jeremy's birth, Dan presumed. A final frame showed Dennis behind the wheel of a grey Porsche, his face obscured by sunglasses as he grinned and gave someone the thumbs-up sign through the window. A key chain with a Porsche tag lay on his desk, casually tossed beside a pen holder.

Judging from the photographs he seemed to be a man of many moods, all of them smiley. Currently, however, Dennis's facial expression had just undergone a change from smiley to uncertain when Dan told him about the ransom request.

"Well, that's a game-changer," he said, tapping a pencil against his laptop. "To put it mildly."

"I understand you were asked to add Jeremy to your insurance policy as his legally adoptive father, but you declined."

Dennis's eyes shifted to the view outside where a window washer dangled precariously on a narrow ledge on the building directly across the way. He leaned over to reach one last corner of the window.

"That's one way of putting it."

"Is there another?"

Dennis turned back to Dan and regarded him for a moment before he spoke.

"There certainly is. My wife tried to con me into thinking that Jeremy was my kid. That's definitely something she neglected to tell me."

"You didn't know about Eli Gestner?" Dan asked, feeling a little surprised himself.

"No, I didn't. But then my wife is a natural-born liar." Dennis shrugged. "Janice and I split when the kid was born. Naturally, I assumed it was my kid, but later when I learned about the illness, it didn't make sense. Nothing like that runs in my family."

"By illness, I assume you mean Jeremy's autism?"

"Yeah — that little detail. It's genetic, right?"

"Only partially, as I understand it."

"Whatever. She tried to convince me to have him covered through my company health insurance. Said I had to take some responsibility, blah, blah, blah. But I was suspicious, you know? So I did a bit of checking around and found out he wasn't mine."

"How did you feel about that?" Dan asked.

Dennis eyed him blankly. "How would *you* feel? I'd barely talked to her in three years and she suddenly shows up asking for favours."

Across the way, the window washer walked from one end of the platform to the other. Dan felt his stomach clutch as the bucket of cleaning fluid shifted uneasily with each step he took.

"You didn't keep in touch with her after you separated?"

He thought of Ked and how he'd anxiously awaited news from Kendra while she went off to California to stay with an aunt during the final months of her pregnancy to keep it from her family.

Dennis shook his head. "She made it clear she didn't want to stay in touch when we split."

"But if you thought he was your son … ?"

"He wasn't, but even if he had been she made it clear she was taking him with her. It was her little experiment. I never really wanted to be a father anyway." He made a dismissive gesture. "Anyway, up to that point I still thought he was my son, but when Janice told me he was autistic, I knew he wasn't mine. Not to mention the curly, black hair. I mean, Janice and I are both blond." He shrugged. "He's cute as hell, but that kid does not look like me."

"So that's how you discovered he was Eli Gestner's son?"

A frown creased his brow. "Hey — Eli's a good guy, don't get me wrong. And I'm glad the kid has a father to turn to. But the deception hurt, I have to say."

Dan's eyebrows rose. "Not to mention how you got stiffed for the fertility clinic payments."

Dennis shrugged. "That was the least of it. What I objected to was that she lied to me about my son." He shook his head sadly. "Or the kid who was not my son, as it turned out. My insurance would have covered him if he was, but since he wasn't mine I wouldn't take the chance of lying to my insurance company on top of everything else."

"Is Jeremy's treatment expensive?" Dan said.

"From what Janice tells me, yeah, it's extremely expensive. Schooling, treatment, medication. It's a good chunk, all told. Probably twice as much as I paid the fertility clinic. But if you're thinking I'm a heartless bastard who wouldn't help out a sick kid, I'm not. I'm just a bit of a prick when someone lies to me again and again. Especially when it's my wife."

"It must have hurt when she went off with another woman."

"Right — Ashley. Don't get me started. Sure, it was a kick in the head. But I'm over it now." Dennis shrugged. Water off a duck's back. "We weren't that well suited to one another anyway. Me, a lower-class boy climbing the corporate ladder in any way he could, and her, the spoiled little rich girl."

Dan glanced at the photos. "But you still keep her picture on your desk."

Dennis shifted uncomfortably. "Yeah, well … I just brought those back out a while ago. I hadn't really looked at them till recently."

The window cleaner spat over the edge of his platform and looked down.

"Janice mentioned she had a difficult relationship with her mother," Dan ventured.

"Huh!" Dennis smirked. "That's putting it mildly."

"I understand she thinks her mother may help with the ransom money."

"Her mother? Well, good luck with that. She's a piece of work. And pretty ruthless, too. I never had a problem with her, but then I gave her what she wanted: a front for her disreputable daughter. When Janice was with me, Clarice didn't have a thing to worry about. I may have come from nothing, but I dress up pretty well. I made Janice look respectable. When she left me for a woman, well ... the old lady went nuts. At first she suggested I was to blame, but then I wised her up about how lesbians don't need or want men. I honestly think Janice knew what she was before she married me. I mean, I knew what I was. Didn't you?"

"Not at first, but it didn't take me long to figure it out."

"Exactly. I mean, if you're lying to yourself about something as basic as that, what other lies are you capable of telling yourself or anybody else?"

"True enough," Dan said. "Can you think of anyone who might have had a grudge against Janice or anyone with a reason to believe that Jeremy might make a good target for kidnapping?"

Dennis gave him a blank look. "Not a clue. Why should I? I mean, it's not as though we stay in constant touch. I don't even know who her friends are, to tell the truth."

"Do you know anything about the nanny she fired recently?"

He shook his head.

"How about the surrogate? Do you know much about her?"

"No, not a thing. Really. I wasn't even consulted. She took it for granted that I would accept whatever she did and pay up when it came time to shell out." Dennis sat forward and clasped his hands together like a man about to make his best offer. "My wife's life is a mystery to me. I barely know who she is anymore. That's God's honest truth."

Dan nodded. "By the way, would you mind telling me where you were on the weekend? Specifically, where you were Saturday evening, July twenty-eighth, going into Sunday morning of the twenty-ninth."

"Why?" Dennis sat back and gave him a hard stare. "Am I a suspect?"

Dan shrugged. "Just eliminating the possibilities. I'm sure the police will get in touch sooner or later to ask the same thing."

"Yeah, they already did." He smiled, but his expression remained grim. "I worked on Saturday afternoon. I had a bit of catching up to do. Afterward I headed over to the gym, probably got there around seven. My routine takes me a couple of hours. I'm pretty devoted to it."

"I can see," Dan said. "That kind of a build takes constant work."

"Oh, yeah!" Dennis smiled. "You work out?"

"Yes, but not as intensively as you. I've got a son at home. He requires a different kind of attention."

"Right. Fatherhood. Don't remind me." Dennis rolled his eyes. "Anyway, it's Mega-Fitness on Queen near Victoria. I checked in at the desk with my membership card. I was also chatting up another member at some point. She gave me her number. She'll remember me."

"Her name?"

"Soledad Somebody. Shouldn't be hard to find. I can ask when I see her again." He laughed. "*If* I see her again. People come and go around that place."

"What about Sunday? What did you do then?"

Outside, the window washer cinched his belt and released the rope to lower the platform. Dan felt a sickening lurch as the winch slipped and everything tilted precariously. The man looked around in surprise, as though someone had tried to trick him by rocking his platform.

"I got high," Dennis said with a smile. "Sunday's my chill day. You gonna report that to the police?"

The washer examined his rig minutely but showed no fear. He picked at the knot that had resulted in the slippage. Suddenly everything resumed its original position and he started in on the next window, waving to someone inside. Dan gave a sigh of relief. There had to be better ways to make a living. Despite the drawbacks, he was glad to be a private investigator.

"No," he said, turning back to Dennis. "I won't report it. That's your business. But Jeremy went missing sometime overnight on Saturday. It's just a three-hour drive from here."

"A little less if you drive fast." Dennis's smile persisted. "Anyway, I don't know why the fuck they didn't just stay at the cottage."

"What cottage?" Dan asked.

"Mine. The one at Lion's Head. Didn't Janice tell you about it?"

"I don't think she mentioned it, no."

Dennis picked up the photo of himself and Janice in the Muskoka chairs and held it out for Dan to see.

"We used to spend all our weekends up there in the summer. She texted to ask about using it that weekend." He shrugged. "I said sure. I mean, why spend the night in the woods when you can sleep indoors, right?"

"Right."

"Then again, if I'd known Ashley was going to be there I would never have offered. I mean, she stole Janice from me. In fact, she did her best to tear us apart. It was like a non-stop campaign once she started. And it worked."

"Maybe if you'd been a better husband it wouldn't have."

Dennis set the frame back on his desk and looked at Dan. "Is there anything else I can enlighten you about?"

"Thanks," Dan said. "You've already been extremely helpful."

SEVEN

The Edge of the Universe

ELROY JAMES STILL HAD NOT RETURNED Dan's call by the time his meeting with Dennis Braithwaite was over. Dan was only mildly surprised, however. Usually a veiled threat about illegal activity elicited a quick response, but maybe Mr. James thought he had nothing to worry about. On the other hand, a text from Donny was waiting for him when he got back in his car: *Prabin says he's busy this weekend*. Dan trashed the message as he pulled out of the underground garage. *Sure, blame it on the boyfriend*. At least it freed him up to take a drive to the Bruce Peninsula.

The afternoon traffic was already a bitch. He'd overstayed the three o'clock cut-off and the entire downtown core was flooded with drivers, most of them irritable. By four, the city would be almost unnavigable. But if you couldn't avoid it, it was a good time to relax and get caught up on calls.

Janice picked up on the first ring. Dan heard Eli talking loudly in the background. It hadn't occurred to him that the three of them might all live together.

"Your ex-husband wasn't very helpful when I asked about possible suspects," Dan said.

"No surprise there." He heard something that sounded as if she were sucking on ice cubes. It was followed by a tinkle, as though she had just spit into a glass. "Sorry, just rinsing my mouth out. No, Dennis was never very helpful unless it would benefit him in some way. The things you learn about people when you live with them, right?"

"Right," Dan said. "On the other hand, he did mention he was surprised to learn only recently that Jeremy isn't his biological son. He said that's why he turned down your request to put him on his insurance claim."

"Oh, that. Well, yes. He could have helped, but he decided not to. Did he really tell you about that?"

"He did," Dan said. *But you didn't.* "Did you expect him to lie to his insurance company?"

There was a pause. "I didn't want him to lie, I wanted him to *believe.* That's why I didn't tell him. What exactly did he say?"

"He said he had someone look into it and discovered Jeremy wasn't his son. He asked how I would feel if it had been me. Frankly, I'm glad I know I'm the father of my son."

"Smart." She made another gurgling sound.

"He also said you asked him to let you use his cottage that weekend."

"Right — I texted to ask him."

"So why didn't you use it?"

"He never replied." She snorted contemptuously. "Just as well. If you knew Dennis ... everything has a price tag. I just assumed he was being his bitter, vengeful self. He won't admit it, but he still hates me."

Dan thought of the photographs on Dennis's desktop. Hate wasn't the word that came to mind.

"Listen," Janice said, "while I've got you — there's something else we should discuss. That strange woman I told you about? I didn't want to say anything in front of Ashley, but it's possible it could be her mother."

"Wouldn't she recognize her own mother?"

"It's doubtful. Ashley hasn't seen her for the past sixteen years. She had mental problems. I don't know everything about the family history, but it's pretty messy. The father was abusive and abandoned the family when Ash was just a kid. That was when the mother had her first breakdown. Then, when Ashley was twelve, her twin sister died. It was the mother's fault. That's when they put her away. It was devastating for Ash. After that she went to live with her grandmother."

"Any reason she would try to come back now?"

"Not that I can think of. Ashley doesn't even know if she's still alive. I just thought it might be a possibility."

A thought occurred to him. "Would she have known your real name is Katharine?"

"I don't know how."

"All right. I'll look into it."

Janice seemed to be in a mood to talk. "It's hard to explain, but in a way it brought us together. Ashley and I have these dark things in common. Things we never discuss."

"Tragedies can do that."

"That's true. She talks tough sometimes, but she's a sweetheart. I feel like I owe her my life."

"How so?"

"She helped put me back together. After Dennis, I was a mess. When we found out Jeremy has ASD, Ashley gave up everything to help me take care of him. She was very successful when we met. She was a photography model."

Dan thought of her quiet, good looks. "I can see that."

"So far I haven't given her much in return," Janice said with a rueful laugh. "Life, right? It never turns out the way you think it should. What are you going to do now?"

"I thought I might go up to the Bruce Peninsula and have a look around the area where Jeremy vanished."

"You won't find anything. We packed up everything at the campsite after the police came. They did a pretty thorough search."

"What about the farmer who found you passed out?"

"What about him?"

"I'd like to talk to him. He might have seen something. If you have his number, I'll give him a call before I go up."

"I don't think he has a phone, but I can tell you how to find him. He's a bit out of the way, though." She paused. "What if we get another call from the kidnapper while you're gone?"

"I've got my cell. I'll keep it on."

"Suit yourself. His name's Horace McLean. He's off Highway 6. Turn right at the three wind turbines and follow Cemetery Road toward the North Shore. The sign says McLean Farm." She paused again. "You'll find him a bit odd, though."

"Odd how?"

She paused. "Odd as in, he lives way out in the middle of nowhere. Odd as in, he doesn't have a phone or believe in the internet. Just odd in general, though he may have saved my life, so I shouldn't be rude, I guess. Anyway, you'll see for yourself if you go up there."

Dan stopped off at home long enough to eat and pack a bag with a change of clothes. He wasn't anticipating being gone more than a day, but it was best to be prepared. He took Ralph out for a quick walk and left a note for Ked.

He had Nick on the phone as he got in the car. "I have a question for you."

"Shoot."

"Have you read the file on the kidnapped Bentham boy?"

"I scanned it briefly."

"Was there anything on the family histories of the two mothers?"

"Such as?"

"One of them — Ashley Lake — had a mother who seems to have gone AWOL for the past sixteen years or so. She had a history of breakdowns. Her partner, Janice Bentham, told me Ashley's twin died and the mother was at fault."

"I recall seeing something about that. Is it relevant?"

"Possibly. Janice mentioned a strange woman who was hanging around in the weeks before the boy was kidnapped. She thinks it might be Ashley's mother come back from the dead."

"Let me look into it for you. It'll have to be discreet, of course."

"I am the soul of discretion. And while I've got you, was there anything about the farmer who rescued Janice Bentham up on Georgian Bay?"

"Anything in particular?"

"Just wondering — is he a crazy person? Anything like that?"

"I didn't get that sense from the report. He checks out as a regular, routine sort of recluse. Grows strawberries, apparently. Though that might be a bit odd. Why are you asking?"

"I thought I'd pay him a visit."

"When?"

"Now."

"I thought you said we were having dinner guests tomorrow night." It was Nick's cross-examiner's voice.

"Nix on the guests. I dropped in to see Donny. He got back to me saying Prabin declined, but I don't think it was Prabin's choice."

There was a pause. "Is it my body odour?"

"More like your uniform. He finally admitted he doesn't want to get to know you because you're a cop."

Nick laughed. "He's not the first."

"Piss on him. He doesn't even know you. And he doesn't seem to want to make the effort, despite the fact I keep telling him what a first-rate guy you are."

"You don't have to defend me. At least he's being honest."

"If you can call it that. He's taken all this time to be honest about it, so I'm not sure it counts."

Dan braked abruptly to avoid an altercation between a black BMW and a Lycra-clad cyclist who had stopped in the intersection in front of the car, refusing to move while he exchanged a few choice words with the driver. Their voices carried over the noise of the traffic.

"Don't start any fights with your friends on my account. We'll both regret it. You've already lost one recently."

Dan's friend Domingo had died of breast cancer the previous year, closing the circle down on an already small number. The social rewards of middle age were proving slim. "Yeah — you're right. But I resent being put in this position."

"Just give it time. When you're ready you can talk to him about it. I'm sure it'll clear up."

The car's driver, who had apparently had enough of the cyclist's harangue, began to beep his horn insistently. Dan wanted to step out and tell them both to shut up.

"All right."

"When will you be back?"

"If I leave now, I'll get there by early evening. I might be back tomorrow afternoon, but I don't know how long it will take to check things out. I don't even know if this farmer is going to be there. No phone or internet."

"How is that possible?"

"It's called a lifestyle choice, Nick."

"Okay. Not one I would make. But don't rush. I don't want you driving down that highway tired late at night. Take your time and do whatever you need to do. I'll see you when you're back."

"Thanks. For understanding."

"My pleasure. Just remember — I love you. And you will never find a more understanding, caring, devoted mate than me."

Dan smiled to himself. "I know that," he said, wondering why it was so hard to say "I love you" back.

The GPS informed him that his drive would take three hours and thirteen minutes. That was a conservative estimate, he knew. At Chatsworth, he caught the 6 and continued north to Owen Sound. Once famed for its brothels and taverns, the Sound had been nicknamed Little Liverpool due to its reputation for obstreperousness. Back then it boasted an intersection known as Damnation Corners, where four pubs offset four churches a block away on Salvation Corners. Now, however, it claimed to be a quiet retirement town. But for Dan, it was the last stepping stone before you hit the Bruce.

He made the drive to the Sound in just over two hours. Lion's Head was still another forty-five minutes up the road. Travelling at night and speeding most of the way, he could probably shave off a bit more time. So it was more than possible to get there and back by morning if you were desperate enough.

It had been years — no, decades — since he'd made the journey, back when Dan was a kid and summer weekends meant the possibility of driving from Sudbury over to Manitoulin Island then taking the ferry across to teacup-sized Tobermory, and beyond that to Lion's Head.

The last time he'd made the trip, his parents had been testing an uneasy truce between them. The arguing started in earnest as soon as they were on the road, bickering about sleeping arrangements and forgotten provisions. It was as though they couldn't agree on anything more than the plain fact of being husband and wife, and that only reluctantly. They were nearly always at odds with one another. Even catching the ferry had been a near miss, as they got lost on the way and had had to backtrack down barren country byways, all the while fighting over who was at fault and whether a road map that took up so much space when unfolded across the dashboard was even worth the bother.

"Just stop and ask someone," his mother ordered, angrily slapping the chart to one side as though wiping away a potential future for them all.

His father glared out at the passing landscape. "Where do you see someone to ask? Should I ask one of the trees?"

But they were already laughing again by the time they reached the ferry lineup, taking secretive sips from the bottle in the brown bag stashed at their feet, with sideways glances at their son.

With the blue swath of Georgian Bay spread out before him, Dan had climbed to the top deck to gaze at a smudge on the far horizon, focusing on the fantastically twisted shapes of Flowerpot Island approaching, then looking down beneath the waves to discern the outlines of shipwrecks, their vanished worlds taking shape in his four-year-old mind like tales of hidden treasures.

He wandered up and down the boat with his curly-haired terrier, Sandy, while his parents spent their time in the bar, coming out to check on him now and again. Seeing him happily engaged, they eventually left him on his own till the whistle sounded.

Once off-ship they followed single-file in the line of cars headed past Tobermory. A song played on the radio, soft and beguiling, the singer urging them to walk before trying to run. Someday, she sang, they would live in a land of white lace and promises. Ironic, in fact, as his mother's death lay just up ahead, not long past Christmas. There would be white lace in the coffin, though Dan would not remember what the promises had been or whether she'd kept them. For years afterward, he would wonder where she had gone and whether there was a ferry to get there, the memories of that final trip inextricably intertwined with her death. Once, he dreamt she was waiting for him on Flowerpot Island, but sadly he couldn't get there.

His reveries were interrupted outside Wiarton when a livestock carrier approached from behind. In the mirror he saw the driver checking the distance from Dan's car to the oncoming traffic. Dan slowed to let him pass. The driver gave him a thumbs-up as he pulled alongside.

The vehicle was long, with open-slatted sides. As it sped by, Dan was startled to see dozens of eyes staring at him. Pigs pressed against the bars, looking terrified, as if they already knew what would happen to them at the end of the road. The truck zoomed past.

On that last trip, his parents had rented a low-ceilinged cottage outside Lion's Head. They'd stayed up drinking each night, rising late each morning and speaking in hushed voices as though unaware of the rocks and trees, the beckoning landscape just beyond the windows. Dan didn't wait. He crept out of bed and washed his face, knowing there wouldn't be a cooked breakfast as there would have been with his Aunt Marge and cousin Leyla. He sidestepped the empty beer bottles and pushed aside the ashtrays stuffed with butts, scrounging in the fridge for cheese and stuffing a handful of cookies into his knapsack before setting out.

Fired by tales of the Ojibwa and spirits of Manitoulin, Dan had taken Sandy and wandered for hours along the rocky terrain that unfurled outside the cabin door, searching for remnants of teepees and lost arrowheads. Even now, it looked as though little had changed in all those years.

Another truck passed, more eyes appealing to him, snouts quivering in the wind. If it had been a van full of joy-riding kids, half drunk and returning from some party, Dan would have told them to turn around. *Go on home before something bad happens*, he'd have said. *Before your worst nightmares come true.*

He saw a vacancy sign and turned in the driveway. It was a strip motel with a long line of identical cottages. No need for distinction. You stopped for a few hours before moving on, every one all the same.

The desk clerk, a thin, nervous Asian, turned out to be the owner. He grinned when Dan asked his name, as though no one had ever done that before. Sonny, he replied. He'd been here for five years since coming to Canada from mainland China. The Bruce must have seemed like the far end of the Earth to him.

Dan took his key and got back in the car, driving slowly till he found his cabin. The lot was nearly full, with cars parked up and down the asphalt strip. He was lucky to have found a place.

A lone cyclist headed his way, a woman sitting upright on an old-fashioned bike with high handlebars. She wore a large sunhat and veil. Just before she reached him, she turned and headed back.

Dan parked and unlocked the door. The cabin smelled of disinfectant. As he retrieved his bag from the trunk, the cyclist rode by again. She was Asian, too, but she looked much older than Sonny. Maybe she was his mother.

Inside there was a mini-fridge, dresser, and queen bed. Everything in the room was beige or brown. Each time Dan turned on the bathroom light it was accompanied by a loud whirring overhead. *I'm just washing my hands*, he wanted to say. *I don't need a whirlwind to accompany me.*

He went back outside and stood on the stoop, looking up and down the lot. Farther along, a television blared through one of the windows, but the lights were off. Dan checked his watch: just before nine. It would be dark soon. It struck him that he hadn't thought to bring a book to pass the time. That was dire for an inveterate reader who disliked television on principle. He was also hungry. His last meal had been breakfast.

He locked his cabin then got in his car and headed for Wiarton. The town had one main street with three traffic lights from end to end. He stopped at a red light and waited. An engine gunned behind him. The signal turned green and Dan moved forward, keeping his eyes open for a diner. He passed a Chinese place and a pizza parlour. Both were shuttered and dark.

The second light turned yellow before he reached it. When he stopped, the driver behind him honked. Dan looked back and saw a burly man with a beard shaking a fist out the window of a black pickup truck. He honked a second time, but Dan just sat there. Seconds later, the truck zoomed around him and tore through the intersection. The driver's words were garbled, but their intent was clear.

"Got places to go, buddy?" Dan murmured.

He headed to the next light — red again. A large *For Sale* sign filled the window of a hotel on the corner. There was nothing open further down the strip. He slowly turned around in the intersection, disregarding the light, as that seemed to be the local custom, and headed back to the motel.

The sunset was in tatters, orange and red bands threaded through with purple. It clung from one end of the horizon to the other, lending a sense of impending desolation to the view. A mistake, really, especially if you wanted to avoid thinking of things you'd rather forget. Like life, like loss.

He watched the colours changing as he drove. The sky seemed vast, almost too wide and open due to the peninsula's flatness. It felt as though he was perched on the edge of the universe. If he let go of the steering wheel, he might just float off in the distance.

The motel entrance lay just up ahead. He signalled and turned in, though there was no one behind or in front of him as far as he could see. Just empty roads.

Yes, he could have done without the sunset.

Back inside his room he turned on the television, texting a belated *I love you too* to Nick.

EIGHT

Into the Lion's Den

DAN WOKE EARLY, while it was still dark out. He stretched and discovered he'd slept well. Far better, in fact, than he slept at home most nights. There were no messages on his phone, nothing from Janice saying that the kidnapper had called again. He showered and shaved then stepped outside for a walk. By the time he returned the sun had risen; the sky looked far bluer than it did in the city.

Back in the room his phone showed a text from Nick in response to his uncharacteristic, late-night love note. *Who is this!!! Do I know you?* it read. *Cheeky bastard,* Dan shot back. *You get to say I love you all the time. For me it's not that easy.*

When he looked out the window, the old woman was still riding her bicycle. Or more likely she had resumed her riding from the previous evening. She held herself erect as she sailed past his room and headed along the asphalt strip, turning neatly just before reaching the end.

"Your mother enjoys her bicycle," Dan told Sonny when he dropped his key off at the office.

"No — wife. She lonely. Speak only Chinese. No one talk to her."

Dan tried to imagine how it would feel to be the only non-English speaker in a sparsely populated land. You would probably want to ride your bicycle all day long.

He got in his car and headed up the highway. Twenty minutes later he came to a junction where three wind turbines rose on the right just before Cemetery Road, exactly as Janice had described. A pine forest edged the horizon. Somewhere out there his childhood memories had been formed. He recalled them so vividly it was as if they had been flitting around in the woods all that time, just waiting for him to return.

His phone signal died right before the entrance to the McLean farm. He turned down a long dirt road where a smartly outfitted farmhouse sat like a welcoming beacon at the far end. Red and green, with gingerbread trim. He half expected to see fairy lights lined up along the drive.

Instead he saw a bull, probably the one Janice had just managed to avoid. Fat, sleek, and reddish-brown, it stood in a field all by itself. It turned its huge head to eye him.

A heavily bearded Santa Claus came out to watch Dan's approach, scratching his head in surprise at seeing a visitor. As he came down the stairs, Dan noticed his strange walk, as though he had to propel his legs forward one at a time. A frantic barking came from inside.

†

They were seated next to the kitchen window. A vase crammed full of daisies sat on a linen tablecloth. White lace and promises. A rifle leaned up against a wall.

"Horace — call me Horace," the man said.

An idyllic setting in the middle of nowhere. Apart from the gun. A moment earlier, three small dogs had been hounding the visitor. Now they lay curled on a brown sofa, licking one another's faces.

"Thank you, Horace. Please call me Dan."

"Dan … Daniel. Meaning 'God is my judge.' Your lineage is well proclaimed. Firm in your adherence to the law despite being surrounded by enemies." He gave Dan a sly look. "Is that you?"

"Some would say so."

Horace nodded. "The lord saved Daniel in the den of lions, sending an angel to close their jaws, finding no fault in the man. Feast day, July 27." He looked off to the window then back to Dan. "You've got the lions on your side. I like you, young man."

"Thank you, sir." It had been a long time since anyone had called him young.

"She was lucky, that girl," Horace continued. "Old Dobbins" — he nodded to the bull outside — "don't take too kindly to strangers." He laughed a deep, hearty laugh. "Hell, he don't take too kindly to me half the time either! 'For it is impossible for the blood of bulls and goats to take away sins.' Hebrews 10:4."

He turned his gaze back to the table. Dan had at first declined his offer of food, but he was glad when the old farmer insisted, sliding a plate of eggs and bacon in front of him. The yolks were bright yellow, the bacon crisp and crinkled tidily on the plate. He was starving.

"Best eggs you'll ever taste," Horace told him.

Dan nodded after a single bite. "You're right."

"Most excitement we've had up here for a long time," the farmer continued. His gaze was far off as he recalled the emergency vehicles and police cars that arrived after he found Janice passed out on his farm. "She all right, that girl?"

"For the most part, yes."

"The boy?"

"Still missing."

"Local talk says now it was a kidnapping." He stared intently at Dan, as though daring him to say different.

"Yes, it looks like it."

"Doesn't surprise me, I suppose."

"Why is that?"

"Too many crazy people in the world," Horace concluded, as though a simpler outlook would solve all the world's problems. That and a plate of farm-fresh eggs. And who was to say he wasn't right?

Dan folded the eggs over onto his toast, the yellow oozing out from the centre. Definitely the best eggs he'd had in a very long time.

"More coffee?"

"Please."

Dan watched as Horace poured a long, black thread into the cup.

"That's why I'm up here," Horace said.

For a moment, Dan thought he meant for the coffee.

"Used to live in the city," Horace explained.

"In Toronto?"

Horace gave him a scornful look. "Not Toronto. The Sound. Nasty place."

He had that faraway look in his eyes again, as though he were looking past him to the sin and wickedness that lay at the core of all human beings. Dan was beginning to regret having driven three hours to meet a full-on eccentric. He'd be giving Nick his assessment when he returned: *A regular, routine sort of recluse, my ass.*

"'I saw three unclean spirits like frogs come out of the mouth of the dragon, and out of the mouth of the beast, and out of the mouth of the false prophet.'" Horace sighed. "So I moved up here when my doctor told me it was this or pushing up daisies."

"Happier?" Dan asked.

Horace snorted and shrugged his big shoulders. "Nope. Everywhere I go, there I am. Still the same me. But now I got daisies far as I can see."

Daisies for crazies. Dan resisted the temptation to laugh. He took a moment to savour his coffee then set the cup down.

"Can you tell me what happened when Janice Bentham arrived on your property?"

"Sure!" He scratched his head and smiled. "It was a little strange, to say the least. People normally don't just end up here by chance. Hard to find. No Wi-Fi, eh?"

Dan thought of his dead phone signal.

Horace continued. "The dogs were making a fuss and I looked out the window. I saw Old Dobbins was getting a little restive." He patted his hip. "Takes a bit of effort to get around, so I don't hurry. Accident with a tractor a few years back. I waited, but the dogs didn't stop, so I thought for a moment there might be a wolf hanging around. We get them sometimes. That's why I keep a gun." He nodded to the shotgun. "Don't like killing, but I wouldn't hesitate to use it. So when I looked out and saw that little girl stumbling alongside the fence, I knew I had to get her out of there before Dobbins decided to take matters into his own hands, so to speak. I called her Rachel then. That was before I knew, of course."

"Knew what?"

"How the child was begotten of another. It just made sense in my head, so I went with it. But there it was, true all along."

Dan took a moment to follow his logic. "She told you her son was a surrogate baby?"

"Nah, she didn't tell me. Couldn't talk, could she? Had the breath knocked out of her good. Didn't even know about the boy then. I heard it all later. Anyway, she was passed out when I found her. I waved Old Dobbins off then made sure she was safe and come back to call 911. I tell people there's no phone, but I got a land line. Can't remember the number half the time though." He winked. "So that's about it. Then that other girl came along about ten minutes later. First I took her for an angel. Then I thought to myself, what would an angel be doing up here? I called her Leah."

Ashley, Dan thought.

Horace nodded as though all was clear. "Rachel was jealous of her sister, you see. That was Leah. Couldn't stand that her sister had babies and she didn't. Especially after Leah stole her husband on their wedding night. So she made the servant girl bear children for her." His expression darkened. "When I heard the boy was missing, I was worried. There's bears out there. And wolves that would tear you apart." He shook his head. "Shame. A real shame. I hope they find him."

Dan took another bite of egg and considered Horace's words. "If someone were to kidnap a child, where would they take him, do you think?"

"Up here?" Horace scratched his beard. "If it were me, I'd put him on a boat and take him somewhere far from here."

Dan considered. "Where exactly?"

"From here you could sail up and be away to the northern shores of Superior. Head up to Nunavut, if you wanted. Or if you went west and south, you'd end up in the States. For all the talk about border patrols, it'd be an easy thing to sneak over in a sailboat. At night, say. Take the boy out and hide him away somewhere." A thought occurred to him. "Or caves. If I didn't have a boat, I'd hide him in one of the caves till the coast was clear then head out late at night when no one could see."

Dan finished his meal then let the older man show him around the farm briefly. He had no interest in the livestock, but Horace seemed to want his company.

"What are your people?" Horace asked as they stood outside the door to the barn.

It took Dan a moment to understand the question. "Calvinist," he said.

Horace nodded. A weighty reply that took some consideration. "That's predetermination," he said at long last. "Who gets saved and who doesn't. You believe in that, Daniel?"

"I believe in the law."

Horace laughed long and hard. "Oh, that's good. Yes sir, that's good! 'Render unto Caesar the things that are Caesar's.'"

Dan slowed to let the older man keep pace with him, propelling himself forward with each step.

"Well, you've come to the right place then."

"How's that?"

"Lion's Head. That's where you're headed, young Daniel."

Afterward, as Dan got back in his car and turned back down the long drive, he looked in the mirror to see Horace waving.

"Caves," the old man called after him. "It's the caves you want. Watch out for the lions, though."

He laughed a high, snorty laugh.

NINE

Caves

DAN HEADED AWAY FROM Horace's farm, along the coast, till he came to a sign reading *Caves: next three kilometres.* They lay somewhere up ahead in the shadow of the formidable limestone outcrop that gave the peninsula its name, towering over the water like some mythical protector from the *Iliad.* He pulled over to the side of the road, turned off the car engine, then got out to stretch, enjoying the warmth of the sun on his shoulders and back.

He stowed his belongings in the trunk with a city boy's wariness of leaving anything exposed through car windows, prepared for a long walk over difficult terrain. A winding, mossy trail led him to the first cave in less than twenty minutes. There wasn't a lot to it, just a forbidding-looking entrance opening onto a shadowy space bounded by damp rock on all sides. That the human race had evolved from cave-dwelling ancestors seemed almost beyond comprehension. Then again, he reasoned, everyone had to start somewhere.

He emerged from the shadowy indentation and followed the path again, stopping to peer into several shallow depressions others might have accepted for caves, but which were of no interest to him as they would have been impossible to hide or take shelter in, even if you were a four-year-old boy.

As the path descended Dan heard a low rumbling ahead, a sound as old and amorphous as the trees and rocks surrounding him. He skidded down an incline, clutching at cedar branches until he came out suddenly onto a beach, its pebbles caught in a restless eddy.

He stood looking out where the waves crested white before tumbling over themselves to reach the shore. Seagulls glided along, waiting to catch a glint of fin and scale. He felt something formidable and uncompromising here. It ran through his veins, a force as strong as love or the protective urges he felt when he thought of his son. It seemed to come from deep in the earth and rise up all around him.

He knelt and trailed a fist in the water, iron-cold despite the air's warmth. The last time he'd been here, just up the coast, had been four years after his mother's death. By then he was living with his Aunt Marge, a large woman with a big heart, and his cousin Leyla, who was like a sister to him.

His father had convinced Marge to let Dan come with him for the weekend. Stuart Sharp had got it into his head that they should try to recapture something of the carefree time they'd had the summer before Dan's mother died. Not that it had been carefree to Dan, but his father seemed to think it was. There had been talk that they might even live together again. If everything went well on the trip then they would see.

Dan hadn't felt comfortable being alone with his father. The one good memory he had was of stopping at a roadside diner for ice cream and eating it as quickly as he could before it melted down his fist in sticky rivulets. Not really much of a memory as these things went.

He stood and headed back along the trail where it veered off right before it began to climb again. A weathered sign said *Gun Point*.

He was conscious of having been alone for nearly half an hour before he spotted other people. He came upon them suddenly, a young couple walking slowly and talking quietly. The boy slid his arm lightly over his girlfriend's shoulder. Dan watched as she reached around and gripped his back pocket, hanging on tight. *Ownership*, it said.

He smiled and thought of Nick. They'd been lying in bed one morning, not long after they first met, all sexed out. When Nick tried to get up, Dan had held onto him.

"Don't move," he said.

"Feeling insecure?" Nick asked.

"I like this," Dan said.

"I like it too. But I'm just going to the bathroom."

When Nick returned, they'd had a serious discussion. To Dan's surprise, they both voiced a desire for a monogamous relationship.

"You mean just me and you?" Dan asked.

"That's usually what monogamy means," Nick had replied. "I get the feeling you wouldn't mind if I got possessive about you."

Dan thought about it. "Strangely, I feel as though I want to be owned by you. Like I need to belong to just you."

Nick laughed out loud. "That's how I feel about you, which makes us pretty old-school in our thinking. Imagine, in this day and age: two monogamous cis males. We're ancient history."

"Very ancient," Dan agreed. "Did the dinosaurs have good sex lives?"

"Let's find out."

The relationship had grown from there. It seemed to obliterate the assumptions Dan had harboured his entire life that all pleasures must eventually be paid for and all joys must end, if not in grief then in loss or disappointment. A lifetime of hard work did not necessarily lead to the promised rewards of sanctity and grace. Wheels turned and people got ground under. The only lessons were those of privation and regret, life's sad souvenirs. His father would have agreed.

He grasped a branch and pulled on it, suddenly finding himself at the top of the promontory with a long blue vista stretching before him. Up here everything was alive: rocks, wind, and clouds. Far below, waves scribbled a corrugated surface over the lake while all around him tree branches stretched blindly, restlessly searching. Then, for one solitary moment, there was no wind, only stillness and a silence that seemed to pour down from the sky before it all started up again.

He walked carefully out to the edge where the ground fell away in a sheer drop to the water. Looking west, past the limestone cliffs, he saw the town with its cottages and colourful rows of sailboats bobbing in the wind. He'd last seen his dog, Sandy, out there somewhere. The last summer his mother was alive.

It was a mistake to have gone back. Even at eight Dan knew that. His father had parked in the long gravel drive outside the cottage and just sat there. Dan waited, wondering what was going through his head. He seemed overwhelmed on seeing it again, unable to comprehend what it all meant till he faced it.

The cottage had one long main room, with bedrooms and a kitchen partitioned off in back. The rafters were stuffed with life jackets and fishing rods and paddles. An oil lamp hung suspended from a hook over a wooden table. The pot-bellied stove still worked. Water was pumped via a long hose into the sink. The floorboards left splinters in your feet if you went barefoot. Dan remembered all of this. There had been an outhouse with a sun and crescent moon carved near the top of its door.

The evening of their arrival was chilly. Dan sat wrapped in a blanket, the wool scratching his arms and the back of his neck. They'd been roasting marshmallows, watching the outer coats turn from white to brown then slowly start to blacken and blister. The trick was to remove them from the heat before they caught fire. Half of them slid off and landed in the flames with a sad plop before you could eat them.

His father had gone inside to cook supper. Despite Dan's pleas, he'd decided to boil the hot dogs rather than roast them on the fire.

"Too easy to lose," Stuart had pronounced. "Then we'll have to go to bed hungry."

The next time he came out, he was holding a stubby by the neck. The case of beer had gone into the trunk along with the rest of the groceries. Dan didn't like beer. It fizzed like pop, but it was for grown-ups and tasted rotten the time he sneaked a mouthful from an open bottle left on the kitchen counter. His Aunt Marge didn't like it either. It was the only time he ever saw her lose her temper with her wayward brother, who could hardly be bothered to pay attention once he'd reached a certain point in his alcoholic downslide.

Dan and his father sat listening to the call of a distant whippoorwill while the fire crackled. His father went back into the cottage again, only this time he didn't return for quite a while. When he finally came back out he made his way uncertainly, holding two paper plates, nearly dropping one as he placed them on the wooden table. The hot dogs were swollen and flesh coloured, the buns loose and flappy. He looked down at his plate and rested his chin on his hands, then he slowly lowered his face.

At first Dan thought his father was saying grace, but after a moment he realized he was crying. A vein beat thickly in his father's neck, his skin glinting in the firelight. He smelled of alcohol.

Dan knew better than to disturb him when he was drinking. He dug into the beans and wolfed down his hot dog after covering it with ketchup and mustard and relish. When he looked up again, his father's face was resting on his plate. Slowly Dan finished his supper, picked up his leftovers, and dropped them in the fire.

"Dad," he called, "I'm going to bed." He said it again a little louder when his father didn't stir.

After a moment Stuart Sharp raised his head. Traces of beans stuck to his cheek before sliding down and falling onto the table. In the firelight, he looked like a creature with a melting face that Dan and Leyla had seen in a horror movie a few weeks earlier. Every time the monster appeared onscreen, they'd screamed till it became a game. Now, it seemed less like a game. Dan felt a revulsion for his father, watching him as he got to his feet and staggered over to the fire.

It happened quickly. One second he was lurching forward then the next he went down into the flames, throwing sparks into the night air. Dan was never sure what took control of him. Suddenly he was no longer an eight-year-old boy, but a fear-driven adult grabbing his father by the sleeves and pulling until he had him safely away, the older man batting the embers and sparks from his clothing, examining his damaged hands.

Young Daniel left him there and went off to bed. In the morning, his father sat drinking coffee at the picnic table, his hands bandaged, burn marks raw on his cheeks. Neither of them mentioned the incident then and it was never spoken of.

Now, the adult Dan turned from the view and continued down the far side of the promontory. Horace had said the largest and deepest of the caves was off the main trail and not easily found. Nevertheless, Dan found it. It was larger and more intricate than any of the others. The chill hit him as soon as he entered. He was able to walk upright for nearly half a minute before the ceiling lowered, forcing him to crawl as the stone bit into his hands and knees.

The rock seeped and glistened around him. He took out a mini Mag and pointed it upward. Shadows flitted across the roof, childhood monsters coming back to haunt him.

The drive back home had been marred by his father's drinking. They'd had a fender-bender. His father was hungover, the highway nearly empty, but Stuart Sharp had still somehow collided with another car. Both men pulled over to the side of the road. Dan waited, tension knotting his stomach as the other driver swore at his father for weaving onto the wrong side of the road. It took an hour for the OPP to show up. From that day on, Dan had understood that his father was a failure of a man living a failure of a life. Why had he even bothered to try? He still couldn't answer that question even now. For years afterward, he had chastised himself for being so uncharitable that he felt no sympathy for a man trying to recapture a bit of past happiness.

The feeling of being in the cave surrounded by darkness was seductive. Suddenly he seemed a long way from everything: home, work, family. It almost felt as though they might start to matter less the longer he stayed. If he had a blanket, he could imagine stretching out and drifting to sleep. Comforting. Like death.

He continued till there was no further space left to explore, then he headed back. Daylight hit him like a hangover. It was tempting just to crawl back inside, but he had things to figure out.

He heard a ragged cry and looked up. Four crows swooped past in a game of chase, disappearing over the lip of rock, then reappearing after a moment, so close he could hear the snapping of wings. They stayed with him while he continued along the trail.

The next cave was shallow, but the one after it was deceptively deep. It started off as a vertical crevice. He crawled down into it. A sign warned climbers not to attempt to go too far. After a long passageway he came to a space that opened up into a small chamber. There at last he was afforded a glimpse into what might have been a real hideout. The floor was littered with debris. Someone had spent time here, though nothing told him that a boy had been held against his will. Then again, it might not have been against Jeremy's will.

Dan's eyes caught a tinselled glitter among the rocks, something shrinking from his Maglite as he moved forward, trying not to hit his head on the low-hanging ceiling.

A thin chain.

He took off his T-shirt and wrapped it around his fingers, then began to pull. At first the chain resisted, then it slowly unwound from the rock it was caught on. It was a rosary, a thin circlet of beads ending in a silver crucifix.

Redemption.

He pocketed it and headed back to the entrance, blinking in the light.

For a moment, the sky seemed grander than he remembered. It blinded him, as though he'd lost all perspective underground. When his sight returned he dipped into his pocket and pulled out the chain. On back of the tiny cross someone had carved the initials MV. *Marietta Valverde.* He remembered the dismissed nanny's assertion that the two women were going against God's will by raising their child together.

I never ignore people who hate, he'd told Janice. *It's too dangerous.*

Dan recalled Horace McLean's comments on Calvinist doctrine, the long, dark night of human thinking fastening onto the concept of predetermination. Who gets saved and who doesn't. Then he thought of his father. Maybe that was why Stuart Sharp hadn't fought harder for a better life. He'd already known he was damned.

TEN

The Return

DAN WAS GRATEFUL for the long drive home. By the time he reached the outskirts of Toronto he felt altered, as if a subtle transmutation had occurred, a reordering of his senses. He had needed time to regress to his habitual self, the one that Nick and others knew him by. Otherwise they might have found him unrecognizably changed by his encounter with the past.

After thinking about it, he had decided not to turn the rosary over to the local police, as he knew he ought to have done. If they hadn't bothered to check all the caves as thoroughly as he had then it was their fault for missing a substantial clue to Jeremy Bentham's disappearance.

In the meantime, he had plans for it.

Heading down the Don Valley Parkway, he got Janice on the phone. The crucifix glittered in the light where it hung from the rear-view mirror.

"Any further calls from the kidnapper?" he asked.

"No, nothing. But Jeremy's surrogate called to complain that you'd been there interrogating her. Sarah Nealon. She sounded afraid. She didn't even ask for money this time."

"Let me know if she calls again."

He asked if she was free for a visit.

"Sure, we're here," she said, without sounding the least bit curious. "How did you find Mr. McLean?"

"Odd, as you said. I saw his bull too. You're lucky to be alive. I'll fill you in when I get there."

The Junction was an old neighbourhood of well-tended lawns and staid brick homes. Despite rampant gentrification, however, it still maintained an urban edge for the boho crowd with its residential lofts and an abandoned railway track put to better use as an off-road cycling path.

As Dan turned down Janice's street, a copper-coloured Volvo pulled away from the curb and cut sharply into the roadway. Swerving to avoid it, he glimpsed an older woman with a worried expression behind the wheel.

Janice looked panicked when she opened the door. She was jittery, her words rushed.

"She was here again. Just now. I saw her."

"Who was here?"

"That strange woman I told you about." There was panic in her eyes. "I — I think she might be the kidnapper. I took her photo and she ran off."

She held up her cellphone. The image matched the description she'd given him on their first meeting: mousy looking, brown hair fading into grey. Sad eyes. Her face was set in a grimace of pain. It was the woman he'd seen driving the Volvo.

"Stay here. I'll be back."

He jumped into his car and tore down the street, grateful there were no strolling grannies or kids on bicycles flying out of driveways.

He headed in the direction the woman had taken, hoping she wouldn't be that far off yet. Instinct made him turn west on Dundas.

He'd been driving for a couple of minutes, cursing himself for not having gone east instead, when he caught sight of the Volvo at a stoplight two intersections ahead. He edged forward, bypassing drivers who looked anxiously out their windows, honking at him as he zipped in and out of the lanes.

He'd nearly caught up, pulling into her lane four cars behind, when she glanced in the side-view mirror. Her expression was still worried. Dan couldn't tell if she'd seen him or not. Without warning, she veered right.

With a quick look over his shoulder Dan turned, almost sideswiping an oncoming van. The driver laid on the horn, giving him the finger and blocking the intersection. Dan ignored him, hoping he would drive on, but this was an angry driver. He rolled down his window. Dan did the same.

"Yeah, you're right. I'm a dickhead," Dan said to expedite the situation.

"You nearly smashed into me," the outraged motorist shouted.

"Yes, sorry. I didn't see you."

"It's not a turning lane."

"You're right."

By then, others began to ply their horns and edge around them.

"Got the message," Dan said.

The other driver drove on, leaving Dan to ease ahead, but the light was red again. He waited impatiently for the signal to turn. By then the copper-coloured Volvo had disappeared. He pressed the gas and the car surged forward.

He didn't know where he was. Richview, possibly, or maybe Weston. The neighbourhood was sheer sprawl. Block after block of manicured lawns and split-level homes. He trolled the nearby streets, but there was no sign of the Volvo.

After twenty minutes he gave up and headed back.

Janice met him at the door. Her eyes flitted up and down the street.

"Did you catch her?"

"No. She was headed north, but I lost her at an intersection about ten minutes from here."

She let him in. It was an old house, more functional than comfortable. Certainly not beautiful. Stripped of anything decorative. The light wattage seemed unusually low. No doubt that was because of Jeremy's ASD, Dan realized. The boy's needs had come first.

He followed her into the kitchen. A white cat looked over disdainfully from a countertop.

Ashley sat at the table, dressed in jeans and a T-shirt. Despite this, Dan was struck again by her looks. Dennis Braithwaite must have been bowled over to lose his wife to such an attractive woman.

"Are you okay?" he asked.

"Absolutely," Ashley assured him with that clipped delivery. "But it was a shock."

"She's not okay," Janice contradicted. "We're both distraught."

Her cell lay on the table with the woman's photo displayed.

"Any idea who she is?" Dan asked.

Janice looked over at Ashley. "I asked her. She doesn't know if it's her mother."

Ashley shook her head. "Impossible to say. It's been years."

Janice reached a protective arm around her. "The last time Ashley saw her mother the police were taking her away in handcuffs."

"It's okay," Dan said. "I've asked a personal favour of a police officer to put a trace out on her. When I find out what there is to know I'll get back to you on it."

"No, don't." Ashley looked startled. "She ... she's a monster. I never want to see her again."

"You won't have to. I promise," Dan replied, though she didn't seem reassured. He turned to Janice. "You said you advertised for a new nanny when Marietta left. Is it possible she's someone who applied for the position and got turned down?"

Janice shook her head. "She's definitely not anyone we saw. I'd remember. I suppose it's possible she was someone we didn't see. There were quite a few applications."

"When you posted the ad, was it online?"

"Yes."

"Did you specify that Jeremy has autism?"

Janice nodded vigorously. "Oh, yes. It takes someone with special qualifications to look after him. It couldn't just be a regular nanny."

"And did this woman come by after you started advertising for the position?"

Janice paused to think. "Yes — the first time was not long after that. Do you think there's a connection?"

"I'm not sure," Dan said. "But there must be a reason for it."

"I thought she was on the verge of speaking today, but I surprised her by taking her picture. Then she ran off. But why would she come here? I mean, if she has Jeremy then why would she come back?" She pressed a palm to her forehead. "This is crazy!"

"Is it possible this woman is connected in some way to your surrogate?"

"Why would she be?" Ashley said.

"When I saw Sarah the other day she was high on meth. And she was faking a pregnancy."

"Faking a pregnancy?" Janice looked astonished. "Why?"

Dan shook his head. "That stuff does strange things to your brain. I wondered if she was trying to convince herself she was pregnant so that if she suddenly found herself with a real child, like Jeremy, it would somehow all be justifiable in her mind."

A look of bewilderment came over Janice. "You mean if she took Jeremy for herself? But he's too old to be a newborn."

"When you're high, things don't have to make sense. Sarah wears an ankle monitor, so it would be impossible for her to kidnap anybody without leaving a trail. But if she found someone to help her … who knows? She said her mother was looking forward to having a grandchild of her own."

"She was very angry the first time she came here demanding money. She said it was our fault she turned to drugs. We're still not sure how she found us."

Dan nodded. "She told me that when the agency dropped her she got a look at your file. Your address was in it."

"Unbelievably careless," Ashley said. "We should sue."

"Possibly, yes," Dan said. "Did she ever mention losing a child before?"

"No. Did she say she had?"

Dan shook his head. "Not in so many words, but she said something terrible happened to a boy and it worried her a great deal. She seemed to be concerned about children in general. She said she robbed a bank to start a campaign to solve world hunger."

"Oh, that," Ashley said, rolling her eyes. "Yes, we heard. The gun wasn't even real."

"We knew about the robbery," Janice said. "But we never knew the reason for it. It sounds bizarre."

"I doubt the money would have gone to charity organizations. It was more likely a way of justifying her actions to herself. It's possible she could have thought that by kidnapping Jeremy she'd be protecting him."

"Well, that's just great!" Janice said with disgust.

Dan took a napkin from the table then reached into his pocket and held up the rosary. "Do either of you recognize this?"

Janice reached for it. "Those are Marietta's initials."

Dan pulled it back. "No, don't touch it."

"Where did you find it?"

"Inside one of the caves on the Bruce Peninsula."

"Oh my god! That stupid girl." Janice's gaze was fixed on the chain. "What — what will you do with it?"

"I'll hand it over to the police and let them do their investigation." Dan slipped the chain back in his pocket.

"Do you think they have Jeremy?"

"If they do, they're not keeping him at their place. I was there two days ago. And the police had already been there. How much did you know about Marietta before you hired her?"

"She came highly recommended from an agency that specialized in finding help for children with special needs. Apart from that — nothing."

"The agency cleared her," Ashley said.

Janice nodded. "All we knew was that she was from Manila and was fluent in English. From what she told us, her family is poor. Marietta's father is blind, so she was used to helping people with disabilities. It was hard to let her go, but we had to."

"What about the boyfriend, Ramón? Do you know anything about him?"

Janice shook her head. "Nothing much. He never talked about his family. He was very quiet. Marietta ruled the roost whenever he was around. She only brought him here on weekends."

"Was he still working when you knew him?"

"Yes. He worked at a tile store out on the Queensway. The Tile Factory, I think."

Dan made a note of it. "With her parents moving to Canada, they'll be in need of cash." He stood. "I'd like to take a look at Jeremy's room while I'm here."

"Sure."

Janice led him down the hall to a room filled with stuffed animals and cut-out paper hearts on the walls. A small dresser and bed took up most of the space. The walls were painted bright blue, a colour that soothed Jeremy, according to Janice. It looked like any child's room.

"We do our best to keep him happy," she said, leaning against a wall. "It was a shock when we got the diagnosis. It was about a year ago. He had hit several early developmental landmarks, so we thought everything was normal. Then came the fits and the withdrawals. The doctors said he'd regressed somehow. I still don't really understand it. Each day there's new territory to navigate. The paperwork alone and the applications for funding — it's endless."

"I'm sure it must be difficult," Dan said, looking over a set of plastic dinosaur figurines on a dresser top.

"You have no idea. The meltdowns can be terrible. There are so many triggers — loud sounds, even twinkling lights on a Christmas tree. Other kids taunt him in playgrounds. One little girl hit him with a plastic baseball bat when he wouldn't respond to her. She was only four, but she knew he was different. When I asked her why she did that, she said it was because she thought he was an alien."

"Children are cruel," Dan said, turning to her. "Have you come to a decision about the ransom?"

"The police said we should sit tight and wait for the next call, but I want to be ready. I spoke with the bank. I'm going to meet with them. Though honestly, I was hoping somehow it wouldn't come to this."

"You mean that Jeremy would just turn up?"

"I know it's not very realistic."

"I'm afraid it's not."

"I still haven't talked to my mother." She shrugged, as though to say it was beyond her.

Dan opened a closet. Everything was neatly arranged on shelves at the height a four-year-old would find comfortable. One set of cotton shirts was out of line with the others. He reached down and felt beneath the bottom shirt till his fingers grasped something cool and hard. He pulled it out: a small silver pendant.

"Oh, that's where that went," Janice exclaimed. "I lost it a while ago."

Dan let it slip into the palm of her outstretched hand. He finished his search then left with a firm order to report the strange woman's reappearance to the police.

The Tile Factory was an impressive showroom on the Queensway. Lots of glass and flags on poles around the front entrance. The man who greeted Dan with a big smile settled into a more casual expression once he realized he wasn't a potential customer. He gave Dan's investigator card a quick glance and sighed. Still, he must have decided he liked him for some reason, as he started to talk. Either that or he just liked gossiping about former employees.

He chewed gum while he spoke, exhaling a minty breath and toying with a blue dolphin tie pin.

"Yeah, buddy used to work here. One of our best shipper-receivers. Worked hard at first and gave us no trouble. I was even considering him for management. Then all of a sudden, a couple months ago he starts to be a problem … showing up late, forgetting orders. I knew something was up."

"What exactly did you think it was?"

"Not sure." His fingers stopped their twisty movements, leaving the dolphin pin upside down. "I gave him a chance, had a friendly talk with him, but he didn't improve. In fact, he got worse. He was even kinda surly and belligerent with me. Told me I didn't know what I was talking about."

"Do you think he had a drug problem?" Dan asked.

"Never saw a sign of it, and I'm pretty good at spotting that sort of thing."

"Would you take him for a thief?"

"Ramón? Not a chance. He used to stay late some nights. I never for a moment distrusted him." The man thought about it for a moment. "Tell you what I think. I think he wanted me to fire him."

"But if you fired him, he wouldn't get employment insurance," Dan said.

"Exactly. There was a guy not long before who asked me to lay him off. Said his wife's mother was sick and they needed to move to Victoria, but he still needed a bit of income to tide him over to the next location. I worked out a way for that to happen."

"But Ramón didn't seem to care about that?"

The fingers began their fidgeting again. "Nope. As I said, it was like he wanted me to fire him. So I did."

"Did he complain?"

"Not at all."

Janice had had a crisis of conscience when she fired Marietta because of the timing with her parents arriving from the Philippines. Why would Ramón deliberately jeopardize their financial situation even further?

"Did you ever meet his girlfriend? Marietta?"

The dolphin had worked its way upright again.

"Yeah." The man smiled. "She came to our Christmas party last year. Pretty girl, but tough. Not sure how she ended up with him. He was always kind of a softie. She was the one wearing the pants, that's for sure. No way would he have screwed up without her knowing it."

Dan left, thinking over that curious information.

ELEVEN

Polygraph

DAN WAS PARKED OUTSIDE Marietta's high-rise at eight the following morning, a Sunday. He didn't know what church she went to, and there were far too many to check them all; he just knew mass started early. Although he suspected he would find Ramón at home if he buzzed, he waited to catch Marietta on her return so he could confront them together.

It was a busy building, with people coming and going constantly. He'd have to keep alert not to miss her. Sure enough, at a quarter past the hour he saw her approaching. He waited as she stepped into the elevator then gave her two minutes and followed, making a mime of checking for his keys as the next person arrived.

Upstairs, a bag of garbage had been left outside Marietta's door alongside two discarded shoeboxes. Hiking boots, one pair each of men's and women's. *Interesting footwear*, Dan thought. There were two voices coming from inside the apartment. At first he thought he could make out a few words, something about "today and yesterday," but then he realized they were speaking Tagalog.

Marietta answered his knock. Her eyes betrayed fear on seeing him, but her defiance was well in place.

"I don't have to talk to you."

"No, you don't, but I could talk really loudly right here," Dan said. "If you'd like me to let your neighbours know about Jeremy's kidnapping, that is."

Her eyes flitted up and down the hallway. Ramón came up behind her.

"You need to leave us alone," he said. "We don't want trouble."

"I think you may already be in plenty of trouble," Dan said. He held up the rosary, making sure the initials were visible.

Marietta's hand flew to her mouth. "It's not mine!"

"Then why do you look so frightened?"

"I'm calling the super," Ramón said.

"No, wait." Marietta reached out and took it in her fingers. "Where did you get this?"

"I found it in a cave on the Bruce Peninsula," Dan said, retrieving it and wrapping it back in the handkerchief.

"Who cares?" Ramón demanded. "Even if it's Marietta's, what does it mean?"

"It means that one or both of you were near where Jeremy Bentham disappeared."

Marietta shook her head repeatedly. "It's not true!"

For a moment Dan thought she might collapse.

"You're crazy. We didn't hurt that little boy," Ramón said, putting his arm around her. "Marietta loves him."

For once Dan detected a spark of anger in this quiet young man who had so far been docile and subservient.

"What happened to your job, Ramón?"

"My job at the Tile Factory? I got fired."

"Why? Did you do something wrong?"

Ramón glared at Dan without speaking.

"I had a chat with your boss. He seems to think you were one of his best employees until your attitude changed recently. He said you acted as though you wanted to be fired. Now why is that, if you're so poor? Are you coming into some money, Ramón?"

All his bravado vanished. His mouth quivered. "Please go away and leave us alone. We can't tell you anything."

"Please!" Marietta said.

"I'll go away," Dan told him. "But the police will come back to ask the same questions. I don't think that call to your sister in Manila is going to count for very much."

The door closed on Marietta's frightened expression. Dan almost felt sorry for them.

Nick sat on the far end of the couch, looking out his window to the lake where the afternoon sun spotlit a bevy of sailboats tilting their way around Toronto Island. He was quietly fuming. It seemed to be the theme for the day. Dan had just admitted that, in effect, he was tampering with evidence to a crime.

"It's a grey area. I didn't lie. I just decided not to hand it over to the local police at the time. They can have it now that I'm done with it."

"I don't like this one bit," Nick said.

Over the past year, Dan had learned a little of his partner's views on life. When asked why he became a cop, Nick had replied that it beat laying bricks. That was when Dan gave up trying to outguess him. But one thing he knew for sure — Nick was serious about police work and upholding the law.

"Technically I'm not tampering," Dan said calmly. "I found something and I brought it in. I'm giving it to you, an officer of the law."

Nick's face was pure disgust. "What the hell am I supposed to do with it?"

"Bring it to your superiors."

"You should have left it there and told the local cops," Nick said.

"And what if some happy-go-lucky cave explorer had come along and pocketed it in the meantime? Then there would have been nothing for them to find. Look — it was a lucky strike on my part. I didn't know it was evidence until I brought it out into the daylight and saw the initials, but now at least we know it is. So ultimately I've done someone a favour by doing their job for them."

"Is this what being a private dick means to you? To run a countermand operation to official police investigations?"

"What would you have done in my place?" Dan stared him down. "I mean, if you weren't an officer of the law. Would you have just left it there?"

Nick shrugged. "Probably not. But I would have given it to someone who worked for a law enforcement agency up on the Bruce rather than bring it back here."

"Why?"

Nick's face screwed up in exasperation. "Because they're in charge!"

"Well, they missed their chance. So I'm giving it to you and you're going to give it to them. I saved them the delivery charge."

"This is nuts."

"Talk to Lydia. She's a smart cookie."

Dan waited as Nick had a brief conversation with his boss. He hung up his phone and turned back with a shrug.

"She says, 'Good catch.'" Dan started to speak, but Nick cut him off. "Don't get smug on me. It will still piss me off. I'm not going to support vigilante operations."

Dan waited till Nick's temper abated.

"That's not what I am, and you know it. I've helped the police before. Consider me an extra pair of eyes. I'm not trying to make the police look bad. I want what's best for my clients. Just trust that I will always play fair with you too."

"You're exasperating, you know?"

"Ked says the same thing." Dan cocked his head. "Come to think of it, I say the same thing about him. Could be a pattern there."

"Yeah, I'll say."

"Anyway, I'm glad to know Lydia supports me." He winked. "If you feel the need to apologize, I'd be happy to be taken out for supper."

Nick managed a smile.

Ted greeted them at the café door like an innkeeper welcoming a pair of preferred travellers. "My two favourite customers," he said, beckoning them to their usual table.

"I bet you say that to all the boys," Nick joked, already in a better mood.

"Sadly, no. I wish even half of them were worth the effort." He smiled. "Get comfortable and I'll be back with a couple of menus. We've got some really good specials today. Anything to drink?"

"Soda and lime," Dan said.

"Ditto," said Nick.

"You got it."

It was early. The place was nearly empty. Ted returned with drinks and menus. When he began reciting the house specials, Dan put up a hand.

"Why don't you tell us what we're having?"

"Want me to surprise you?"

"Sounds good," Nick said.

Ted gathered up the menus and headed back to the kitchen. When he'd gone, Nick reached across the table and gripped Dan's wrists.

"Are you taking my temperature?" Dan asked.

"Your blood pressure. It's cool and calm, as always." Nick held on tightly. "You're a hard man to read, but I'm getting to know the signs."

Dan looked down at Nick's fingers. "If I didn't know you better, I might think this was a lie-detector test."

"It is. So be careful what you say next." Nick cocked his head. "First question: do you love me?"

"You know I do."

"Evasive, but correct. I do know you do. You even texted me a love note while you were away. It was short, but very welcome even though you forgot the 'undying, forever and ever' part. We can work on that." He smiled. "Now let's try a harder question. These two kids — Marietta and Ramón — do you think they're the kidnappers?"

"Ah — I knew this was a trick."

"Just answer the question."

"I could make a case for them on the evidence as it stands," Dan said. "It's up to your guys to do a DNA sweep of that cave and see if they were there."

"I need a 'yes' or a 'no.' That's how polygraphs work. My interpretation is that you think they might not be."

"I don't *think* anything. For now, I know two things. First, the nanny was fired after money and jewellery went missing from the home. There's your potential motive. Second, a rosary with her initials was found in a suspicious location. There's your evidence. But it's circumstantial. I still need to know what a DNA search turns up in the cave, then I might think something, one way or another."

Nick's eyes held Dan's. "You're being unusually vague on this."

"Not really. I'm normally undecided until I know things for sure. I learned a long time ago not to make assumptions that could end in a prison sentence for an innocent person."

"I can't argue with that. Do you mind at least telling me who your other suspects are?"

Dan shook his head. "I don't have suspects. I have leads. I follow them up and see where they go."

"Okay, smart guy. Then what other leads are you currently following or looking into?"

"Janice's husband, Dennis Braithwaite, for one. He spent a lot of money on fertility clinics, only to discover the boy wasn't his son. After the fact, that is, because Janice lied. He also just found out that the kid is autistic and it's costing her a lot of money. Not content with the normal lawsuit-type revenge, he refused to include Jeremy on his insurance. He and Janice are still legally married, so he could easily have adopted the boy and claimed him on compassionate grounds. But he wanted to make them suffer."

"Sounds like a prick. I'll make sure Lydia takes a closer look at him. Anyone else?"

"Didn't they give you guys the same list of names they gave me?"

"I'm sure they did, but I have to say your insight is proving a tad more accurate. I'd like to tell Lydia I've done due diligence on my end, and that includes probing your observations as the guy who found the first piece of tangible evidence in the case."

"The first as in the *only* piece of evidence?"

"As in the *only*. That's right. The guys up north haven't come up with a thing. As far as they're concerned, this kid vanished into thin air."

"How is that possible?"

"Exactly." Nick released Dan's wrists just as Ted came back with a basket of bread.

"I like the lovey-dovey stuff," Ted said, grinning.

"I was being interrogated," Dan said.

"That's always fun too." He set the bread on the table. "I've got a couple of ace specials coming up for you guys in a few minutes."

"Tedster, we are everlastingly grateful," Nick said.

"No prob." Ted grinned. "Has anyone ever told you that you're a pretty cool cop?"

"Not often enough, but thanks for the compliment. How often do you get told you're a top-notch waiter?"

"Yeah, just about never."

"Well, you are. So thanks for that too."

Ted retreated. Dan eyed Nick over his soda. "A pretty cool cop, eh?"

Nick shrugged. "You gotta take compliments where you find them." He waited. "So who else?"

"The surrogate mother needs a closer look. She's a meth-head who wants people to believe she's pregnant again."

"But she's not?"

"No. But she seemed worried about some kid. She said something terrible happened to him."

"Not Jeremy?"

"I don't think so. She's on probation after a bank robbery she committed while high, but the judge was lenient."

"It happens," Nick said. "Especially if they think it won't happen again. Who else is there?"

"There's also the mysterious older woman who keeps showing up. Ashley got a good look at her this time. She can't say for sure if it's her mother. One thing is clear, she never wants to see her again."

"Can't say I blame her. I looked into the mother, Miriam Lake. Alcoholic, depressive. At thirty she was deemed not criminally responsible in the death of her own child. The breakdowns looked legit. They put her in an institution."

"Is she still there?"

"No. She was released a few years ago. 'Not a danger to the community at large,' was the decision. I've heard that one before. After that, she moved to New Brunswick and just dropped off the radar."

"So she could be anywhere. Even here."

"It's possible."

"Thanks for that. I'll keep her on my list," Dan said. "Any other guesses who the woman might be?"

"I wondered if she might be connected to the surrogate, Sarah Nealon."

Nick tore a piece of bread in half and lay half on his plate. "Why?"

"Sarah blames her pregnancy with Jeremy for her drug addiction, though that was just an excuse to ask for money. On top of that, she said her mother was looking forward to having a grandchild. What complicates things is that she wears an ankle monitor."

"Pretty unbreakable as an alibi."

"I know. I'm just trying to tie this older woman into the kidnapping. Sarah happens to be a convenient hook for now."

"Anyone else?"

"There's an ex–business partner who got angry with Eli — the biological father — over a bad business deal. Apparently death threats were uttered."

"That's Elroy James. The guy's a biker. Comes from up north. Your territory, I believe."

"So not a legitimate businessman? I called his number and his secretary said he was on his way to Hong Kong."

"Secretary — right. Depends what you call legitimate, I guess. He operates a few clubs here and there. What happens on the side is what I'm interested in. He was up on a money laundering charge a couple years ago, but he got off. Slippery guy."

"Which makes me wonder what sort of deal Eli had with him."

Nick paused, bread in hand. "I guess it's only natural to want your money back, but kidnapping's a pretty drastic way to go about it. If you're going to chase this guy down, be careful. He's dangerous."

"I'll keep that in mind."

"That would be wise. Okay — so who else is there?"

"I keep coming back to Dennis Braithwaite. Maybe it's just because I don't like him. But he's familiar with the Bruce. He has a cabin up there. He claims he was at the gym last Saturday evening, but he hasn't got an alibi for Sunday after midnight."

"The gym checked out, but it closes at 10 p.m. He could have driven up to the Bruce and been back here by Sunday morning." He bit into the bread. "Speaking of, you never said how your trip went, besides the tampering-with-evidence part."

"The farmer's an interesting character. Your description of him doesn't begin to cover it." Dan thought back to his conversation with Horace. "He said if you really wanted someone to disappear you just had to get in a boat and head over to the U.S. The shorelines are thinly covered, especially at night. You could cross without anyone noticing. It sounded like he knew what he was talking about."

"And what do you think?"

"I think it would explain why the Bruce OPP hasn't found anything yet. Not to mention that their search-and-rescue resources are woefully inadequate, if I found the only clue."

Nick shook his head. "They're not inadequate — they're inadequately funded. The Bruce is covered by a volunteer SAR team, apart from the fire department in Lion's Head." He shrugged. "You get what you pay for. That's not to denigrate the volunteers. They're well trained, just not full-time."

"How much of a search did they do?"

"Moderate. Because there were no signs of violence, they assumed he wandered off on his own. It was a passive search using flares and whistles. It was followed by a fairly thorough search with boats trawling up and down the coastline. Still, nothing came of it. By the third day they rounded up a dozen volunteers and formed a grid search. They covered most of the peninsula in and around Lion's Head."

"No dogs or helicopters?"

"I think they had a couple of hounds out. The choppers would have been next. Then they got the report about the call from a kidnapper and things took on a new dimension."

"So they just stopped looking for him?"

"Not entirely, but the search was less aggressive. It surprised me when you turned up the rosary. It's odd they didn't find it earlier."

"That's what I thought."

Nick caught Dan's eye. "You think it's a plant?"

Dan took a long time to answer. "I'm not sure."

"What purpose would that serve?"

"The obvious one: to throw suspicion on somebody other than the kidnappers. In this case, Marietta and her boyfriend Ramón."

Ted came up to the table with a worried expression. "Guys, I'm afraid I have to leave. Elaine's taking over for me." He nodded to the bartender who gave them a quick wave of her hand.

"Anything wrong?" Nick asked.

"I just got a call. It's my grandmother." His voice caught. "Sounds like she might have had a stroke."

Dan exchanged a look with Nick. "Anything we can do? Do you need a ride somewhere?"

Ted shook his head. "Thanks, I've got a cab coming. I'll be okay. You stay and finish your meal."

Nick watched him exit. "Hard luck. Kid could use a break."

TWELVE

Straight Up, No Chaser

THE HELICOPTER GAINED ELEVATION faster than Dan expected, zooming upward like a scrap of paper caught in a twister. The blades whirled, grinding the air to smithereens, and then they were off to the Bruce. Clearly, this was a lot quicker than going by car, though Dan doubted Marietta and Ramón would have had the funds to rent a chopper in any case.

The officer who called made it clear that Dan's co-operation now would mean a lot less hassle later if he took time to point out the cave where he'd found the rosary. Which was precisely what he intended to do. At the very least, it meant Nick would be less irritated with him.

They were four in total with the pilot: Dan, the police officers, and one of Jeremy's large stuffed animals, a kangaroo that had been allotted its own seat. It leered at him through its protective wrap.

Conversation was limited due to the noise. The cops talked amongst themselves. Dan was tempted to start a conversation with the kangaroo but decided not to risk the officers' ire. Instead, he contented himself with looking out the window, watching the cityscape shift from familiar to almost unrecognizable once they'd passed over the downtown core. His visual memory depended on a horizontal POV, he realized, not a vertical one from a thousand metres up.

Twisting to look out the other side, he knocked his foot against a metal support rod connected to the seat ahead. The whole contraption felt oddly jointed together as it jarred and shuddered. The 401 appeared below like a long black ribbon, joined by the 407 and the tangled offshoots of smaller highways leading in all directions. Light glinted, needles of brightness reflecting off lakes and rivers, only to be succeeded by patches of green and swaths of exposed earth.

Smoke rose in long plumes from lumber mills and incinerators, the lines of civilization following zigzagging shorelines, with the instinct to situate near water for ease of transportation or communication. Below, the grid of roadways divided a patchwork quilt of crops. The terrain looked increasingly hostile the further north they got, though Dan recalled that he and Sandy had had no compunction about exploring whatever they encountered. He often wondered what fate Sandy had endured — wolves or bears, possibly starvation. Any of which could turn out to be the fate of Jeremy Bentham, he reminded himself.

There were still many unanswered questions. Had someone woken the boy and enticed him out of his tent or had he simply wandered off and been taken by waiting opportunists? The campsite was secluded and required a climb over the escarpment, so an unplanned kidnapping was unlikely. In any case, he hadn't cried out. Despite being non-verbal, Janice said, Jeremy was more than capable of voicing his disapproval. Which could mean he wasn't afraid of his captors. But if it was Ramón and Marietta, why bring him to the cave before taking him elsewhere? Nick had informed him that the police were now focusing their attention on the pair. So far, however, all they had was a rosary with a pair of initials on it. There was still no Jeremy. Maybe he'd risen from the cave on the third day and gone off on his own.

A thin trail of smoke floated outside the window, grey wisps buoyed up on a jet stream. Below, the chopper's shadow passed fleetly over trees and rocks. Helicopters could reach around seven thousand metres before the air got too thin. Dan estimated they were flying less than half that, staying well within ground effect.

Looking down, he thought of his father, who'd spent his adult life riding the shaft between the earth's surface and the vein of ore that provided his livelihood. Sudbury had been a mining boomtown back then, a place of hard work, with only the relief of a Saturday night to break up the monotony. It had been a man's world down there, just as it was a man's world up here in the helicopter.

An hour later they were descending. Dan watched the terrain change from low-lying scrub to forested mountains after a brief foray over open water until they touched down near the field where he'd parked while exploring the caves. The blades whirred and slowed as the wind threw everything into turmoil, then came to rest and let it all snap back to life.

They were met by the handler, a tall thin officer with a self-important demeanour. Dan could imagine him running alongside his hounds. The dogs were noisy, excited by the prospect of a chase. The cops introduced themselves before turning to Dan. They joked with one another, but their exchanges with him were humourless. Closing ranks. As an outsider, he was a threat. He would let Nick know, once his rancour died down, that cops treated civilians the way he claimed civilians treated cops: with a scarcely disguised condescension.

No doubt they saw him as a guy who would prefer to do what they did had he made the grade. A wannabe cop. Or could they sense that he'd never want to be part of their insider club? What he lacked wasn't ability, but the instinct to conform. He looked them over. Navy pants and jackets, square-toe boots. Uniform. Meaning *same*. Erasing individuality and encouraging conformity. No, Dan couldn't do that. He sometimes wondered how Nick put his true identity aside each day when he went out the door and became a police officer. But then Nick marched to his own drum.

Dan took them through the undergrowth, sure-footed where they were cautious, uphill and along the trails he'd followed till they came to the cave. It wasn't till he turned to look back that he realized he had a clear sightline to Horace McLean's farm.

"Are you sure this is the right one, sir?" the handler asked, as though he might be smart enough to find a clue they had missed but not smart enough to recognize one cave from another forty-eight hours later.

"I'm sure."

The cop's expression said he wasn't willing to take his word for it. "Can you show us where you found the evidence?"

"Yes, no problem," Dan said, already slipping down into the crevice where a chill blotted out the sun and the day's warmth.

Once Dan and the other cop were in place, the handler followed with his hounds. The dogs moved in a slow frenzy, sniffing the air and baying while scampering unsteadily over the rocks. The sound was almost painful as they took their bearings before clambering back out again.

Outside they rushed in circles, noses to the ground, seemingly at a loss as their handler held out the rosary, encouraging them to find the invisible trail that would take them to where the kidnappers had gone. But each time they stopped dead. It was a short paragraph in a story that didn't continue beyond that page.

When the handler let them sniff Jeremy's kangaroo, however, suddenly they were decisive, baying and bounding over the rocks toward the campsite. The handler followed as the dogs fixated on the trail. When he switched back to the rosary, it was as if the scent had vanished.

"They're not finding the girl," one of the cops told Dan. "But the kid was here for sure. They don't seem to have a problem with that at all."

"It's definitely her scent on the rosary," Dan said. "I can guarantee she was the last person who touched it. I made sure of that."

They followed the dogs down to the water, where Janice and Ashley's tent had been pitched alongside Jeremy's. Yellow tape fluttered between the trees. Blackened ash showed the remains of a fire. A plastic Big Belch cup lay on its side, half melted, yellow and pink stripes running together as though two roads had converged. Dan thought of the fire pit where he and his father had toasted marshmallows.

For a moment he felt a stab of anger against his father, followed by an immediate twinge of regret thinking of how Ked had returned to Centre Island for the first time after eight years. At least Stuart Sharp had attempted some sort of communion between father and son and their shared past, as pathetic as that had been.

They headed back to the cave with the hounds and started over again, but the results were the same. The dogs fixated on Jeremy's scent; Marietta's held no interest for them. The ground was slightly damp. It had rained since Jeremy's disappearance. Then again, dogs were supposed to be able to follow a trail even after torrential downpours.

"Could something have erased the scent? Or disguised it?" Dan asked, thinking of the empty shoeboxes outside Marietta's door. "Like new footwear?"

The handler shrugged. "It would take more than that. It might confuse them a bit to have too many different people coming through here, but if they can't find the girl's scent then that's because she was never here. Smell is like an elixir for them. Straight up, no chaser."

Giving the dogs freedom to run brought them no closer to an answer. They found plenty to sniff and ponder, but Jeremy's scent was all they could fasten onto that afternoon. Again and again it led them back to the campsite, coming and going in both directions.

THIRTEEN

Cagey

NICK SAT AT DAN's kitchen table. His fingers twitched as he gripped his coffee cup. He'd just finished his night shift and was reading over a copy of the police report Lydia had given him to be handled "with utmost discretion."

"In other words, I'm supposed to let you know what's in it without telling her I did," he said, looking up at Dan.

Dan held out a hand. "So let me see it."

"Not so fast," Nick said. "I can't just hand it over to you. Maybe you overheard me reading it." He ran his eyes over the first page. "Marietta Valverde says she gave the rosary to the boy as a keepsake when she was fired." He eyed Dan. "Conclusion: *He* left it in the cave. She was never there." He set the file on the table and shook his head. "You see, this is why you need to leave these things to the police. You showed her the rosary and she immediately began to concoct an explanation for why it was there."

"And you think it would have been different if a police officer asked her first?"

Nick watched him warily. "What are you getting at?"

Dan shrugged. "It seems to me a police officer would have been looking for evidence that proved her guilt. I was just asking a question without anticipating an answer."

"And the difference?"

"The difference is I saw two people who were very uncomfortable with what I showed them even though I had no power over them. They may not have been in that cave, but I guarantee they know something about it, whereas the police saw two people who were afraid of their authority, but have now concluded based on the evidence of a couple of dogs that they can't be guilty."

"So you still think they are?"

"I told you my first thought was that the rosary seemed like a plant. But planted by whom and for what purpose?"

"Maybe they planned the kidnapping but didn't execute it in person and now a third person is trying to double-cross them."

"That's one possible explanation. I'd hang onto that theory for the time being, but I'd still look for another explanation."

Nick frowned. "Like what?"

"I think the boy stole the rosary from Marietta and lost it in the cave. Because clearly, from what the dogs showed us, he was there and she wasn't. That's why she was surprised to see it. He may also have stolen the things that went missing from the house before Janice fired Marietta."

"Why do you think that?"

"When I searched his bedroom, I found a locket hidden under some shirts in his closet. Pretty and shiny, but not expensive. Janice said it was hers and that it had been missing for a month. Ergo, Jeremy stole it."

"Then why not just say that? Why did the nanny tell the police she gave it to the kid?"

"Two reasons: one, because she loves that kid and wants to protect him. Two, because in the Philippines you learn you can't always trust the police. Even if she's lying, there may still be a rational explanation for where the rosary was found. Okay, sure. The kid stole it and the kid dropped it. I can buy that. But she was terrified when I showed it to her even before I said where I found it. She knows something. What about their phone records?"

Nick nodded. "They check out. Same call, same time every week to a sister in Manila. No surprise."

"Exactly my point. If you wanted to concoct an alibi, you'd plan a crime for around that time to make sure you could prove where you were if anyone looked into it. The rosary is the only thing telling us otherwise. On the other hand, Dennis Braithwaite checked into his gym on Saturday evening, but then has no alibi for the rest of the weekend. It's not that all the others have iron-clad alibis, but his seems especially loose."

"What do you make of him?"

"On the surface, he's an up-and-coming exec with promotion written all over him. He's ambitious and gets a check mark for being a good corporate citizen." Dan shrugged. "On the other hand, he says he's over the wife even though he keeps not one but two pictures of her on his desk. Happy memories? Sure, why not. This despite the fact that he refused to help pay for her son's medical treatment."

"You think he's lying about being over her?"

"That's how I read it."

"So his motive could be revenge."

"Or to pressure her to come back. In any case, he's no great shakes as a human being. What about Sarah Nealon, the surrogate?"

"Ankle bracelet report shows she never left town. She couldn't have done it. Even if she managed to remove it, the monitor would show it had been tampered with."

"Okay. Again, no surprise there. How about Eli Gestner's hard-to-find ex–business partner, Elroy James? He still hasn't returned my call. Hong Kong must be keeping him busy."

"There's something about him in the report." Nick flipped through the pages. "Right here. Elroy James. He was out of the city. Montreal. The records check out. Hard to fake, but not impossible. We just got the hotel CCTV footage. We're looking at it."

"He wouldn't have grabbed the kid himself. If he's a criminal then he's got affiliates, that sort of thing."

"Sure. People to do the dirty work for him. His file makes for pretty colourful reading. Numerous charges, but zero convictions. He's got a convincing lawyer."

Dan stood to refill Nick's coffee. Peering over his shoulder, he caught an address in the west end. A four-by-eight photo showed an angry, bullfrog face. The eyes were flat, predatory.

"Is that Elroy? Man, he's ugly."

"Hey!" Nick looked up, surprised. "That's not exactly being discreet."

"Tell Lydia I couldn't restrain myself," Dan said, grabbing his car keys. "Make sure you get some sleep. You look rough."

Elroy James's house was tucked among a row of warehouses, sandwiched between a welder and a stone cutter who specialized in grave markers. Angels danced alongside marble urns under the gaze of sad-eyed saints.

The property was fenced in by an electrified grid, with security cameras placed strategically around the front and back. Dan passed it by then parked and watched from down the block. No lights showed from outside.

He waited fifteen minutes before driving around to a rear laneway. The house was tall, with a single window high up near the roof and a basement walkout directly below. A long, narrow hut sat near the back. On most city properties it would have served as a garage. Only this one lacked a door.

An in-law cottage? Possibly.

Dan drove past and parked a block away. Stuffing a pair of gloves in his pocket, he headed down the lane on foot till he reached the welder's yard. From inside came the hiss of acetylene flames and loud banging. He sauntered along, thinking of something to explain his presence, but no one challenged him.

Emboldened, he made his way farther down till he stood between the warehouse and the fence. He could see Elroy James's house clearly. The windows on the lower levels were covered in tinfoil. Two more cameras pointed along the near side. Clearly, Elroy had faith in security surveillance. *Always a way around that*, Dan thought.

Halfway down the lane he spotted a tree that had grown through the wire, obscuring the view near the back. He reached out with a gloved hand. No sparks. He pulled. Two nails popped from the tree trunk. The fencing opened wide enough for him to slip inside.

The hut was solidly built, with just one window on the yard side and a padlocked door facing the house. Despite being in the heart of the city, it felt isolated. It would, in fact, make a perfect bunker to hide something in. A four-year-old boy, for instance.

Dan made his way toward it, listening for sounds from inside. Nothing. He tapped gently on the wall. To his surprise, he heard movement, something secretive and surreptitious. It lasted a few seconds then stopped.

He knocked again, only louder. The sounds were repeated. This time Dan heard someone throw themselves against the wall in response. It occurred to him it might be Jeremy, unable to respond verbally. Or possibly gagged.

He was tempted to leave and contact the police. To explain his actions he could say he'd heard a cry for help, but if someone in the house had seen his approach the hut would be empty by the time they returned.

He tapped a third time. Now there was a frenzy within. Emboldened, he went to the window and peered in, but pulled back immediately as a large dark shape leapt at him. Massive paws crawled over glass and a pink mouth bared a ferocious set of teeth that would have torn him apart had they reached him.

His heart thudded, but only an eerie silence emanated from inside the walls.

I know why the caged bird sings, he told himself, *but why doesn't the caged dog bark?*

"It was a very large Doberman," he told Nick when he got back to his car. "Gigantic. He keeps it locked in a small cottage on the back of his property."

"And this is where I tell you off for being such an idiot for getting close to it."

He could almost hear Nick glowering over the phone.

"Yeah, there's that," Dan said. "What I can't quite figure out is why it wasn't making any sounds apart from moving around when I knocked on the walls. How come I didn't hear barking? Is there such a thing as completely soundproof glass?"

Nick thought it over. "It probably had its vocal cords snipped. It's a drug-dealer special. A lethal weapon if ever there was one. No one would hear it coming."

"Scary."

"And you're sure no one saw you?"

"Not as far as I could tell. Sorry for disturbing your sleep."

"Sure. Now get the hell away from there."

"I like it when you're bossy."

FOURTEEN

Panic

He was nearly home when his cell rang.

"Sharp."

It was Janice. Dan heard panic in her voice.

"He called again."

"He?"

"Yes, this time I'm certain. That distortion thing was still on, but every once in a while I could make out the tones of a male voice."

Dan didn't contradict her, though he knew the point of a voice modulator was to make unrecognizable whatever came through it.

"What was the message?"

"I have till nine this evening. Then there'll be another call telling us how to make a donation. In cash. He actually said 'make a donation.'" The panic was back. "But I still haven't got the money!"

"Okay, try to keep calm. That gives you" — he looked at his watch — "ten hours. I'll come over now."

†

Ashley let him in. Janice and Eli were in the kitchen, their faces sombre. The phone sat on the table. A quick call to the provider confirmed that the number was untraceable.

"Was there any kind of threat mentioned if you don't come up with the money?"

Janice shook her head. "No, but I guess that's implied, isn't it?"

"Yes, it's implied. But so far nobody has actually said they want money for Jeremy's release, just that they want you to make a donation. Is that correct?"

Janice looked at him, eyes wide. "Essentially, yes."

"Not that it will make any difference if kidnapping is proved."

Eli stared at him. "What are you saying?"

"I'm saying they're avoiding any reference to this being a crime. Nobody has ever actually said that they have your son."

"What do you mean?" He sounded on the verge of tears. "Whoever it is has to have him!"

"I have no doubt of that," Dan replied, "but all we're dealing with here, technically speaking, is someone asking for money. It could be a political party asking for private donations or a charity asking for a contribution. In which case, nobody has done anything illegal."

"But why?" Eli demanded. "What is this all about?"

"I don't know," Dan admitted. "It's all very curious. Did you hear the conversation?"

Eli nodded. "We all heard it. It was on speaker."

"Any chance it could have been your former business partner, Elroy?"

"I — don't think so."

Dan heard the hesitation, but whether it was from actual doubt or fear of pointing the finger at Elroy wasn't clear.

"What about an associate or friend of Elroy's? It could have been someone calling for him."

Eli shook his head. "I have no idea. I never met his associates."

"Did anyone tape the call?"

Janice shook her head. "No. We didn't authorize it with the police."

"We said minimal interference. For Jeremy's safety." It was Ashley who spoke.

"Okay. How did you leave things with the caller?" Dan asked.

"When he asked if I had the money I said it was coming." Janice fought back tears. "Only it's not true. When I went to the bank, they said it could take a couple of weeks to approve the second mortgage. I asked about a line of credit, but they turned me down when I told them how much I wanted. I couldn't tell them why I needed it." She looked imploringly at him. "This is where we really need your help."

"How?"

"I spoke to my mother last night. I think she was on the verge of giving me the money, but she said we should resist the demands. I told her if we resist then Jeremy will never come home. To her, he's barely real. She's never even met him. I think if you come with me she'll understand this is for real and that it's the only way to negotiate with kidnappers."

"You realize that paying them doesn't guarantee you will get your son back?"

"What else can we do?" Janice wailed. "We've got no other options."

"All right," Dan said. "I will come with you to talk to your mother. Just tell me what you'd like me to say."

Janice's eyes narrowed. "You can say she owes me, the selfish bitch."

Eli and Ashley watched uncomfortably.

"I doubt that will help convince her," Dan said. "I seldom find that family debts are repaid in the way we want them to be."

Janice teared up again. "I'm sorry. I shouldn't have said that."

"Call her now and tell her you're coming over in an hour. Once she gives you the money, we still need to discuss how you're going to deliver it to the kidnappers."

"Won't someone just tell us what how to do it?"

"Presumably they will have it worked out. But it would give you some leverage to ask to see some proof they have Jeremy before handing over the cash."

"You mean he won't just be there when we pay?" Eli asked.

"Probably not. It would be too risky for the kidnappers to have Jeremy with them."

Janice looked startled. "Then how —?"

"You tell them you want assurance that Jeremy is alive. Once you know he's all right, you agree to make the drop."

"How will I know he's all right if I can't see him?"

"They might put him on the phone."

"He doesn't talk!"

Dan smacked his forehead. "Sorry — I wasn't thinking. Then they might agree to put him in front of a camera. Skype, maybe. Although that would risk leaving their location open to tracking, so they might not agree."

"And if they don't?"

"Then we play it their way." He waited. "The most you can hope for is that they keep the location public, but chances are you won't have a choice. If it's just a cash handover, anything can happen. It could be dangerous. Unless they specify who makes the drop, I will do it. But you have to do everything they say."

FIFTEEN

Beauty

DAN WAS SURPRISED TO LEARN that Janice's mother lived at Harbourfront in a condo not far from Nick's. In fairy tales, beauty queens lived in inaccessible castles on mountain tops. But this was a modern version of the story. And where Nick's building was modest, Clarice Bentham's was palatial.

The guard who challenged him when he drove up to the gate looked like an overgrown Brazilian muscle boy minus the beach. He squared his shoulders and made it clear this was his territory. It was like getting into an embassy.

He scowled at Dan, prepared to resist all inquiries, but his expression turned to pleasure when Janice's face appeared in the window.

"Hey, Lou!"

"Miss Bentham! Didn't see you there. Just a moment."

He turned back and made a show of pushing a button that lifted a flimsy bar any car could have driven through without much effort. But it was the show that counted, Dan knew.

"Good to see you again, Miss Bentham," Lou said as they rolled past his small hut.

Dan counted three Porsches and four Jaguars on the first parking level. He snagged the last visitor spot and followed Janice up to the lobby, where she was recognized by desk staff and buzzed in without question.

In the elevator, she turned to him. "My mother has a strong personality. Please be ready for anything she throws at you."

"Most of my clients have strong personalities," Dan said. "I'll do my best."

The doors opened onto a subdued hallway with soft greys predominating. It managed to suggest epic proportions without being overly intimidating. Dan followed her to the single door on that floor.

He was surprised when a maid wearing an actual maid's uniform answered Janice's knock.

"Hello, Eunice. I'm here to see my mother."

"Yes, Miss Janice. Your mother is waiting." Her expression was restrained. She held out a hand, indicating a long hallway to the right.

Dan followed Janice down the corridor, past an oversized portrait of a woman with boyish grey hair and startling blue eyes that seemed to catch everything in their gaze. The hand-drawn eyebrows and sculpted cheekbones suggested an advertising campaign by a modern-day Rembrandt. At the bottom Dan caught a name: *Francesco Scavullo*. Donny would have had a thing or two to say about that, he knew.

Janice reached out and touched the wall, caressing its rich brocade.

"Hello, home," she said softly.

They moved on past poster-sized portraits, advertisements with blush sticks and eyeliner pencils placed cunningly alongside the models' faces. Each bore the legend, *Clarice Magna — la belleza cuesta!* One of the faces looked familiar, but Dan had no time to examine it closely.

They entered a room facing the lake. A woman stood with her back to them, gazing outward. She turned. It was the woman in the Scavullo portrait, looking much the same as in the photograph, except she was even more commanding in person.

"Janice."

The voice was soft. Dan couldn't read her expression. She could have been quietly angry or simply stating a fact: *This is my daughter come to ask for money.*

"Mom."

The older woman approached and hugged her daughter. Her shoulders slumped. Years of pride seemed to evaporate in the gesture.

"It's been too long."

"I know. I'm sorry." Janice wiped a tear from her cheek.

Clarice Bentham turned to Dan. "Who is this?"

"Mother, this is —"

"I'm Dan Sharp. I'm here to help your daughter facilitate the ransom transfer. I understand you've agreed to put the money in her hands."

The older woman shook her head. "I haven't agreed to anything yet."

Dan nodded to a table where a large hat box sat wrapped. The motif: red poppies bound with yellow ribbons. *La Belleza Cuesta*. "I must be mistaken. I thought that was the money there."

Anger flitted across Clarice's face before being replaced with something that might have been admiration.

"You're correct. That is the money. If it leaves here — and I haven't yet decided whether it will — I have a man who will be going with Janice."

"No — this can only be done one way and there's no room for a third person. I will accompany your daughter and make the arrangements."

Her eyebrows shot up. "It's my money and it will be done my way."

"Then you will be responsible for the death of your only grandson. A grandson I understand you haven't even met." Dan turned. "Good day."

She let him reach the doorway.

"Wait."

Dan turned, his look focused directly on her. "There's no time to waste. You need to decide now."

"Let me speak." She looked him up and down as though assessing his ability to complete the task. "What assurance do I have that you can do what you're saying?"

"The fact that I'm even here should tell you I intend to do the job I've taken on. If you want to read my professional qualifications, your daughter can direct you to my website."

"It's a lot of money."

"And your grandson has only one life. It's a gamble, but I suggest you go through with it. There is a deadline of nine o'clock tonight for Janice to have the cash in hand."

"Tonight?" For the first time her voice faltered. She looked sharply at Janice. Her daughter obviously hadn't informed her of the fine print.

Janice nodded. "Yes, it has to be tonight."

Clarice reached out a hand to her. "Will you be there?"

Janice looked at Dan. "Mr. Sharp and I will go together."

"And what will happen then?"

"Mother, we don't know. We aren't the ones running this operation. I'm grateful that Mr. Sharp — Dan — is going to do this for us."

"And where does all this take place?"

Dan stepped forward. "You can't know that, Mrs. Bentham. But I will agree to the exchange only so long as it's done safely."

"Meaning?"

"Meaning no vigilante operations. It has to be a straightforward handover of the money — hopefully in return for the boy. No weapons."

"What if the kidnapper brings a gun?"

"I assume he will. But I also assume a kidnapper does not want to become a murderer, so unless someone does something desperate, he won't use it."

Her eyes flashed with concern. "Can you guarantee that Janice and Jeremy will be safe?"

"I can guarantee I will do my utmost to protect them."

"Even if it means risking your own life?"

Dan wondered if her concern was for the money or the safety of all involved. Perhaps both, if he were to be charitable.

"Yes."

"Mom, please! We need to do this now."

Clarice Bentham sighed. Emotion flitted across her face.

"Just be careful."

"I will."

Dan picked up the box and tucked it under his arm. The maid reappeared and held out a hand indicating the hallway they'd entered by. Janice turned back to look at her mother.

"Thank you," she said.

"Take it — it will all be yours one day. All that and more."

Janice nodded. "I'll call to let you know what happens."

In the elevator on the way down Janice slumped against the wall. She breathed with relief.

"You handled her perfectly. How did you know what to say?"

"Practice," Dan said.

SIXTEEN

Ransom

THE HAT BOX SAT ON THE KITCHEN TABLE, two full cups of coffee beside it and a third cup nearly empty. The tablecloth was a colourful Mexican weave, long streamers of red and purple flung outward from its centre. Like fireworks or artillery flares. Explosive. Dangerous.

"I've never seen a million dollars all in one place before," Eli said excitedly. "It's actually quite impressive looking."

"Well, don't get used to it," Janice snapped. "It won't be around long."

He screwed up his face. "All right — relax! I won't." He waited a while then asked, "How's your mother, by the way?"

"Still a cunt. By the way."

They all sat around trying to ignore the telephone that adamantly refused to ring. Ashley's eyes went back and forth between the other two. Her taciturn demeanour was overshadowed by the constant bickering between Janice and Eli. It made them seem more like fractious siblings than friends.

Eli pulled out a joint and turned to Dan. "Do you mind?"

"Go ahead."

"Cool." He lit the joint and held it out to Ashley. "Ash?"

She shook her head. "Not me."

"I'll have some," Janice said.

He passed it to Janice, who toked then handed it back without a word.

Dan watched him closely. "You never said what your business deal was with Elroy."

Eli looked over. "Do you have to ask?"

"I don't. I just wondered why you never told me."

Eli shrugged. "It's not something I'm proud of."

The smoke rose in loopy, blue-grey strands around his head.

"What went wrong?"

"They caught the stuff at the border. It never got here. I set it up. Elroy pitched in half. I lost my money and his. It was one of those stupid things you agree to in the moment then regret later."

Eli took a final toke then stabbed out the joint. He stood and wandered restlessly around, looking in cupboards and corners.

Janice glared. "Eli!"

He whirled as though he'd been struck. "What?"

"Sit down and be patient."

He looked warily at the chair he'd just abandoned. "Why?"

"Because you're making us all nervous."

"I don't care! This is making me crazy."

He sat anyway then popped up again after five seconds and turned on the TV, muting it as the images streamed into the room. News, weather, sports. Nobody spoke. Their nervousness was palpable.

Silence invaded the room. The three of them were glued to their phones, tapping and scrolling incessantly. It was catching. Dan checked his own phone before sending off a note to Ked saying he'd be home late and not to wait up. His son responded immediately: *Got it, Dad. I won't wait! Have fun whatever you're doing.*

They had been sitting around for nearly half an hour when Eli lifted his head and looked at Dan. "Is it all right if we order a pizza?"

Dan gave him a curious look. "Sure. Go ahead."

"Any preferences?"

"I'm fine, thanks," Dan said.

He'd heard of the self-absorption of millennials, but he couldn't for the life of him imagine what it would be like to be the autistic child of such parents.

Eli turned to his phone and dialed. There was a bit of inadvertent comedy as he kept getting put on hold. Finally, after a good deal of pot-addled confusion, he placed his order. They sat back and waited.

After another minute, Eli cast a baleful eye at the others. "What do we do if he doesn't call?" he asked no one in particular.

"Then we don't do anything," Janice explained, like a harassed mother to a difficult child. "We can't do anything until he phones." She rolled her eyes at Dan as though to say, *You see what I put up with?*

"I meant, what do we do with the money? We can't just keep it here all night."

"We'll worry about that when it happens," Janice snapped.

Silence took over the room again as the three turned back to their screens. It seemed only a few minutes later when the doorbell rang. There was a moment of panic before they realized it was the pizza delivery.

"I've got it," Janice said, and headed to the door brandishing a credit card.

A minute later the smell of warm pizza flooded the room. Janice pushed the money aside and placed the Domino's box on the table, lifting the cover. Dan was struck by how casual they were. As if there weren't a million dollars sitting in the house. As if a child's life wasn't at stake.

"Pepperoni and mushrooms." Janice looked around at the others. "Who wants a slice?"

"I think everyone does," Eli responded, with a look to Dan.

"I'm good," Dan said.

Janice brought out plates, passing the box around. They ate in silence, barely looking at one another.

A phone pinged. Licking her fingers, Janice picked up her cell. Her expression turned from curiosity to terror.

"Oh, shit!" She dropped the phone.

Dan reached across the table and grabbed it. A text message lit up the screen. *We're playing with the lions. Come and join us. Bring presents.* The screen went dark.

"They're at Lion's Head," Dan said.

The others crowded around.

"What number is it from?" Eli asked.

"It doesn't matter. It'll be untraceable. Prepaid phone, prepaid minutes. You won't catch them that way. The signal will be traceable only when it's on, which is going to be minimal. Once they text you, they'll turn it off again. After they use it a few times they'll throw it away and buy a new phone."

Dan called Nick, who phoned back a minute later to confirm that the number was untraceable. All eyes were on Dan.

"It's to be expected," he said. "They'll do everything they can to get you to deliver the money while evading any sort of trace. It only makes sense. They didn't come this far only to invite capture."

Eli shot Dan a baleful look. "Why do you keep saying 'they'?"

"This is a coordinated effort and that generally means there's more than one person behind it." He nodded to the box of money. "For now, let's just make sure Jeremy gets home safely."

"Yes, that's all that matters," Janice said.

"What you do next is of the utmost importance." Dan eyed the others. "From now on you need to do everything they ask. No surprises, just submission to their demands. That means heading up to the Bruce Peninsula tonight. Who's coming and who's staying here?"

"We're all coming," Janice said without hesitation.

The others nodded.

"All right. Grab whatever you need. We'll take two cars. It might be too late to find a motel, so we may have to sleep in them."

"We can stay at the cottage," Janice said. "Screw Dennis. I still have a key."

"We should still take two cars," Dan said. "In case we need to split up at any point."

"Why don't you and Eli go in your car? Ashley and I will go in ours." Janice looked at her. "Are you okay to drive?"

"Of course," said Ashley.

Janice gave Dan the address. "So do we try to drive side by side or just meet you up there?"

"I may be a little fast," Dan said. "Let's meet up there."

Eli looked as though he was trying to clear his head. "Let's do it," he said.

Dan picked up the hat box by the handles. "I'll take the ransom."

He texted Nick as he was leaving: *I'm off again for another day at least. Sorry to abandon you.* His phone rang a few seconds later. He turned off the ringer. Nick would have to forgive him.

Ten minutes later they were on the highway, heading north.

SEVENTEEN

Things That Go Bump in the Night

Dan kept sight of Janice's car in his rear-view mirror until they reached the 401. After that, he lost them. Eli was silent till they were out of the city. His buzz seemed to be wearing off. His words came slowly, ruminatively.

"You have a kid, right?" he asked, looking over at Dan.

"Yes," Dan said. "A teenage son. He's in university now."

"Did you ever think he wouldn't get there? Or maybe that you wouldn't live long enough to see it?"

"Sure," Dan said. "That sort of thing passes through every parent's mind, I think. It's not rational, but you stop and consider it once in a while. Then you move on and trust that it will happen."

"I think about it all the time."

"You'll get there," Dan said. "And you'll get Jeremy back."

"He still won't go to university. His prognosis isn't good." He trailed off and looked out the window. "It's expensive to treat autism. The government programs are useless. We had to put him in a special school. It costs. A lot."

"It can't be easy," Dan said.

"You know what I think?"

"What's that?"

"It's just …" His voice trailed off. After a while he said, "This ransom. We have to do it, right? You're helpless when a kid needs you. It's the ultimate love. I was completely selfish before Jeremy, but now it's as if nothing else matters. Is that how you feel about your son? I mean, still?"

"Still," Dan said. "No matter what else is happening in my life, I always think of Kedrick."

"Jeremy's a beautiful boy. Smart and funny. Once you get to know him, you see that. He responds to you. He really does. And your heart goes out to him. I'd do anything for him." He paused. "I think sometimes I love him more for his troubles. It breaks my heart to think he'll never have a normal life."

"I can understand that."

"You just want so much for them. You want everything for them." He took a deep breath. "And Janice too. I sometimes think it's my fault Jeremy has ASD. Genes, you know? They say there are between two hundred and four hundred genes responsible for the disorder."

"Chances are only half of them are yours. Does Janice blame you?"

"No, thank god. It's just my way to take the blame for things. Not smart, I know." He laughed lightly. "Even back when we were kids, Janice was always a hell-raiser. I used to take the blame for her. She got me in far more trouble than I can remember."

Silence took over, broken only by the humming of the car.

"What are you going to do about Elroy?" Dan finally asked. "To pay him off?"

Eli sighed. "Jesus — he threatened me with a knife. He said he would cut off my balls and I'd never have another kid. Not that I want to. One's enough. But I've got a plan." He trailed off again.

Dan looked over to see him slumped against the side of the car, eyes closed. He preferred him asleep, so he kept the car steady so as not to wake him. After twenty minutes, he turned his phone back on. Nick's message was waiting: *What the fuck, Dan! I hate it when you vanish like that. I want to know what's happening.* Dan smiled. He'd said he wanted to feel possessed by Nick and that's what he was getting.

There was nothing but empty highway for the next two hours. Darkness followed darkness, with a burst of light now and then as a town slid past. Farther north, his hometown would be one of those ghostly glows in the distance. He'd never go back, apart from the odd visit. *Leave it in the past,* he always said. *Like an old love. If you drag it into the present it will destroy what good there is and sour what's still to come.* Did anyone outrun their demons?

Behind him, flashes of lightning lit up the sky like a fire-breathing dragon, then vanished again. Nothing more than a conjuring effect, a magic trick. Sleight-of-hand. *An autistic child gets up in the middle of the night and vanishes in a dark wood. Where does he go?*

The rain started when they were half an hour south of Owen Sound, coming down in sheets. He was going too fast, hydroplaning all the way. With each flash of lightning he saw how nature tortured itself, fire cauterizing the rocks and trees, wipers slashing at the rain.

Half an hour to go.

The Bruce was a very different place by night, distinctly different from the city. Instead of cars and buses flanked by the facades of condos and office towers, here there was dense forest, a fog-bound coastline, the rush and claw of the water and its impenetrable depths.

The giant arms of the turbines rose and fell in the darkness, flailing endlessly just before he turned onto Cemetery Road. Dan checked his watch. Once again he'd made it in under three hours. Not bad driving considering.

Passing the McLean farm, he saw lights at the far end of the driveway. It looked as though Horace kept late hours, but then he was more of a hobby farmer, Dan reminded himself. Strawberries and daisies.

Dennis's place lay just up ahead. He found the sign on the mailbox and turned into the drive. Eli slept on.

The cottage was set back from the road, surrounded by pines and elms. Lion's Head crested in the distance, its bulk a long dark outline against the sky. He heard the water close by.

The other car showed up ten minutes later, its headlights flashing up the drive behind him. Ashley was a good driver too, it turned out. Dan woke Eli, who seemed surprised to find himself there already.

Janice let them in. The place was spartan but comfortable. Dan had expected more of a show from a wealthy investment banker; then again, maybe this was the other side of Dennis Braithwaite.

Once they were inside, Dan examined the lock. It was sturdy enough.

"Is this the only door?" he asked.

Ashley's eyes grew wide. "Do you think someone might try to get in?"

"Just being sure," Dan said. "I don't like surprises."

They watched as he went room to room, examining everything, opening closets and looking around before returning to the main room.

"I'm going to put the money right here," he said, placing the box on the floor beneath the table.

The others followed him with their eyes.

"That way we'll know where it is at all times. I'm not anticipating any danger. I doubt anyone will try to steal it before we deliver it, unless they suspect a double-cross and want to take charge of things early to surprise us."

"How would they even know we're here?" Janice asked.

"It's possible there's a trace on your phone."

"Are you kidding me?" Janice wailed. "This is crazy!"

"It's best to be safe."

"Great." She slumped into an easy chair. "What do we do?"

"We need to set a watch." He pointed to the couch. Beside it was a side table covered in magazines. "We'll all take a turn. When it's your turn you simply sit on the couch and read. If you see or hear anything the least bit odd, you wake me. Got it?"

They all nodded, wide-eyed, like children being told a ghost story.

"Who's first?" Eli asked.

"I'll go first, unless anyone has objections," Dan said.

"I'm good with that," Janice said.

Dan checked his watch. "It's past midnight. You should get as much sleep as you can."

"No argument with that," Eli said.

They were all exhausted from the drive and the adrenaline rush that had by now subsided. Janice and Ashley took the bedroom at the front; Eli and Dan each claimed a room at the back.

Dan waited till the others had gone to bed then sat on the couch. An article on teeth whitening came closest to having an appeal of all the reading material within reach. Most of the magazines were fitness-oriented. *Not surprising,* Dan thought, remembering Dennis Braithwaite's well-honed physique.

The wind had increased. After a while, Dan put the magazine down and turned off the light. From time to time, lightning crept into the room. He watched the glow as it crept up his arms and torso, as though he were a ghost appearing out of the ether.

He was tempted to text Nick to say they'd arrived safely, but without saying where. In the end he decided against it. It was always at the back of his mind that with all the technology at his disposal Nick might succumb to the temptation to track him.

Just before two, he knocked on Eli's door. Eli came out scratching his beard and looking bewildered. His eyes were stark and his skin splotchy. Dan couldn't shake the notion that he was still an adolescent.

"Can you do this?" he asked.

"I can do it." Eli nodded.

"All right. You can wake one of the women in two hours. Remember — if you hear anything, call me."

Dan headed to his room. He hung his shirt on the back of the door but left his pants and shoes on. He caught a glimpse of himself in the mirror. Sleek, no extra flesh. His chest was hard, his shoulders pronounced and bony. He wished now he'd had a bite of that pizza. Breakfast was a long way off.

He stretched out on the bed and looked at his watch. A lone mosquito buzzed across the luminous dial. Outside, the leaves made a shushing sound. His head dropped onto the pillow, but he knew sleep wouldn't come. It promised to be an exhausting night.

An hour went by. He hadn't heard a thing from the front room. When he looked out, Eli was sitting up reading with his back to Dan. *Good for you,* Dan thought. *You stayed awake after all.*

He lay back down with his arms behind his head. He was just drifting off when a splintering sound sent him bolt upright. For a moment, he held completely still and listened. Outside, the wind thrashed around the eaves. Something thudded against the cabin wall. He was out of bed and racing for the living room.

Eli looked up, stunned. "What's going on?"

"I don't know. It came from outside."

A moment later, Janice and Ashley emerged from their room.

"Stay here. I'll go out," Dan said.

"I'll come with you," Eli said.

"No, you're still the watch. Keep your eyes on the box. I'll call if I need you."

Rain lashed his face and chest as he opened the door and headed out. At first there was nothing to see. Then he saw a branch fallen across the drive, just missing his car. It would have to be moved before they could leave.

He came back in, dripping rain. The box was still beneath the table.

"It's okay," he told the others, who stood watching anxiously. "Just a branch. It came down in the storm."

"I was sure someone had come for us," Eli said.

Dan shook his head. "We're safe," he said, though he wasn't as certain of that as he would have liked. "Everybody okay?"

"Of course. We're fine," Ashley said.

Janice rolled her eyes. "Ashley's fearless. But I'm terrified. "

"If you want, I can stay up the rest of the night and let you get some rest."

"No," Janice said. "You need to rest too."

"All right then," Dan said, heading back to the bedroom.

This time he removed his pants and shoes.

EIGHTEEN

Deliverance

Morning brought a sharp knock at the door. Dan leapt out of bed, cursing his lack of foresight as he raced out of the room wearing only his boxers. Ashley glanced up from the couch with a curious expression just as Janice and Eli exited from their rooms.

"Who knows we're here?" Janice demanded.

Dan pulled the door open. Horace stood on the step holding a large tote bag.

"Thought that was your car, Daniel of the Lions."

"Horace. Good morning." He felt absurdly naked.

His expression must have been comical. Horace laughed a belly laugh. "Didn't mean to scare you!"

"No, of course not. What brings you up here?"

"Saw you folks had a branch down. Just being neighbourly."

"Right," Dan said, trying to make sense of things. "It came down last night in the storm."

"Lost a couple myself. If you want, I can come around with the tractor and help haul it from the driveway."

Dan looked over at the fallen limb. It seemed less daunting by daylight. "Thanks. I think we can manage."

Horace glanced inside past Dan and caught sight of Janice and Ashley. Eli stood beside them, all three staring out at the farmer.

"Hi, Horace," Janice said timidly, holding her dressing gown together by the edges.

"Ah, the young misses." His manner softened. "I saw young Daniel's car here and thought I'd bring him some fresh eggs and homemade bread, plus a few leftover strawberries. Season's long done, of course."

He held out the bag. Dan took it from him.

"Thank you, Horace. It's still a bit early for us."

"I understand." He looked disappointed, as though he'd expected to be invited in for coffee. "I won't bother you folks. I hope things are okay. That boy of yours come back?"

Janice shook her head without speaking.

"No, of course not. Excuse my speaking out of turn. But he will." He raised a finger. "'Can any hide himself in secret places that I shall not see him?' Jeremiah 23:24."

Janice stepped onto the porch and grasped his hand, squeezing it. "I never got a chance to thank you properly before, but I am so grateful for your help."

"It's my pleasure, miss. I won't keep you. Enjoy those eggs."

He turned and walked away, a forlorn figure hobbling down the drive.

"Thank you, Horace," Dan called after him.

He shut the door and stood there holding up the bag. The others were watching.

"Creepy," Ashley said.

"Who was that?" Eli asked.

"That was the farmer who rescued me after I fell on my way back to the parking lot," Janice said.

Eli made a face. "That was him?"

"Him," Janice echoed. "A strange man."

Dan looked out the window. Horace had reached the end of the driveway. He turned and waved.

"Very strange," Eli agreed.

Dan emptied the bag, placing the eggs in a bowl and a pint of berries on the table alongside a loaf of bread.

"At least we have breakfast," he said. "I'm glad to see we all made it through the night. Did you check to see if there were more texts?"

"I checked," Janice said with a shiver. "Nothing yet. This is crazy."

Ashley put an arm around her. "We'll get through it. Jeremy will be home soon."

"I hope so."

Janice sat at one end of the couch, contracting her body and wrapping her arms around her knees like a child.

"I suggest we all eat so we're prepared for whatever the day brings," Dan said, nodding to the table.

A Bible-quoting, egg-delivering farmer and a two-and-three-quarter-hour ride across the country in a rainstorm to deliver a hat box full of money. Nothing makes any sense here, he thought. But he was prepared to see it through at any cost, short of loss of life. Maybe it would all make sense afterward.

He went to his room and dressed while the others fixed breakfast. When he returned they ate in silence, their expressions set, then cleared the dishes.

Afterward, Dan went out to survey the branch lying across the drive. There was a dent in the siding where it had fallen against the cottage. He grabbed an end and pulled. At first it resisted then suddenly swung around and moved slowly, a foot at a time.

At last he had it pushed aside so it no longer blocked the drive. It was only when he turned back to the car that he saw the envelope tucked under the wiper.

Thinking about it later, he was sure it hadn't been there in the middle of the night when he went out to check for damage. Someone had taken a big risk leaving it.

The note was addressed to Jeremy Bentham in a childish purple scrawl. Crayon. Dan brought it in and laid it on the table.

The others stood watching as he slit it open with a knife, taking care to keep his fingerprints off the surfaces. *Donations go to 36 Whippoorwill Road. Eight thirty sharp.* And a smiley face.

Dan looked at his watch. It was ten past eight. They still had time.

Eli and Janice looked surprised, but Ashley was angry. "Who the hell could do this?" she demanded of no one in particular.

Dan's mind was racing. "Who knew we were here?"

"That farmer did," Ashley said.

Janice put a hand to her mouth. "I texted Dennis last night, just in case he might be at the cottage. I didn't tell him why we were coming, just that I needed it for one night. He said it was okay."

Eli turned to Dan. "You said yesterday you thought Janice's phone might be tapped. Do you still think that?"

"Anything is possible," Dan said. "The kidnappers know her number. The fact that she even texted to say where we were going could have tipped someone off."

"This is unbelievable," Janice said. "I feel so vulnerable and exposed."

"That's how they want you to feel," Dan said.

Eli set the hat box on the table then sat and watched it, as though afraid it might disappear if he took his eyes off it.

"Shall we?" Dan asked.

"We're ready," Janice said.

"We'll go in my car." Dan hefted the box. For a moment, he thought it felt lighter, though he couldn't have said for sure. "Have you counted it?"

"My mother wouldn't lie," Janice said.

"Then let's go."

The town of Lion's Head hugged a natural harbour at the base of the peninsula. Its population, under a thousand during the peninsula's cold, squally winters, swelled to far greater numbers than it could contain with the influx of tourists each summer. The grey-white cliffs unfurled along the promontory, providing a backdrop to the town.

Traffic slowed noticeably as they approached the town limits and passed a makeshift cabin that constituted the local LCBO. Dan tried to recall if it had been there when he was a boy. More likely back then you would have had to drive south to Owen Sound or north to Tobermory for alcohol. The good old days, when Sunday shopping was illegal and bootleggers did their best business after hours.

There was always an eager entrepreneur waiting to make a buck on someone else's backward laws.

The downtown core bustled and crackled with people heading to the marina and its rows of tethered masts. Here, all roads ended at the water. Dan turned onto Whippoorwill Road. The street sign was riddled with holes. It might have been a woodpecker's dream or somebody's idea of a shooting gallery.

The pavement curved out of sight up ahead, but the promontory across the way stayed with them as they drove. Janice began to call out lot numbers as they passed. Some of the lots were empty and overgrown with weeds and evergreens. Dan slowed as the numbers increased, keeping an eye out for signs they were being followed. So far, nothing seemed out of the ordinary.

He didn't recognize it at first. But there was something about the curve in the road and how it gave onto a view of the bay. Even then he still wasn't sure till they were passing the drive and he saw the outhouse with the sun and crescent moon carved into the door. Some things stayed with you forever. For Dan, that was one of them.

He still recalled that final trip with his parents. The details came back effortlessly. On the fourth day there'd been an argument — over what he was never sure. The result was that they were leaving immediately. *This very moment!* his mother screamed. *Get your things and get ready, Danny. His royal highness wants to go home, so we're going home.*

That morning on their walk Sandy had stopped to sniff at something on the ridge behind the cottage. When Dan called him he'd taken off, enjoying his little game of hide and seek. He'd done it before and always showed up later, but now here was his mother telling him to get his things as his father packed the car.

"Sandy's not back yet," Dan wailed.

It had been a mistake to defy his father.

"We're going with or without that damned dog," Stuart Sharp declared. "Too stupid to know what's good for it. And that's final."

Dan packed slowly, pretending to forget where he'd put one thing or another. Every now and then he went to the window and whistled, hoping Sandy would hear. But Sandy hadn't returned by the time they were ready to leave. Against Dan's protests, his father gunned the motor and headed down the road.

Dan felt a sickness in his gut as he cried silently in the back seat. His dog was out there somewhere in the bush behind them, only he didn't know where.

It was the last time he saw Sandy. Then, just after Christmas, his mother had died. Both of them gone. Now here he was back again. For a moment he held his breath, feeling the same tension in the pit of his stomach, the remnants of the cottage floating past as the car headed around the curve.

Number 36 lay just up ahead, a white, family-style cabin with a wraparound porch. The drive was obscured with tree branches. Dan parked on the side of the road. For a moment no one moved. They all sat there looking at it.

"I'll check it out," Dan said. "I want you all to wait here."

"What about Jeremy?" Janice asked.

"He won't be here," Dan said. "They'll be keeping him somewhere safe till they get the money."

He stepped out and shut the car door, looking carefully around as he headed up the drive. The air was still. Nothing moved in the morning's slowly accumulating heat. He climbed the stairs and tried the door handle. It opened easily onto a darkened interior. He stepped inside. The place smelled as though it had been shut up for years.

It was a shadowy world cut off from everything. Time, people, places. As if it existed on its own, beyond good or bad. He turned at the sound of footsteps following behind him on the stairs.

Eli came up carrying the hat box. "This it?" he asked softly, as though afraid of being overheard.

Dan resisted the urge to snap at him for disobeying his order. Instead, he said simply, "Looks like it."

They wandered from room to room. In the kitchen, avocado-coloured appliances gleamed. Seventies retro. With a start Dan realized these were originals, barely touched. Mint condition. Somehow, the past had stood still. It was as though he were four again.

They waited there, hardly daring to breathe. The feeling was intimate, like being so close to another person you felt the warmth of their breath on your skin. The silence pressed in, suffocating where it should have felt comforting.

Dan couldn't shake the sense that someone might suddenly spring out from a closet or behind a closed door. A note on the table in the same purple scrawl read: *Gifts to be left here. Thanks for stopping by. Your present will be delivered by the time you get home. Don't think about sticking around.*

"Put it there," Dan said, pocketing the note.

Eli placed the box on the table as carefully as if he were setting down a newborn baby.

He stepped back. “Now what?”

“Now we do exactly as we're told. We leave.”

“What if Jeremy's around here somewhere?”

“He won't be anywhere near here,” Dan said. “Trust me. We're probably being watched.”

For a moment Dan thought he might have to take him away by force, but finally Eli submitted with a last troubled glance around the room.

Back in the car, no one spoke. Dan turned to Janice and shook his head: *No Jeremy.* She understood. Her face fell.

As he drove away, Dan looked in the rear-view mirror until the place was swallowed by trees. All roads led to the water. Someone in a boat would never be seen from the road. *That's how they will come*, he thought.

He stopped at a curve up ahead and turned to the others.

“I'm getting off here. You drive on up ahead. When you get to the highway, find a place to stop and wait for me.”

Eli grabbed his shoulder. “What are you doing?”

“I'm going back to see who shows up. I don't want any of you with me.”

“I'm coming with you,” Eli said.

Dan turned and jabbed a finger in his face. “You stay *here!*”

Eli froze. For a moment no one spoke.

Dan turned to Janice and Ashley. “Don't let him leave this car. When I'm ready, I'll text you to come for me.”

“You'll get killed,” Janice said in a voice laced with panic.

“They won't see me. Now drive before it's obvious we're here.”

Ashley slid behind the wheel as Dan stepped out of the car.

†

Dan ducked into the brush and made his way back to the cottage. Crouching low, he could see the shore while staying hidden by the trees. Any abrupt movement on his part, however, and he would be seen by anyone watching from the water.

It was another ten minutes before he heard the outboard motor. A small craft, it moved sleekly toward him across the bay. There were two men on board. One of them had a pair of binoculars. Dan watched him scan the shore. He'd brought his own binoculars, and noted the lack of identifying markers on the boat, no doubt making it handy for running cigarettes and alcohol across the border.

The men wore caps and sunglasses. They were dressed in lightweight tracksuits, just a couple of pleasure riders out for a spin. From their movements, Dan could tell they were young, late twenties or early thirties. He snapped a couple of shots with his phone, holding as still as possible.

The one behind the wheel directed the craft in to shore while the other secured it with a loop around a piling.

It was all over in minutes. The man on shore made his way to the cottage and returned in less than thirty seconds with the box. Taking a quick look around, he slipped the rope off the piling and stepped back into the boat. They sped off. A minute later they were no more than a speck heading for the far side of the promontory.

Dan traced his route back through the brush, texting as he went. A minute later he saw the car coming toward him.

The mood was solemn.

“Did you see anything?” Janice demanded.

“Two men in a boat,” he told them. “I’m sorry. There was no sign of Jeremy.”

“You always said it was a ‘they,’” Eli said.

“Had to be. It was all too well coordinated. Let’s go. No sense sticking around here.”

They stopped at Dennis’s cottage for the second car.

“I’ll drive back with Janice and Ashley,” Eli said.

“Okay, but be extra careful driving.” Dan looked at Ashley. “We’re all tired and a little tense.”

She nodded. “I’ll be careful.”

He let them get a head start as he checked his messages. There were three unanswered calls from Nick. Nothing in his voice mail. *On my way back*, he texted. *No boy yet, but the drama’s over*. The reply was immediate: *You better be all right.*

He would have to get used to Nick worrying about him.

He had just passed Owen Sound when his phone rang. *Unknown number, unknown name.*

“Sharp.”

“Is this Mr. Dan Sharp?”

“That’s the one.”

“This is Elroy James.”

Curious timing, Dan thought.

“Thank you for returning my call, Mr. James. I was beginning to think you didn’t exist.”

“Oh, I exist all right. I understand you’ve been trying hard to get in touch. I’ve been out of town. What is it I can do for you?”

He sounded unusually pleasant for a man who kept his home surrounded with security cameras and a voiceless guard dog in a hut in his backyard.

"I'm a private investigator. I was hired by one of your former business partners, a man named Eli Gestner. I understand there was a disagreement when you parted company last year."

"Oh, that. No, there's no problem. Me and Eli are on quite good terms."

Dan snorted in disbelief. "I'm surprised to hear that. I understood that he owed you a lot of money."

"You're out of touch, Mr. Sharp. That's all been taken care of. Ask Eli."

"I will do that."

"Please, by all means ask him."

"And so the death threats you made to him at the time were just what — a little joke?"

"Nothing to get concerned about. It was all a misunderstanding."

"Glad to hear."

"Is there anything else I can help you with?"

"Not at the moment. Thank you."

NINETEEN

Beautiful Boys

IT WAS JUST PAST NOON when Dan reached the city. He was headed down the parkway when Janice called, excited, to say that Jeremy had been safely delivered to his grandmother's condo around the time the box was picked up at the cottage.

"Great! When did you hear?"

"Just now."

"I'll meet you there."

Dan waited outside the condo until she arrived. He watched as she stepped out of her car and hurried over to him.

"Where are the others?" he asked.

"I dropped them at home. I need to do this myself."

Dan wasn't sure how Ashley felt, but he suspected it must have been hard for Eli to be told to wait.

"They found Jeremy wandering on the grounds with a letter addressed to my mother."

"What did it say?"

"It just said, 'Hello, Grandmother. My name is Jeremy.'"

Dan pondered this. Perhaps it was Clarice Bentham who had been targeted after all. She had provided the ransom money. Was that why the boy had been sent to her?

"They left him outside to avoid security cameras. Maybe there's something on the grounds that will show them arriving. Chances are there will at least be footage of a vehicle."

"All I care is that he's back and safe. Thank you. A million times, thank you. If we hadn't had your help, things might not have gone this way."

"Of course. It's what you hired me to do."

They took the elevator to the penthouse. The maid opened the door.

"Oh, Miss Janice —! He's here. Your son is here!" She was nearly in tears.

"Thank you, Eunice. I'll see myself in."

They went into the windowed room overlooking the harbour. A small boy sat on the floor. Still, silent. His eyes were focused intently on the sky outside the glass. He seemed to be listening to something no one else could hear.

His skin was pale, his features delicate. A beautiful child trapped in his own private world.

Janice ran over and knelt. He made a keening sound when she hugged him. It might have been pleasure, it might have been sorrow.

"Hello, Jeremy! Hello, Jeremy!" She was ecstatic. "I'm so glad you're back, Jeremy!"

Clarice Bentham stood at the window, watching them. She was immaculate, her hair done and wardrobe perfectly coordinated. Her slip-on bangles made a clinking sound as she wrapped her arms around her chest.

"He seems to like it here," she said. "At first I was worried when they brought him up. He didn't speak, but you warned me he wouldn't."

"Not in words, no."

"He's a beautiful boy. And he does communicate — in his own way."

"Of course he does," Janice said, without lifting her eyes to her mother. "He knows exactly what he likes and what he doesn't. He lets you know in his own way. Don't you, my baby?"

"He let me hug him. Just once, briefly. I never knew," Clarice said, shaking her head. "I couldn't imagine —!"

Her eyes glistened. Dan sensed an underlying fragility, as if the proof of her grandson's existence had exposed something vulnerable in her.

"You never knew because you never met him," Janice said, still cuddling her son. "He's the most beautiful boy in the world."

She looked up, tears streaming down her face.

Clarice stood watching them. "I understand now what you meant when you said you couldn't help loving him. In an odd way, I'm glad all this has happened. It makes me understand something I would never have known if I hadn't seen him with my own eyes."

"Yes, I knew you would." Janice looked at her mother. "Have the police been here?"

"No. I waited till you arrived. As you asked. I thought you would want to handle that in your own way."

"Yes — that's probably for the best." She stood and held out her hand. "Come, Jeremy. We need to go home."

Dan watched as the boy took hold of her hand and got unsteadily to his feet.

Janice turned to her mother. "Thank you for providing the money for his release."

Clarice shook her head and smiled at her daughter. "It's you I care about, Janice. The money doesn't matter in the least."

"You're right. It doesn't matter at all. It never did. Not to me, anyway."

Clarice's smile faltered. "I did it to bring you back to me. And now this delightful grandchild."

Dan watched the two of them. Something was happening here he didn't yet understand. But he felt it. Something intricate and bitter.

Janice's expression had turned cold. "Well, don't get used to it, mother. You won't see either of us again."

Though the words were addressed to Clarice Bentham, Dan felt as though he'd been slapped.

Clarice put a hand to her mouth. "What? No!"

"You had your chance. Thank you for the money, but it was my money after all. So don't think I'm going to be grateful for it."

Clarice's face crumpled. "Janice —!"

"You've manipulated me for the last time. I can't hear you anymore."

"Janice, please! What are you saying?"

Janice took Jeremy by the hand and headed down the hall. She brushed past the maid, who stood watching with a muted expression.

"Good day, Eunice."

"Good day, Miss Janice."

At the door Janice stopped and pressed a hand against the brocaded wall.

"Goodbye, home. You won't see me again."

Clarice's voice reached them from down the hall. "Janice! Please!"

It was all Dan could do not to turn around and apologize for her daughter's behaviour.

In the elevator, Janice turned to look at Dan. "I suppose you think I'm being cruel. That I've been lying to my mother."

"There's always a reason when people punish one another."

The boy stood by her side, focused on the lights of the elevator panel. He made the keening noise again. She leaned down and put her cheek to his.

"That was only the second time I've seen my mother in three years," Janice said, looking up to watch the numbers as they descended. "The last time was the other day when we came to pick up the money. It's all for appearances. She doesn't really care about me."

Dan thought otherwise. "You said she disapproved of Jeremy's complicated parentage."

"You can say that again." She let out an exasperated sigh. "Look — there's a lot more to it than that, okay? My father died when I was eleven. He was no great loss. He was an emotionally frigid monster. All he cared about was business. My mother remarried a year later. He was a creep. He used to come into my bedroom at night. He would tell me, 'Pretend you're a tree, silent and strong. Just don't make a sound.' In my mind I pretended I was inside the walls and that they were protecting me. I went someplace else where he couldn't touch me."

She stopped talking for a moment. Dan said nothing, waiting as the elevator hurtled downward.

"My mother knew, but she refused to believe it. She didn't want to know. I endured him till I was old enough to leave. By then, of course, I knew what he was doing was wrong."

"I'm sorry," Dan said at last.

"Not as sorry as I was."

The elevator came to rest. The doors opened and they headed through the lobby to the parking lot.

Outside, she stopped and gave him a sad smile. "I'm free of her forever. The money she gave me the other day was going to be legally mine once she died. I just asked for it a little early. And now, as far as I'm concerned, she can go ahead and die."

She stood beside her car, fidgeting with the keys, holding tightly to her son. Still, Dan waited.

"Once when we were out camping — Ashley, Jeremy, and me — Jeremy was behind our tent when I heard a crashing sound in the bush. I ran out and found myself staring at a bear. It was huge. Jeremy just sat there, oblivious. I picked up a branch and swung it with all my might. The bear took off before I could take a second swing. That's the kind of mother I am, Dan. My mother was never like that with me."

She left him standing in the parking lot.

He headed east, over the Don bridge. The cityscape was reflected back at him, as though it led a double life, one on the surface and the other below. With all the excitement, he hadn't called Eli to confirm Elroy's claims about his debt. He called now, but it went straight to voice mail.

"Eli, it's Dan Sharp. I've just come from Clarice Bentham's. I'm sure you're revelling in the good news. I'm very glad it turned out well. Sorry for bothering you, but I had a call from your ex–business partner on the way home. He seems to feel you no longer owe him anything. Can you enlighten me? Thanks."

Ked was in the living room watching television with a beer in his hand. He waved when Dan entered. Ralph shook himself upright and looked at Dan, then decided to stand his ground rather than come to him. Dan went over to his son and hugged him so hard he was afraid he might hurt them both.

"Whatever stupid things I may have done in the past, I apologize for. Whatever stupid things I may do in the future, I apologize for those too."

Ked pulled back and looked at him with surprise. "Okay."

"It's not easy being a parent," Dan told him. "But I try. I think at some point all parents try."

"Dad, you're kind of scaring me right now."

Dan was surprised to feel tears forming in his eyes.

"I just want you to know that, no matter what, I will always love you and be there for you."

Ralph whimpered.

"You too, Ralph."

Ked gave a little choked cry then hugged his father back. "I don't know what this is about, but I will always love you too."

"Good," Dan told him. "We're all good then."

He left Ked there shaking his head in bewilderment.

Ted stood over them, clasping a couple of menus to his chest. His grandmother had been transferred to the ICU at Toronto East. Her prognosis was good. He looked ecstatic.

"That's great news," Dan said.

"Very good," Nick chimed in. "We're happy for you."

"She's the only family I have left. She has to pull through." He seemed to take stock of his surroundings and held out the menus. "What can I get you guys?"

"Anything you care to recommend."

"In that case," he said, tucking the menus under his arm, "I recommend the pasta special. It's a spinach and cheese gnocchi. I had it for lunch. It's devastating. And maybe a couple of Caesar salads."

Nick nodded. "Sounds great."

"Me too," Dan said.

"Okay! Two house specials coming up."

Nick toyed with the candle on the table. It was set in a short, red cup. The flame flickered as Nick turned the glass. This was the first time they'd seen each other face to face since the previous morning.

"All good?" Dan asked.

Nick looked up from the flame. "Time will tell. They're still checking out the boy. He seems to have been well treated. Of course, he can't tell them anything about where he was or who was with him."

"I meant with us," Dan said.

Nick's face darkened. "Well, since you're asking, I think you're too much of a daredevil. If one of those guys in the boat had seen you, you could have been killed. They could have had a watch set up long before you arrived." He shrugged: *duty done.* "There, I said it."

"Okay. For the record, I never intended to be reckless. I considered the possibility that someone might have been watching and probably armed. I took every precaution. In any case, my clients made it clear they wanted to deliver the money and get their son back with minimal police involvement. That was my job and I did it to the best of my abilities."

"Yes, you did."

Dan studied Nick's face. "I'm not going to apologize."

"I don't expect you to."

"Then what?"

Nick scratched his head. "I don't know. It just seems like we're on opposing teams on this."

Dan thought of Donny's distrust of Nick. *It's like you're dating the enemy,* he'd said.

"There are no sides, Nick. We both have jobs to do. You've done yours and I've done mine. Things might have turned out very differently had the police been there."

Nick nodded brusquely. "My point exactly. We could have had boats in the harbour waiting to pick up the trail."

"And the boy might not have been returned if there had been any interference," Dan said, his eyes searching Nick's face.

Before he could say more, Ted was back with a covered basket. Steam rose as he pulled the napkin aside and placed it on the table.

Nick reached for a piece of bread, pulling it apart and wafting it beneath his nose. "Now that's heaven."

"Not enough of that going around these days." Ted gave them a devastating smile then left them alone again.

Nick reached for the butter, his eyes on Dan. "You're right — it could have gone either way. I guess there's no telling, is there? We might have saved the money but lost the boy. So it's all worked out for the best then."

"Seems so, doesn't it?"

Nick's hand paused. "Am I missing something here?"

"I wish I knew."

Nick laid the knife aside. "What then?"

"I watched a woman whose kidnapped son had been returned to her tear her mother to shreds for the abuse she suffered from a stepfather when she was a teenager. I thought tragedies were supposed to bring families closer, but in this case it just ripped one apart."

Nick shrugged. "Not your fault."

"Maybe. I don't know." Dan shook his head. "It's just a feeling I have that there's more to come. And somewhere out there is someone with a million dollars that doesn't belong to them."

"Maybe there will be fingerprints on the notes. Thanks for handing them over, by the way."

"I won't hold my breath waiting on the fingerprints, but you're welcome."

"Anything else I should know?"

"I had a call from Elroy James on my way back. When I asked about the money Eli Gestner owed him, he said it was taken care of. As for the death threats, he says it was all a misunderstanding. Poof — no problem! Everything's fine. Please forget the nasty words I uttered."

"Meaning what? You think Elroy just collected his earnings?"

"Something like that."

Nick sat back. "That's for us to worry about now. But I can tell you this: unless he has a twin, the Montreal hotel CCTV puts him there at the time of the kidnapping."

"All that says is he didn't do it himself. I'd make sure I was far away too when the time came if I was involved."

"Sure. Whatever. But it's behind you. You're the man of the hour again. Why not enjoy it? You always want to question everything just a little beyond what's decent."

"It's my nature."

"Yeah, it is," Nick agreed. "But even cops let go of a case once it's solved."

"So do I."

Nick watched him. "So when will you let this one go?"

"As you said. Once it's solved."

TWENTY

A Separate Deity

In Dan's experience, most drug addicts stayed awake all night and slept all day. Like vampires. But Sarah Nealon was already dressed when he showed up on her doorstep early the following morning. He put his foot in the door when she opened it, just to make sure she let him in. She looked surprised, but then again she looked surprised by nearly everything.

The sun-catcher whirled overhead as Dan sat at the table watching Sarah move around the kitchen. Light splintered in all directions, catching the hidden corners of the room. A crystalline world of beautiful, shiny pieces. He waited patiently as she served him tea with the same exaggerated graces as previously.

"You were here before," she said, seating herself across from him.

"Yes, I came to ask about Jeremy Bentham."

"Oh, yes — I remember now."

"I thought you'd want to know someone found him and brought him home yesterday," Dan told her.

She clasped her hands. Her face was filled with glee. "That's such good news!"

"Do you know where Jeremy was staying while he was missing?"

"While he was —? Oh, no!" Panic flooded her features. "I would never —"

"It's all right." Dan smiled. "I just thought you might have known. The last time we spoke you said you were worried about a boy who got hurt."

"I ..." Her hands made fluttering motions around the pillow she had strapped to her belly. "Every child is precious. Did you know there is a separate deity for every single thing in existence?"

"I didn't know that," Dan said. "How do you know?"

Her eyes roamed the room. "I can hear them. They talk to me."

"When you're sober or just when you're high like today?"

"Oh, I'm not —" She covered her mouth with both hands.

"Speak no evil," Dan said. "Do you want your baby to grow up to be a drug addict?"

She shook her head sadly. "No — that would be a crime."

"Then why don't you get off drugs, Sarah?"

"I try, but he won't let me."

"'He' being the baby's father?"

"He says we're destined to be together, but we can only be together if I listen to him."

"How old are you, Sarah?"

She looked at him with a childlike expression. "Twenty-eight."

"If you want to see thirty, you need to stop doing drugs. Isn't that what the doctors have told you?"

"Yes, it is. And I do want to see thirty, only —"

"Only what?"

"Only it's so hard to stop. Whenever I try, he gives me more."

"More crystal?"

Her fingers reached up and turned the sun-catcher again, but she didn't answer.

"Where does he live?"

She turned away so abruptly it was as if he'd slapped her across the face. "I can't —"

She turned back to face him, smiling as though they were both in on the same secret.

"You can't what?"

"I mean, I'm not really …"

"Pregnant?"

Her face was a mask of sorrow. "It's just that — when you lose one the others are so precious."

"Who did you lose, Sarah?"

She shook her head. "I don't want to remember."

"Was it someone you cared about?"

"There is a god for everything." She reached out a hand and stroked Dan's face. "Even for you. And for me. It makes me happy when I remember that. And even if someone dies, there is still a god for them. It doesn't matter how they die. It could be hunger …"

"Like the children in other countries you were trying to save."

"Yes!" Her face lit up. "You know about that?"

He took her hand and held it gently. "You told me."

Her smile was heartbreaking. "Because I trusted you."

"I won't betray you."

She put a finger to his lips. "Please don't tell anyone else."

"I won't."

"What I did was a mistake. I won't do it again."

"That's good," Dan said. "Otherwise you would have to go back to prison, and this time it would be for a good deal longer."

"Oh, no!" Her wail cut through the air. "Please! I was in jail when my father died. They wouldn't let me go to his funeral."

"What about your mother? Have you seen her recently?"

"My mother?"

"Are you in touch with her?"

"She doesn't like it when I ..." She looked off.

"She doesn't like it when you get high?"

"No — when I call. She doesn't like it when I call. I told you — I'm not high."

"How is your mother these days?"

A pained expression crossed her face. "She's fine. Why do you keep asking me about her?"

"I just wondered how she was. Did she look after Jeremy for you while he was away?"

"What? No!" She gave him a strange look. "Oh-ho! You're trying to trick me." She wagged a finger at him. "It's not nice, you know."

Dan held up his cellphone, showing her the photo of the woman in the copper-coloured Volvo.

"Is this your mother?"

Sarah looked at it then looked down. She shook her head. "No — I — no."

"Look again. Are you sure it's not your mother?" Dan pressed. "Or someone else you know?"

"I'm sure." She pushed her cup aside. "I think you should leave now. Marjorie is coming. That's my social worker. She's coming and I have to get ready. I'm going to have a baby soon. Everything needs to be ready."

"I'm so glad for you. Whose baby is it, Sarah?"

"I can't!" she cried. "I can't tell you."

Her hands fluttered around her. An anxious nun caught in a paroxysm of apostasy. But she would not betray the man she loved.

"Why can't you tell me?" Dan asked.

"Because — I couldn't save him. I wanted to, but I couldn't."

"Who couldn't you save?"

"The boy. He fell and … I didn't mean to."

"You wanted to save him but you couldn't," Dan said.

"No! Yes!" She sat there shaking her head. "It wasn't my fault."

"Was it the baby's father?" Dan asked. "Did he make someone fall?"

"Of course not! It was before I even met Elroy."

Her shoulders shook as she laid her head down on the table and sobbed into the tablecloth.

"Elroy James?"

She turned her sad, gentle face toward him. "I couldn't save him."

"It's okay," he said, running a hand softly over her head. "You don't have to save anyone. Do you want me to call Marjorie to come over?"

"No." She shook her head from side to side. "I'll be fine."

"Why didn't you tell me Elroy James was Sarah Nealon's boyfriend? Or should I say her pimp?"

The traffic was in a snarl. Dan stopped at River Street.

There was a pause before Janice spoke. "It's sad, but I didn't think it was worth mentioning."

Dan tried to keep calm. "How could it not be worth mentioning when they're both suspects in a kidnapping?"

"It didn't occur to me," she said. "I wasn't thinking."

"Did you tell the police about their connection?"

"I must have. Yes, I'm sure I did."

"So it was worth mentioning to the authorities, but not to me?"

She sighed. "Look — why are you doing this?"

"Because I want answers. How did Sarah meet Elroy?"

"Eli introduced them."

"Eli?"

"Yes, Eli. And don't ask me how Eli and Elroy met, because I have no idea."

"Did Sarah and Elroy ever have a child together? A child who might have been hurt?"

"What? No! Not as far as I know. Just leave it alone, Dan."

"I can't. I don't like it when my clients have selective amnesia. First, you didn't tell me you tried to con your husband into thinking Jeremy was his child, then you neglected to mention that Eli's business venture with Elroy was a drug deal, and now I find that you didn't think it worth mentioning that two suspects in the kidnapping know each other. Why is that?"

"That's really no concern of yours now."

"Now that I've done what you wanted me to do?" She was silent. "Remind me again. How do you and Eli know one another?"

"Why are you giving me the third degree? We met in a stupid posh school for rich kids. I got him expelled for something I did there. All right? Anyway, it was a long time ago."

That was their sibling-like relationship right there. Rich kids growing up together, complaining their rich-kid complaints about how hard life was and how their parents just didn't understand them. Dan knew exactly what that meant.

"It strikes me there are a number of things you didn't bother telling me that would have helped had I known them earlier."

"Fine — I'm telling you now. Eli and I go back a long way."

"And Ashley? How long have you known her?"

"I told you that. We met when I was still married to Dennis. We had to keep it quiet at the time, but we all know each other's secrets now."

"There are far too many secrets here. Only I seem to have been left in the dark about some of them. What else haven't you told me?"

"Oh, Dan! I don't know. I told you what you needed to know. You brought Jeremy back. That's all that matters."

"Is it really all that matters?"

"Yes. It is. And you did a great job. So thank you, but it's over. You need to let it go."

So everyone keeps telling me.

She hung up.

TWENTY-ONE

Cruise Control

NICK'S CALL CAME THROUGH just as Janice hung up. The good news was that Jeremy Bentham had been examined by child psychologists and forensic investigators, all of them concluding that he showed no signs of having been mistreated in the time he was missing. The bad news was that they could shed no light on where he had stayed or who had held him captive. Turquoise fibres on his clothing indicated he'd been sitting or sleeping on a couch with worn polyester cushions, but that could have been anywhere. All they could say for sure was that someone had looked after him and fed him. He seemed to have no idea that anything out of the ordinary had occurred. Then again, that was the nature of autism, especially as severe as Jeremy's. Kids like him lived largely in their own minds. The report concluded by saying he had been taken care of and may never for a moment have felt threatened.

Case closed, at least as far as Dan was concerned. It's what everyone was telling him. *But for the missing million dollars. And the kidnappers still at large.*

As he crossed the Don Valley, he tried the number for Elroy James. It went straight to voice mail. He dialed again. This time someone picked up. He recognized the voice of Elroy's secretary, or whatever she called herself.

"Elroy Enterprises."

"My name is Dan Sharp. I'd like to speak to Elroy."

"What's it about?"

"Extortion and kidnapping."

"Oh, right. You called before. He's not here."

"Remind me. What is the nature of your business?"

"It's on the website." She hung up.

He called his son. When he had Ked on the line, Dan asked him to look up the business address.

"Hey, Dad! It's near your office. On Matilda Street near Broadview."

"Does it say what kind of business it is?"

"Shipping."

"Thanks, pal."

He set his GPS then turned his car around and headed back toward the river. He was cruising along when an incoming call caught his attention. The number wasn't blocked this time: *E. James. Speak of the devil.* He picked up.

"Sharp."

"What the fuck do you want now?"

Not nearly as friendly as the last call, Dan noted. He wondered if Sarah had called him.

"How's your girlfriend?"

"What?"

"Your girlfriend. Sarah Nealon. I was a little worried about her last time I saw her."

"Sarah's fine," he snarled. "Is that a concern of yours?"

The blue arrow on the GPS showed him homing in on Elroy Enterprises in one minute.

"At the moment, it very much is."

"Why is that?"

"Because anything that might concern the kidnapping of Jeremy Bentham concerns me."

There was a pause. "I heard the kid came back. It was on the news. All is well, no?"

"I don't think all is well. Not by a long shot."

"Well, that's too bad." He paused. "If that's all you called about —"

"And Eli Gestner — is he still fine too?"

"Eli's got his own problems. He'll have to deal with them. Listen — don't waste my time. I'm about to board a plane."

"For Montreal or Hong Kong?"

Elroy's laugh was harsh.

"Neither! I'm on my way to Kauai. That's in Hawaii."

Dan had never been to Hawaii. Never wanted to. "Aloha then," he said and hung up just as the GPS announced his arrival.

He looked up at the red brick building. A sign in the second-floor window read *Elroy Enterprises.* No outward indication of what their enterprises consisted of. It could have been a real shipping company. It could just as easily have been the offices of paid assassins.

A large man bustled out the front door, locking it behind him. As he turned, Dan glimpsed the bullfrog face in Nick's file. He was a mountain of muscle in a leisure suit. Not someone he'd want to tangle with, fair fight or not.

Elroy carried a slim, black briefcase. As he raised his arm to signal a waiting car, there was a glint of metal: he was handcuffed to the case. A limousine glided over. The car door opened and Elroy disappeared behind tinted windows.

Dan waited till the car pulled away from the curb then headed after it. The driver kept up a leisurely pace as he made his way down to the expressway. Dan stayed several car lengths behind. Their route took them directly to the airport. Maybe Elroy had been telling the truth about going to Hawaii.

He was about to give him the benefit of the doubt when the limo veered toward Terminal 1. Dan slowed and pulled up to the curb. The big man got out of the car and made his way to the sliding doors. Through the glass, Dan watched as Elroy headed to Air Canada domestic departures. *Kauai my ass*, he thought, as a terminal cop waved him on.

He set his speed at 120 and cruised along the 401, mulling over Elroy James's words. All had been good, but now it was: *Eli's got his own problems. He'll have to deal with them.* Dan wondered what those problems might be. Eli still hadn't returned his call. In fact, he was beginning to think Eli was avoiding him. He tried again, but the call went right to voice mail. He hung up without leaving a message.

He got Nick on the phone, updating him on his airport run.

"You'll need to do a quick check to find out where he's going," Dan said. "Assuming he's used his real name, that is. Then give his luggage a proper search when he lands to see what's in that briefcase."

"You're suggesting I haul a guy in for no obvious reason and search his personal belongings?"

"He's a suspect in a kidnapping and I just helped hand over a very large ransom. Can't you guys do that sort of thing?"

"You're kidding, right? You don't really believe we can just go in with guns blazing and make a search like that without proper warrants."

"I'd find a way."

"I'm sure you would, but my way is a lot more bureaucratic than yours. No wonder people think cops can't get anything right, they're all so sure we do things the way they do them on television."

"So you're willing to let a million bucks slide away on a technicality?"

"How can you be sure the money's in the briefcase? He could be making a legitimate business trip."

"In case you need any added incentive, I just learned that he's the boyfriend of the surrogate and drug addict, Sarah Nealon — who also happens to be a suspect."

"Well," Nick said at last, "I wasn't expecting that." There was a moment of silence. "Oh, and by the way —"

"Yes?"

"Lydia says thanks again for the photos of the guys in the boat. Impossible to get a fix on their identities with those sunglasses they're wearing. Same goes with the boat. It couldn't be more generic."

"Best I could do without risking getting shot."

"Not complaining, just letting you know Lydia is grateful for the help. Also for the notes. There were no fingerprints, but we didn't really expect there would be."

"I hear you. I'll leave it in your hands."

"Wait. Where are you off to now? Not heading up to the Bruce again, I hope?"

"No such luck. You'll see me when you get home."

On a whim, he turned off the highway and down Black Creek Drive to Lawrence. An image of the copper-coloured Volvo floated through his mind. He could still see the panicked look on the driver's face. Why would she make herself so obvious if she had intended to pull off a crime like kidnapping? You'd want to stay as far away from your victims as possible rather than give them a chance to take your photograph. Unless, of course, you had another reason for being there.

He headed to the intersection where he'd lost sight of the Volvo, his mind on other things. Like the box of money they'd left on the table at the cottage in Lion's Head.

As they'd headed back, Dan once again caught sight of the place he and his parents had stayed at. The mornings were still vivid in his memory. Each day he'd awakened to the sound of waves, the crying of gulls, and white clouds piled like meringue, making everything look pristine and perfect. The happy time had just begun and the drinking not yet started, for his parents woke slowly and moved like rusty machines till they got their bearings. Young Daniel had hoped to catch some perfect moment and hang onto it, to find the fulcrum before it tipped over into the abyss of drink and retribution.

He thought of Sandy again. When they drove away that final day, he'd been heartbroken. His mother had tried to distract him by telling him dogs were able to sniff their way home over hundreds and sometimes thousands of miles. She reminded him of a movie they'd watched together, *The Incredible Journey*. Two dogs and a cat, separated from their owner, had returned home after months. All that fall Dan had wandered up and down the railway tracks each day after school looking for Sandy, waiting and hoping he would return.

Persistent, his Aunt Marge had called him. When he told her about the movie she offered to buy him a cat, but he wasn't interested. After all, Sandy would be coming back. He felt in his heart he was right. All the while, his father had stayed silent on the subject.

The suburbs flashed by. It was close to lunchtime. Dan was about to turn around and head home when he saw it. A copper-coloured Volvo, sitting in a driveway like any ordinary car. Not like something that should have been kept hidden and out of sight.

TWENTY-TWO

A Telegram for Death

THE STREET WAS PERFECTLY ORDINARY. Split-levels and clipped lawns. Pleasant Valley. One house just like another. A dream of perfection with nothing but uninterrupted boredom and the comforts of presumed security. Dan wondered which was higher in the suburbs — the divorce rate or the suicide rate.

He pulled up to the curb. Without the licence number he couldn't be sure, but it was definitely the same model. He looked over the house. Curtains pulled open, a few daisies in the beds. Quiet, solidity. It was the home of someone who was confident she wouldn't stand out in a crowd. Or perhaps never worried she would be looked for.

Dan parked a few doors down then got out and walked back. From a distance, he noted the flyers bulging in the mailbox. Through the living room window he saw a large plump sofa with a paisley pattern pushed against a beige wall. A bookshelf was crammed with photos and knick-knacks. The sort of things normal people filled their shelves with every day.

It was all so ordinary.

He followed a paved walk around back where a wire fence enclosed a tidy yard. No dogs, voiceless or otherwise. He lifted the latch and let himself in. Grass, daylilies, a few shrubs out of season. A white blouse fluttered on a clothesline. No nosy neighbours peering at him over the fence or from behind the curtains.

He tried the door, but the handle resisted his pressure. Pressing his face against the glass, he made out a mop handle and a bucket with a few cleaning products on the inside steps. Suburbanites obsessed with cleanliness. All those television commercials. He let himself back through the gate then closed it and headed to the front.

He paused in the drive, doing a slow three-sixty. The neighbourhood was deserted. It felt peculiar. No dogs, no kids, no cars. It could have been the opening of a post-apocalypse film. Millions of deaths, no survivors, one lone visitor stumbling into town. In which case he might need to grab Ked and make a beeline for the Bruce. Isn't that what Tom Cruise would do? Only there'd be a girl in a T-shirt and cut-off jeans, feisty but in need of rescue, and Tom's uncommon good sense. She'd distrust him at first, until he saved her from her own recklessness, followed by a kiss, the beginnings of love. La-ti-da. It would all work out in the end, apart from the annihilation of most of the world. It occurred to him he'd better warn Nick before heading out of town.

He climbed to the front porch. Cracks had formed along the foundation, weeds growing up around the steps.

A slip-up in the neighbourhood's immaculate façade. Black iron fronted the stoop. Curlicue, ornate. The overhead light was still on. He opened the mailbox and leafed through the flyers. Pizza parlours, roofers, no-job-too-small construction firms. But no letters. Nothing to identify the owner.

He pulled on the screen. The inside door was a wood affair painted in fake wood grain, as though the original had needed improvement. An irregular pattern of tinted windows formed a luminous gold shield when you stepped back to catch the light shining through. A security company sticker peeled away alongside the plastic weather stripping.

He knocked. No answer, no sound from inside.

The sun made an irregular pattern on the stoop, undulating shadows imprinted where it shone through the railing. A robin flitted down to the railing, cocked its head at him then took off again. Two plastic deck chairs were centred beneath the window, an overflowing ashtray on the arm of one of them. A red plastic lighter lay beneath. Dan leaned down, grabbed it, and held it to the light. The fluid tilted back and forth, flaming up on the first try. He released the starter and the flame whooshed back inside. For a moment, he was transported back to the fire pit outside the cottage in the Bruce. More memories of his father. The unquiet dead.

Dan pictured him going up and down the mine shaft every day for years, the toil wearing away at his soul, making him mean and hateful. He tried to imagine him as a young man, his hopes and aspirations, before fatherhood weighed him down. You could quit a job and get a new one, move from one city to another, divorce a spouse and remarry, but fatherhood never really went away. Was that what had turned him into an angry man? Once a father, always a father, with its burden of responsibility.

He was headed back down the steps when a screen door yawned open one porch over. A woman in a flowery blue dress peered out.

"How is she today?" she asked.

"She's not answering."

"That's not like her. I brought her over some soup yesterday and she didn't call to say she'd enjoyed it. Frankly, it doesn't sound good, does it?"

"Not really."

The woman shrugged. "Still, the doctors say she has a good chance if she follows the regimen." She made sympathetic noises. "You're one of the nephews. Jack? John?"

"John."

"Well, John, I have the key. Why don't we just take a look?" Without waiting for an answer, she bustled off inside, returning a moment later.

Dan watched her huff down her walkway and cross the lawn.

"I'm Carole Dawson," she said, huffing and puffing up the steps. "You must've heard your aunt talk about me."

"Many times."

"We go back a long way." She put the key in the lock and turned the handle. The door swung open. "Hello? Theda?"

She turned and looked at him. "Was she expecting you? I mean, her car's in the drive."

"No, she wasn't expecting me," Dan said. "I was just passing by."

She poked her head inside and called again. "Theda? It's Carole. Your nephew John's here with me."

She turned to him with a concerned look. "You don't suppose anything's happened to her?"

"I hope not."

"Why don't you wait here? I'll just go tap on her bedroom door."

Dan nodded. "Good idea."

He heard her timid knocking, followed by more calling. The sound stopped and he heard her give a little gasp.

She was on her way back out as Dan went in. She shook her head. "Don't go in there. We'd better call someone."

"What's happened?"

"It's most unpleasant." She put a hand to her forehead. "I'm afraid your aunt is dead."

It took Dan only a moment to corroborate that fact. Standing in the bedroom doorway he called 911 then turned to Carole. "What's the address here?"

"Nineteen Westonia Crescent."

"What's Theda's last name?"

She looked at him as though he might be deranged. "Your aunt's last name is McPhail. How ever could you forget that?"

"It's McPhail," he repeated to the operator. "Theda McPhail. Yes — police and an ambulance."

Carole watched him incredulously as he looked around the room, stepping over the body to examine the window frame.

His next call was to Nick. He gave the address. "A woman named Theda McPhail. I'm with her neighbour. She found her."

Carole's eyes threw daggers at him. "You don't even know her," she said.

Dan turned back to the body. "Looks like a strangling," he said into the phone. "There are red marks around her neck. Nylon by the looks of the abrasion. No obvious signs of forced entry, but let me know what you find out." He imagined Nick turning apoplectic at the request. "Please."

Dan directed Carole to sit in one of the chairs. A siren could be heard in the distance.

"Who are you?" she demanded.

"Just a friend," Dan said to reassure her.

When the police came, he gave his statement. Then he directed them to Carole. She was trying hard to convince anyone who would listen that nothing like this had ever happened in her neighbourhood before.

Dan looked quickly around the house then came back over to where Carole sat, stunned. Someone had placed an orange emergency blanket around her shoulders.

"It was so strange," she said, regarding him with a bewildered expression. "Just a few nights ago. I thought she said a telegram. A telegram for death."

Dan cocked his head and listened.

"But it wasn't a telegram." She smiled sadly. "She was on the porch with a newspaper in her lap. She'd been doing the puzzles. She held it up and flapped it around. 'It's my name,' she said. 'Theda is an anagram. An anagram for death.' Then she laughed."

Dan took his leave as Carole pondered the mysteries of fate and linguistic puzzles.

He looked around the kitchen. Janice ran a hand through her hair. They were alone. The cat had hissed on his arrival then vanished. Janice had on a white collared shirt and black jeans. A tattooed claw crept out from under her sleeve. With her flat chest and short hair she might have been a teenage gang member.

"Her name was Theda McPhail," Dan said. "Does that mean anything?"

"No, nothing."

At first she'd been angry when she opened the door. Now she looked frightened.

"I showed Sarah Nealon the picture you sent me. I asked her if it was someone she knew, but she said no. Still, it might have been."

"But what would it prove?"

"I don't know. You said she called you Kathy when she came by."

Her blue eyes flashed. "Yes. She called me Kathy. I told you, Katharine is my real name. But how could she have known that? I just assumed she had the wrong person."

"Do you know anyone else who goes by that name?"

She shrugged. "When we moved here the neighbour next door was a Kate. She moved about a year ago."

"Is it possible she confused you with her?"

"Not unless she didn't know her well. She was a red-head. Older than me. About forty."

"Did she have any kids?"

Janice nodded. "Yes, an eight-year-old girl and a three-year-old boy." The frightened expression returned to her face. "Are you thinking they thought Jeremy was someone else's child?"

Dan shook his head. "They phoned you for the ransom. Presumably they knew who they were calling. Otherwise someone else would have got the call and you'd never have heard about it."

A drawing book lay on the table. Dan turned the cover and flipped through it.

"It's Jeremy's," Janice said. "He draws in it to calm himself."

Something that might have been the mouth of a cave loomed, dark and heavy under scrawls of black crayon, and what might have been stalactites or even long, sharp teeth. He hadn't seen any stalactites in the caves he'd explored. On the next page was a bear-like figure beside a face without eyes. Demons or kidnappers? Or maybe both.

"Did Jeremy have this book with him while he was missing?"

"Yes. It was in his knapsack. Why?"

"Just wondering. It would have helped keep him calm while the kidnappers had him." Dan closed the book. "Did Eli say anything to you about having paid back the money he owed Elroy James?"

The question startled her. "What? No! When did he say that?"

"Eli didn't. Elroy did."

"I don't know how he could," she said at last. "Especially not now. We have nothing."

"Where is Eli, by the way? He didn't return my call yesterday."

"He and Ashley took Jeremy out to buy some ice cream. So he can start to feel normal again. So all of us can, if that's even possible. We need to start acting like a family again. I'll tell him you asked."

†

Dan sat in his car outside the Bentham home, the windows rolled up against the heat and the air conditioner blasting. He had Nick on the phone again.

"Retired school teacher," Nick said before Dan could say anything. "*Just* retired, in fact. Sixty-five. Lived in the neighbourhood for more than thirty years. Nothing suspicious in the background. Impeccable record. No charges, nothing."

A small boy went by on a tricycle, wearing a pirate's cap and brandishing a plastic sword. Off to plunder the world.

"Money problems?" Dan asked.

"No, I just told you," Nick said, exasperated. "Nothing. She was the least likely person to kidnap someone, except for maybe you. Though I'm having my doubts about you these days."

"Any possibility she might have been the mother of Ashley Lake, or related to Sarah Nealon somehow?"

"Never married. Nobody's mother unless she gave the kid up for adoption. No obvious link to Sarah Nealon. What did your client say?"

"Not a clue who she was. Janice, I mean. Unless she's lying, which I wouldn't put past her."

"From the sounds of it, I'd say you've got unreliable clients. Not to mention way too many suspects." Nick paused. "But, oh yeah, you don't believe in suspects. You just have leads. So maybe you haven't focused on the right one yet."

The boy on the tricycle returned, his hat askew, one arm held in check by an angry-looking woman as he loudly voiced his objections at being manhandled. The life of a pirate. But Mother was unswayed as she led him back up the drive.

"I'm glad you said that," Dan said. "Because, in fact, I do have another lead. So you'll have to excuse me for abandoning you again while I head back up to the Bruce Peninsula."

Nick's sigh spoke volumes. "You're going back there?"

"I know a strawberry farmer with a strange knowledge of biblical passages who I would dearly love to talk to again."

"Oh, right. The one without a phone."

"Wi-Fi. It strikes me he might know a thing or two about boats as well."

"You want to show him the photos?"

"Thought I might. Any problem with that?"

"Is he cute? 'Cause I may have a problem with all these overnight excursions you keep making."

Dan rolled his eyes. "Is Grumpy the Dwarf cute?"

"All right. You can go."

The boy and his mother vanished inside the house, the tricycle left abandoned on the drive.

TWENTY-THREE

Last Rites

HE'D TAKE THE DRIVE SLOW THIS TIME. It wasn't as if anyone's life depended on it. Or so he hoped. He hadn't called ahead for a motel room either. He'd have to wing it. All his friends had data on their phones and could locate anything anywhere. Dan had struggled with it briefly then given up. He wasn't married to technology, and he hoped he'd be retired before that day came.

It was late afternoon. The outer-borough traffic had started. Like carrion, they swooped in each morning to pick at the city's carcass then turned around and left again each evening. You could hear a horn here and there as someone crept up to make an illegal pass on the right in lanes already clogged with vehicles, impatient to gain an extra car length, but for all they tried there was no use fighting it. One day there would be no more cars, he reminded himself. That day hadn't come yet either. Pity.

It was nearly six by the time he made it out of the city. The scenery was as unexceptional as ever. Unless you found yourself looking down from a helicopter, of course. One day Dan would convince Nick to go camping with him in the Bruce. Maybe not to Lion's Head, though. That was too fraught with memories. Cape Croker, possibly. Live in the wild for a week to remind them how easy they had it in Toronto.

He'd softened since Nick came into his life and he wondered if it showed. On the other hand, he had to acknowledge that he'd changed for the better. The anxiety and the ongoing nightmares were less pronounced. Was that all it took to dispel PTSD? Someone to hold his hand and say everything was going to be all right? Put that in a bottle and sell it.

Before Nick, there had been others to keep the ghosts of loneliness and depression at bay. Some good sex too, though the relationships seldom went to a deeper place of belonging. A place where he felt anchored and accepted, flaws and all.

They'd both had battles with alcohol. Dan's ended the day he saw the effect it was having on Ked. A teenage boy needed to depend on his father, not worry about him. He had let Ked down again and again until he saw the writing on the wall: he was turning into his own father, a man he'd despised most of his life. There was no one he wanted to be less like. And so he stopped.

Nick's drinking, on the other hand, had begun in earnest with the death of his son and the dissolution of a marriage. Ten years down the road he'd started to wonder whether his job was next on the list of things he would soon be leaving behind.

The turning point came through yet another child, one he never met. He'd ended up on a park bench one night when he was too drunk to make it home. Ironic, he said, considering all the times he'd kicked someone else off a bench. Only now it was him. In the morning, he woke to find a lunch pail by his head. Inside it was a sandwich and a note — *Julian loves you* — scribbled in magic marker. He'd cried to think a child had done that for him. He'd cried again telling Dan the story.

Dan had nearly reached the peninsula when the sky darkened. Fog was crowding in from the sides of the road as he stopped at a gas station outside Chatsworth. A single street lamp lit up the place. There was no one in sight. It felt like the loneliest place in the world. He stepped from the car and unscrewed the gas cap. The escalating numbers on the pump blurred as fatigue hit him. He'd been going at it hard, but something wouldn't let him quit yet.

He got back in the car and checked himself in the mirror. His stark features made him look like a prisoner in a detention centre. He pulled back onto the road. Headlights picked out more fog ahead, lapping at it like a giant yellow tongue. *You need to learn how to trust, to let someone else be your strength*, Nick had told him. *That someone is me.* But if he let Nick be his strength and then Nick left him, what then?

Some days he worried Nick had stolen his self-reliance, his ability to be alone and content. Trusting someone was all well and good, but relationships were chance things, the element of doubt always inherent in them. *I have my doubts. Beyond a reasonable doubt. Was there ever any doubt?* How could trust ever win out? Doubt was like sin.

It was everywhere. *Sins of omission. Sins of the father. Easy as sin.* Beside it, trust never had a chance. *Don't take that away from the boy too,* Dan's Aunt Marge had warned her wayward brother years ago. *He's already lost his mother. What else has he got left? You're no good to him.*

It came out of the fog. The first sign was a flash of tawny hide, followed immediately by the bump and heart-stopping crunch of bone as something flew at him and slid over the windshield. The sound jolted him out of his skin. He braked hard, sending the car into a skid, barely managing to keep it from skating off the shoulder.

In the mirror, the road behind him lay in darkness. He backed up slowly, looking for signs of something in the tail lights. At last, he saw it.

The deer lay in the centre of the road, its antlered head twisted backward as if it were looking over its shoulder to see what had happened. Dan stopped and got out. Dark streaks on the fender, the road disappearing in fog ahead and behind.

For a moment, he couldn't think straight. It had come out of nowhere, a shock to his system. One minute there was nothing then suddenly everything was happening at once. His brain hadn't had time to catch up.

The animal's sides heaved. Young. Probably a yearling. Fear and agony reflected in its eyes.

Dan knelt and put a hand on its flank. It quivered at his touch. Its legs were broken. A dark gash on its side showed entrails, the guts of its life force spilling out and staining the highway.

A keening noise split the air. It reminded him of Jeremy Bentham's animal cries. It shook him. There was no sense calling anyone, animal services, whatever. They would just come and haul the carcass away eventually. In the meantime, it would suffer.

Dan was aware of his heart pounding. He'd been lucky. The collision had torn the deer apart, but he was intact. All around him was calm, the fog making everything hazy, the world unreal. As if time had stopped at the fulcrum. Only it had picked the wrong moment to stop.

The deer's cries grew louder. He was miles from nowhere. Soon another car or truck would come around that corner and spin out of control to avoid him.

He looked down at his hands. They were all he had.

He grasped it by the neck and felt around for a grip. Then he began to squeeze. The animal thumped once, twice, three times. It seemed as though it would go on forever before the shaking slowed then stopped. When he was sure it was over, Dan let go.

He stayed there, crouching by its side. He felt as though he needed to stay with it a bit longer, to apologize for taking its life. After a minute he looked up, took a deep breath, and stood. He grabbed the hind legs and pulled. It resisted at first then slowly began to move till he'd dragged its bulk off the road.

He went back to the car and opened his trunk, fumbling around till he found an old T-shirt to wipe his hands on. The blood had left greasy stains across his palms. He spat on them and rubbed again, but the stains remained. He tossed the rag off to the side of the road. No one had passed him in all that time. It wasn't till he got back in his car that he realized he was shaking. Tears ran down his cheeks. He sat there for another five minutes till he was sure he could drive.

That was one of the times he wished he could rely on someone else to be strong.

The motel he'd stayed at the previous week was full, no sign of Sonny's wife on her bike even, so he kept driving. The next two places had their *NO VACANCY* notices lit up. Things were not looking good. He kept going till he passed the giant wind machines marking the turnoff to Horace's farm. Lion's Head was just up ahead.

He drove until he reached the town. It looked deserted, everything winding down for the night. He hadn't expected much, and it seemed as though that was what he was going to get. His mind was already combing through the possibilities. It had been years since he'd slept on a park bench, not since he left his father's house in Sudbury and arrived in Toronto as a homeless teenager. Back then he'd been foolish enough to think he could find a cheap place to sleep, but with little money in his pocket things hadn't turned out that way. Once again, his lack of planning was having much the same results.

He slowed the car and stopped. Tobermory was another half hour up the peninsula, but this was prime tourist season at the beginning of a weekend. If the places he'd passed were already full then Tobermory wasn't going to have a spare room for him either.

The choices were obvious: a park bench or the car. But Lion's Head didn't have many benches on offer. He reached for the lever and leaned back. By staying in the car he could keep the windows closed and the bugs out. That was the only benefit he could think of.

Then it occurred to him. *Right. Why not?* At least he wouldn't be woken by a police car making its rounds.

Somehow he found his way in the darkness and fog, rumbling up the drive till his headlights swept the tumble-down cottage. Crooked beams, worn wood shingles, smashed window panes. A goblin's house if ever there was one. Grimness surrounded it. If he wanted to, he could go inside and sleep, but it seemed safer to stay in the car. There were no nearby lights from neighbours. This was real country. Anyone hearing him drive up would assume he was lost. Why else come here in the middle of the night? No one would break into a place like this or, even if they did, they'd be kids who couldn't do more damage than what had already been done. A car on the side of the road wasn't going to rouse much suspicion from anyone. At least that's what he was counting on. He pulled the lever and leaned back.

In the morning, he woke with a stiff neck. For a moment he couldn't think where he was. The sun was just coming up, filtering through the pines. He'd had a rough sleep, disturbed by unsettling dreams. It hearkened back to the days when he drank and woke disoriented in unfamiliar places. He looked out the windshield and saw the dilapidated wreck of a cottage, the cut-out sun and moon on the outhouse door. One day he'd probably laugh about it, but not today.

He checked his face in the mirror. It wasn't reassuring to think that eventually he'd look like that every morning, not just on the ones when he slept rough.

He released his lock, swung the door wide, and stepped out. The air felt cool and smelled clean. He leaned down to pull his shoes on then walked over the rocky drive to a tree, turning aside from the cottage as he urinated. Modesty held sway even way out here in the middle of nowhere.

He stretched thoroughly, feeling the sun's rays reaching through the branches to touch his face. The only sounds were the songs of birds and insects just beginning to stir. A breeze came off the lake. *If I lived here I could have this every morning*, he thought, though it struck him he'd miss Nick and Ked and Kendra. And maybe even Donny and Prabin too, when Donny came to his senses again. *If* he came to his senses.

He went back and examined the car. The right fender was dented and scuffed. A vision of the deer's fear-glazed eyes came to him. Something — the hooves or antlers — had scraped off a strip of paint before being thrown free. No sense going to an auto-body shop here. It could wait till he got home.

He turned to the cottage. It sat as though waiting for him, silent and dark, like a disapproving parent. It was almost as if it had known he'd be coming back. The outer stairs were rotting through. He climbed cautiously, taking care to step directly over the supports. The porch was even more treacherous. Nail heads stuck up every few inches, as though someone had tried to dismantle it but given up halfway.

The door opened with a light shove. The lock was splintered around the edges. *Kids,* Dan thought. Inside, rain had warped the floor. The uneven planks gave it a corrugated feel. Light shone down in patches where the roof was worn through. The room seemed tilted, the way his backyard had looked after a violent storm one summer. Leaves and branches, pictures and furniture. Everything off-kilter. A mushroom-coloured carpet shrank from the baseboards. He couldn't remember if it had been there on his last visit. What he remembered was the view of the water all the way down to the shore, with Lion's Head in the distance and the clouds leading on to forever.

He stepped across the threshold into the gloom of the kitchen. For a moment, it was as if nothing had changed. The table and chairs were still there. The cupboards were intact. It wasn't till he got up close that he saw the age and decay. The paint, once a milky blue, was cracked and peeling. The vinyl floor curled up at the edges.

There were a few cans on the shelves. The labels were faded, but he saw they had once been soup cans. A cracked jar sat in the cupboard over the stove. Honey had oozed out the sides and hardened. Even the ants had given up trying to transport it away.

In the bedroom, the linen was rotted through with mouse turds dotting a faded quilt. The windowsill was littered with dead flies. Something had burrowed through the insulation in the walls, pink and yellow tufts sprouting here and there.

He looked out the window and had a sudden memory of being carried on his father's shoulders down to the lake. Hadn't that meant there was something between them? Except he'd been terrified, he recalled. No trust even then.

It struck him that he was looking to find a piece of himself, a link leading directly through his memories to the past. Wasn't that how it worked? You discovered who you were through your history — and the dead, whether quiet or unquiet.

He already knew where his parents' bodies were buried, but it seemed as though this was where their ghosts lingered long after they were gone, still searching among the debris of their lives for those few brief moments of joy they once found on a summer's day now long forgotten by everyone but a permanently scarred son who never understood what they had been all about. As hard as it was to believe, he realized, they might actually have loved one another. Better not to judge them. Everyone fell short. Friends, family, loved ones. And falling short, they resented you for seeing it.

He caught sight of himself in a mirror hanging crookedly on the wall. Mildew had scarred its surface. His face looked as though it belonged to someone else. A sad and lonely man he didn't know.

Not long before she died, his friend Domingo had told him everyone was born into the families that could teach them what they most needed to learn. She had become a convert to Buddhism, a believer in reincarnation. *What would that be in my case?* Dan asked, trying to hide his cynicism. *Maybe how to be the parent you never had and the lover your parents tried to be to one another,* she said softly. Dan thought it over. *I can see that,* he'd said.

For a while on that last trip, his mother and father had seemed to get along. He recalled a supper ringing with laughter and singing, something joyous that held them together. He remembered thinking — hoping — that they had finally arrived at that magic place where everything would change. White lace and promises. They'd been so awed by their surroundings that they forgot the petty grievances and dissatisfactions poisoning their everyday lives. Maybe, if only for a moment, they finally saw how their actions and words had consequences, reaching much further and lasting much longer than the immediate sting and wounding of one another that had always seemed their aim. It was as though they'd suddenly found their faith and salvation in one another — their *trust* — however briefly.

Dan looked from the mirror out the window to a stretch of pine trees. Stalwart, silent. He thought of Nick, the pillar he could lean on if he so chose.

When his mother lay dying, his Aunt Marge had sent him in to say goodbye. The pneumonia had been brought on after she'd been locked out in the cold by his father following a night of drinking, though he hadn't learned that till many years later, long after both of them were dead. He'd been four at the time. She lay there beneath the covers, her life force almost spent. He didn't know what dying was. Didn't know what goodbye meant.

She cried and brushed the hair from her Danny's forehead. There had been such urgency in her face and voice. But what did she need from him? Whatever it was he would have given it to her rather than see her sad. Her breath escaped in a long, drawn-out fury, like pebbles on a beach as the waves sucked them in and spat them out again with inexhaustible force.

And then she was gone.

First his dog, then his mother. He'd tried to bring Sandy back and failed. But he would try harder with his mother.

For years afterward he had made pleas: *Bring her back and I will be good.* More promises. Because he knew from the way his father treated him that he wasn't good. Only it hadn't worked with his mother any more than it had with Sandy.

The memory faded as he looked back at the mirror. How long had he been standing here? It seemed a lifetime.

The first time he and Nick had argued, they didn't speak to one another for a week, both too stubborn to reach out to the other. Finally, Nick called. *Would you have called me eventually? No*, Dan said. *That's not who I am.*

Nick sighed. *Then you're lucky it is who I am. I've never missed anyone like this before, except when my son died. There was a hole inside of me I couldn't get past then. I thought, no, I never want to feel this much again. It tore me apart for years. The loss isn't worth it. But for you, Dan, I would risk it all over again.*

Nick, at least, knew trust.

Dan closed the cottage door behind him and staggered out into blinding sunshine, leaving his memories behind. Why would anyone willingly go back to such a place?

As he headed to the car a curious zooming filled the air overhead, like the sound of thousands of insects, only there were no insects flying about. For just a moment, he thought he could smell burning marshmallows and hear the cry of a long-dead whippoorwill once again. As he looked around, he saw the fire pit his father had fallen into that evening, thirty-two long years ago, when Dan had rescued him with all the strength his eight-year-old self could muster then never spoke about it to anyone.

Ashes to ashes.

TWENTY-FOUR

Prophets

THERE WERE THREE UNANSWERED CALLS when Dan checked his phone. The first two were hang-ups. On the third he heard Eli sputtering, trying to formulate his thoughts.

"I, uh … it's Eli. I don't know what's going on. Elroy called yesterday. He sounded angry. I'm … I might be in trouble. I'll call you back. Maybe you can help."

This was followed by a long silence, then a hang-up.

Dan hit redial, but there was no answer. He left a message telling Eli to call anytime.

He got in his car and headed south. His stomach was making grumbling noises. It sounded like a dog that had been neglected.

He knew that if he drove up to Horace's farm and knocked on the door he would be invited in to eat. But he felt hollowed out emotionally. It would be easier to eat alone. Besides, he wanted Horace to answer his questions, not cook for him.

Lion's Head was already bustling at that early hour, tourists on the way to the beach, hikers off to tackle the trails. He headed for the town centre and parked outside Lucy's Diner. A *Cottage for Rent* notice hung in its window. Inside, red-and-white striped chairs, an old Coca-Cola sign, and a black-and-white photo of the Corner Convenience from the 1940s. In it, three men stood between two gas pumps that read *PREMIUM*, while a bicycle leaned against a wall off to the right. The place smelled of fried fish.

Eating alone in a small town wasn't the same as eating alone in the city, Dan knew. In the city, people tended to ignore you. You could be dangerous or desperate or lonely. That sort of entertainment was not at a premium. Most people would try to avoid it. In small towns, however, single diners were a source of curiosity. Everyone stopped to stare as he entered. Even the waitress gave him a hard look. He thought for a moment she was going to tell him she couldn't serve him in the state he was in, but she simply cocked a head over to a window seat.

Two couples, one aged and the other in their mid-twenties, took up booths at opposite ends of the room. They were like bookends: before-and-after snapshots of a life. A family of four ate noisily at a table near the back. Families tended to segregate themselves, Dan had noticed. Possibly to spare others the constant reminder of their presence or maybe to avoid the glares they received every time their kids squawked. Dan's father had just used the back of his hand to cuff him whenever he'd got a little bit rowdy.

He hadn't realized how hungry he was until he opened the menu. The food looked good and surprisingly health-conscious. Gluten-free everything, if you asked for it. If they could only manage calorie-free everything.

The waitress came over holding a notepad. Her hair was scruffy and red. It reminded him of a Brillo pad. The dark lines beneath her eyes said she hadn't slept well. She looked as if she hadn't had a good day in twenty years. Thirty.

A scream came from a kid as the waitress took his order. She turned to the kitchen.

"All right, Hazel! I'll be there in a minute." She gave him an apologetic smile. *Kids, huh?*

Dan's face felt stiff when he tried to smile back. He'd have to practise more.

"Coffee, please."

"Anything to eat? I got two pieces of whitefish left. Fresh caught."

"Sounds good. And some scrambled eggs, please."

"Home fries?"

"Yeah, sure."

"Okay, no problem. It'll be a few minutes. I'm doing all the cooking today too."

"I'm not in a rush," Dan told her.

"Oh, thanks."

A trucker, hair greased like a 1950s baseball player, sat across the room. His dark eyes glanced over at Dan. Heavy shadows on cheeks and upper lip. Nicely formed ears. The tight T and creased crotch put Dan on the alert. He thought of Nick and turned away. Where there was sex appeal there was always the potential for sex. Even if you thought you knew yourself.

From the kitchen came the sizzle of a fryer, like the sound of thousands of little kisses, the clinging smell of vinegar in the air. The kid screamed again. The server looked harassed and unhappy when she emerged a few minutes later with his cup of coffee.

The eggs were good, but nowhere near as fresh as Horace's. Dan ate the fish and half the home fries before he felt full, downed his coffee and stood. He left her a $20 tip. She banged on the window once he was outside, holding up the bill. He turned and waved, saw the astonished smile. Hoped he could get the vinegary smell out of his clothes.

Even way out here sex still smelled the same.

"What brings you back so soon?" Horace called out as he opened the door.

The dogs were on Dan in a flash. He ruffled their ears and petted them till they backed off, satisfied that he'd paid his dues and knew who really ran the place.

"I wanted to apologize." Dan smiled. "I couldn't chat the other day, sorry. I'd also like to ask you a few questions, if you're not busy now."

Horace waved him in and headed to the kitchen. "Welcome any time, young Daniel. You and your lions."

Dan smiled at the reference. Then again, he was a biblical scholar of sorts.

"So the boy came back. Ransom got paid, I heard."

"Yes. They were pretty happy to have him home again."

"That's good news. Some mothers would do anything for their kids." Horace nodded and looked off. "Had breakfast yet? Coffee?"

"I'm good, thanks. I had a meal at Lucy's."

"Hmm," Horace intoned. "She still with that bad one? I wish she'd leave him."

Dan thought of the server's harassed look. The question seemed not to require a reply.

"I'm just finishing up. Come on in while I eat my breakfast."

A sweet, oatmealy smell filled the room. Something was baking.

"Cookies," Horace said. "Not done yet."

Dan waited as he scraped up a forkful of scrambled eggs then slurped his coffee, taking pains not to get any on his beard.

"I don't suppose you get to see too much of what goes on around here," Dan said. "Being so isolated and all?"

"Are you kidding? I saw your car the other day. I see everything." The older man pointed with his fork to a window in the back. "That there looks out onto the county roads coming and going in both directions. On a good day, I can see from here clear to the water. What I can't see, I can hear." He cocked his head to the window. "Right now there's a sixteen-wheeler headed here. Flat bed, but heavily loaded. Probably the supply truck from Owen Sound. Comes up the backroads to see his missus." He winked. "He'll stop at every two-bit town between here and Tobermory then get on the *Chi-Cheemaun* and head over to the Sault and on to Thunder Bay. Where he goes after that I don't know."

Dan cocked his head but didn't hear a thing. After thirty seconds, he made out the low grumble of a big truck coming along the roadway. Sure enough, when it swung into view it was large enough to be a sixteen-wheeler. Horace nodded to a pair of binoculars hanging on the wall.

"If you want to count 'em," he said with a wink.

"I'll take your word for it," Dan said. "How'd you know he goes all the way to Thunder Bay? Can you hear that too?"

"Nope. Guy named Fred. I talk to him. He's up every week this time." He grinned. Country life made easy. "See. You just asked the right question. And what I don't have answers for, the Bible surely does."

"'Ask, and it shall be given you,'" Dan said.

"'Seek, and ye shall find.' Matthew 7:7." Horace stood and went over to the oven, pulling on the handle. "And just look what we have found."

Dan watched as he removed a tray of golden-brown cookies and set it on top of the stove. "Something for every occasion."

"You betcha." Horace grinned. "I like Matthew. He's friendlier than some of the others. Not too crazy about the Old Testament in general, though. All that killing and smiting in God's name. Strikes me it goes a little against the grain, eh?"

"Just a little."

"Where are you staying?" Horace asked, returning to his coffee. "Not up to that rich boy's cottage again. I would've heard you."

"Not this time," Dan said. "I stayed in town."

"Ah, I see."

In fact, Dan wouldn't have been surprised if Horace could see that he'd slept in his car.

"You ever see his boat?"

Horace scraped a knife on the inside of a jam jar, pulled out a dollop of red, and spread it over a slice of toast.

"Lots of times. Big one."

Dan pulled out his phone and flipped through the photographs to the two men in the boat leaving the cottage with the ransom.

"Is that his, by any chance?"

Horace leaned in to take a good look then shook his head. "Nah. Too small. His is fancier, with a metal rail around the front. And a flag. That one's got no flag."

"What about the men? Any idea who they might be?"

Again Horace leaned in, and this time looked longer.

"Hard to say with those glary glasses, but I can tell you they're not local to here or I woulda run into them at some point. No, they're not our boys." He paused and looked at Dan. "They bad?"

Dan nodded.

"I see. Sorry, but I can't say who they are."

"Okay. Thanks for that." He put the phone away. "I have to thank you for something. The other day when I left, I went to the caves you mentioned. I found something in one of them that might help solve the case."

Horace looked impressed. "Is that right? I told you it was the caves you wanted."

"Yes, you did. What I'm wondering is if there might be more caves around here, possibly with stalactites."

Horace looked to the window and seemed to see something on a far horizon, gazing off in the distance.

"Down the road in the other direction, along the shore, there's Greig's Caves. That's private property. No stalactites, though."

"Big enough to hide a child in?" Dan asked.

"To tell you the truth, I don't see how. They're not deep at all. Besides, you can't get in without paying. Charges too much, that boy." He shook his head. "The only other caves around that I heard tell of are in the conservation area near Wiarton. Those are pretty shallow too. More like holes in the rocks than actual caves. No, in my opinion you already saw the best of the best, young Daniel."

Dan smiled.

"What keeps you out here, Horace? If you don't mind my asking? I had a blissful moment this morning where the sun shone on my head and all I could hear was the wind on the lake and the birds twittering in the trees. If I could keep that moment going forever I might move here. But I doubt I could sustain it. How do you do it?"

Horace turned back to look at him and pushed his plate aside. "Come with me," he said, wiping his lips on a napkin.

He struck out across the field in his hobbling walk, managing to outpace Dan as he headed for the trees. Hay bales had been rolled into wheels, standing upright, rather than in flat rectangles. Easier to move, probably.

"Don't worry about Old Dobbins," Horace called over his shoulder. "He's in the other pasture."

Dan could see them before they reached the end of the field. Two mounds. Two crosses. The birth dates were different, but the end dates were the same: February 27, 1999. Florence and Adeline McLean. *Mother and daughter,* Dan thought. Above: *And death shall have no dominion.* Not the Bible. Dylan Thomas.

Horace stood there wringing his hands, making murmuring noises. "My family."

"I'm sorry," Dan said.

"Happened out on the old county road. Drunk driver. I was here waiting for them. They never came home. Some things stay with you forever, eh? I could never leave them. Not till I'm ready to join them, that is."

He closed his eyes and began a low crooning. It might have been a prayer or a hymn.

When he opened his eyes again he said, "'He will wipe every tear from their eyes. There will be no more death or mourning or crying or pain, for the old order of things has passed away.' Revelations 21:4. That's what I'm waiting for — for the old order to pass away."

"Could be a long time coming," Dan said.

"I got patience. 'Blessed are those who mourn, for they will be comforted.' That's Matthew again."

"Don't you get lonely?"

"All the time. Eats at me like acid in my soul."

In the distance, Dan saw the bull come up to the fence and turn its bulky head in their direction. He hoped there wouldn't be any burnt offerings while he was there.

Horace looked up the hill in the direction of Dennis Braithwaite's cottage. "Drives a grey Porsche, that rich boy. Nice little number."

Dan pictured Dennis Braithwaite's desktop, the Porsche key sitting beside the photographs.

"Have you seen it recently?"

Dan waited. Horace was looking off into the distance again, his face an enigma. There was no forcing a biblical prophet.

"'And Lot went up from Zoar, and his two daughters with him. For he was afraid to stay in Zoar; and he stayed in a cave, he and his two daughters.' That's Genesis."

"You seem to know the Bible inside out."

"It keeps me company." He looked off again. "'Thorn and thistle will grow on their altars. Then they will say to the mountains, Cover us! And to the hills, Fall on us!' That's from the Book of Prophets."

He watched Dan out of the corner of his eye, his face a stone.

"There is no Book of Prophets," Dan said. "Even I know that."

"Sometimes I make them up." Horace winked. "Yes. He comes up here. I see him. He thinks I don't see him, but I do."

"Was he here the weekend the boy disappeared?"

"Oh, sure. That car was up here that weekend. Didn't stay long, though. All that way just to leave again? Thought it strange at the time, but not my business really."

He looked back to the house.

"Cookies'll be ready now."

Dan suspected he'd get no closer than that, but it was something. Dennis Braithwaite's car had been up to the Bruce Peninsula the weekend Jeremy went missing. Janice said he hadn't replied to her text asking for the use of the cottage. He, on the other hand, claimed he told her she could use it while he was getting high in Toronto. Why lie unless you had something to hide? The only question was what was he hiding?

He had just pulled off the 401 and merged onto the DVP when he called. Dennis picked up on the first ring.

"You lied, Dennis. You were in the Bruce Peninsula the weekend Jeremy went missing."

There was a long pause. "Unless you have proof of that, you better not make any public accusations. I assure you my lawyers don't scare. They go in for the kill. And mine are the best in the country."

"Your Porsche was seen at the cottage."

"Doesn't mean I was driving it."

It was a feeble response, not even a denial.

"I had every gas station CCTV pulled all the way up to prove you were there that weekend. And guess what I found?"

Another long silence. Dan saw him calculating the odds on that one. He was willing to take the chance. Big engine, full tank, no stopping. But chances were.

"What did Janice tell you?"

A good guess then.

"She said she never got your reply saying she could use the cottage that weekend."

"That's a lie. I sent a text. It's still on my phone, if you want to see it."

"So why did you go up?"

"Am I being taped?"

"No. This is between you and me. Off the record."

"I went up to talk to her. She knows I don't like Ashley — for obvious reasons. I thought from her text that she and Jeremy would be there alone."

"What did you want to talk to her about?"

He hesitated. "About us. Getting back together. I told her before if she wanted to use my insurance for him then she had to come back to me. I thought I could convince her."

Dan thought of the photos on Dennis's desktop. Happier times. Just as he'd told Nick.

"And what did she say?"

"I never saw her. I drove up late Saturday night and left again the next morning. I thought she'd changed her mind and wasn't coming up after all. I tried her cell, but it was out of range. If she was even there. Which I wasn't sure she was."

"But she was."

The city's skyline zoomed into view, the towers rising in the distance as he headed south.

"Obviously. Look — I want her back, all right? I'm not ashamed to admit it. And Janice knows it. But she keeps toying with me. So there you have it. But I didn't kidnap that kid of hers."

"So you keep saying."

"Why would I?" Dennis's reply was a snarl.

That's what I keep wondering, Dan thought. *Why would you?*

TWENTY-FIVE

Flip

KED WAS HEADING BACK TO BC the next day. Kendra had planned a party for him. Barbecue smells pervaded the backyard, laughter and fun. The air was filled with the *doohf! doohf! doohf!* of club music. Dan's choice would have been jazz. *Music ought to have melodies, lightness, lift*, he thought. *Places where people can enter. Not just heavy thuds.* Branding him from another time altogether.

A number of Ked's high school friends were there, along with his girlfriend, Elizabeth. The gang was fleshed out with Kendra, Lester, Donny, and Prabin. All the usual suspects, as Dan liked to joke. All except one.

"You can't force it to happen," Kendra told him.

"I'd hoped he'd be here. It would make him feel more like family. Donny still doesn't want to know him and Ked hasn't really had a chance. They've been like oil and water all summer."

"Well, I like him if that's any consolation." She took his arm and pulled him away from his grill duties. "Come on. Let's take some photos."

They lined up and took turns being odd-man out while taking the shots. Ked and his friends made a pyramid of bodies on hands and knees, the ones on the bottom grunting and groaning as the others climbed on top. They managed three rows before the weight threatened to collapse the entire lot. Dan caught the effort just in time.

"Okay," he called out, handing back Ked's phone. "More burgers coming up."

His cell rang as he strolled over to the barbecue. It was Nick. "Hey — we're all here waiting for you."

"Sorry, I probably won't make it." His voice sounded gravelly with fatigue. "I'm stuck here for at least another hour or two."

"Emergency?"

"No, just a bureaucratic nightmare."

Dan eyed the gathering. "Jesus, Nick. I want them to like you. Can't you get off a little earlier?"

"Hey! I'm doing the best I can."

Dan felt immediate chagrin. "Sorry. Forget I said that."

"They'll get to know me in time. I'm not going anywhere."

No, but Ked is, Dan wanted to say. He held his tongue.

"You're right. It's okay. Listen, things are pretty busy here. I'm holding up the burger line," he said, though there was no one waiting to be fed.

"I'll talk to you later. I'll try my best to get there."

"Okay, thanks."

He was flipping the burgers. Flip, flip, flip. Things happening incessantly, flying out of his control. Flip, flip, flip.

Hard to depend on people. Maybe it was the heat, but he couldn't control his anger. It had stealth. It crept up quietly. Not swift and sudden, like a strike of lightning. It was unpredictable, coming over him like a slow burn, a dull eruption that would last a lifetime, if he so chose.

Flip.

Donny came up to him as he was laying another line of burgers on the grill. "So he's a no-show?"

"Work." Dan avoided looking at him. "He got an emergency call."

Donny shrugged, as though to say that was par for the course when you dated a cop. "Your son's leaving."

"I know that." Dan turned, brandishing the spatula. "Do you think you'll ever give Nick a chance?"

"Whoa!" Donny held his hands up. "It's you I'm worried about."

"And why is that?"

"Because you have a history of dating losers and lost puppies?"

Dan felt himself bridle. "Nick's not like that."

"An alcoholic? Tell me about it."

"*Recovering* alcoholic." Dan fought to keep his anger in check. "I'm a recovering alcoholic too, lest we forget."

Donny crossed his arms and leaned against the railing. "And one plus one makes two. Do you really think it's a good combination?"

"Forget this bullshit." Dan glanced over to the others. He lowered his voice. "You're not worried about me. You know I can handle myself. Why don't you like cops?"

"Because they're one step away from criminals. Because they throw their weight around. Only they do it with impunity. They're really criminals who just aren't brave enough to be criminals. They want the glory, but not the punishment."

"That's so ..." Dan made a face, "stupid. Some of them genuinely want to help people."

"Great. I'm sure there are some good ones. But I'd like to see proof that Nick is one of them."

"Well, if you got to know him a little better, you might. But until then."

"Until then it won't happen. I hear you."

"So what then?"

"Until then, you're going to go on resenting me for not seeing things your way. Because that's what you do. And I'm going to keep on thinking what I think until I see a reason to change my mind. Because that's what I do. So we need to agree to disagree."

"That'll get tired pretty quickly. Do you dislike Nick for some reason I don't know about?"

"Would it make things easier for you if I did?"

Dan didn't answer. He turned back to the barbecue.

"Anyway, you need to trust your judgment and stop worrying what other people think." Donny pushed off from the railing. "If you love him then stick with him. What I think isn't going to make one bit of difference in how you feel about him. Sorry for being a drag at your son's party."

He turned and walked away.

Dan looked over at the crowd. Kendra and Prabin were up on the porch laughing over something. On the far side of the yard, Donny's adopted son, Lester, seemed to be flirting with two people at once, a boy and a girl. Dan saw Lester give Ked a smile and two thumbs-up.

Ked nodded back then headed over to the barbecue with a paper plate held out. "Three more burgers, please. I'm taking orders."

"Will do. Everybody enjoying themselves?"

"Seem to be. This was a fun idea."

"It was your mother's, so make sure you thank her."

"I already did. But as usual you're doing all the work. So thank you too."

"You're welcome."

Dan shovelled three burgers onto buns and piled them on the plate. He glanced over at Lester again.

"Lester doesn't seem to know what he wants these days," he said.

"It's the polyamorous thing," Ked said. "Everybody's experimenting. Elizabeth and I are more old-fashioned." He squirted ketchup and relish on the burgers and squashed the lids closed.

"What's wrong with knowing what you want?" Dan asked. "When I found Lester on the streets, he told me he was gay."

"He is. It's the other two. They're trying to convince him to play with them."

"Ah."

"So Nick's not coming?" Ked asked, chomping into one of the burgers while balancing the plate in his other hand.

"Looks like it," Dan said. "He's stuck at work."

"I don't think you need to worry about it," Ked said. "Though I concur with Uncle Donny."

"What's that?"

"I like him enough, but it's what you want that matters."

Dan closed the barbecue lid and turned it off. "Well, then I guess everything is good."

"Is something bugging you?"

Dan attempted a smile. "It's my problem. Don't worry about it."

"Okay. Try not to look so serious. You might scare somebody."

Dan laughed. "All right."

The barbecue lasted another hour before starting to disband. When the others had gone, Ked offered to help clean up, but Dan sent him off with Elizabeth, who looked grateful for Dan's insistence.

"Have fun. It's your last day together."

"We will!" she said.

His cell rang.

"Sharp," he said, surveying the remnants of the party scattered across the backyard.

The first thing he heard was sobbing. "It's Eli," Janice managed to get out.

"What's happened?"

"He's dead." She sobbed again. "His car overturned on an exit ramp."

"I'll be right over," Dan said.

TWENTY-SIX

The Silent Boy

A MILLION THOUGHTS PASSED THROUGH Dan's mind as he headed to Janice's home. This case was supposed to have been over when Jeremy Bentham was returned alive and well. Instead it continued to eat its victims, right, left, and centre: Janice and her mother parting irrevocably, the strange woman Theda McPhail found strangled, and now Eli dead in a car accident. Whatever was going on, Dan felt sure it wasn't going to end well for anyone.

Ashley opened the door. She nodded a quick acceptance of his condolences then led him to the kitchen, where Janice was filling a knapsack. The lights were dimmed, as usual. Dan looked over and saw the camping gear piled to one side: sleeping bags, tents, a cooler of food.

"You're going on a trip?"

"We're getting out of the city. We're leaving tonight."

Jeremy crouched on the floor over in a corner, scribbling with a crayon on the same drawing pad Dan had seen the other day. His movements were slow and deliberate, as though he had a delicate operation to perform. What he wouldn't give to be able to ask him about the cave-like drawing and the eyeless face. Maybe that was how the boy saw himself: a face without eyes. He pictured himself as a child and wondered how many times he'd done the same thing, turning a blind eye to what went on around him, sitting in silence and hoping no one would notice him. Silence had always been a good, reliable friend when he needed one. Only Sandy had been better.

"Hello, Jeremy," Dan said.

But Jeremy gave no indication he'd heard. His fingers moved in their careful movements across the pages.

"The police called about an hour ago," Janice said. Her voice was low and calm, as though to keep from upsetting her son. "They found his car overturned on an overpass near the 401."

"I'm very sorry," Dan said. "Any idea what caused the accident?"

"No." She wiped a hand across her face. "Well, not that we've been told."

Ashley looked from Dan to Janice. "You have to tell him," she said.

Dan's eyes went back and forth between the two women.

"It's the kidnapping," Janice said. "We think it was Eli and Elroy."

"What makes you think that?"

Before she could answer, Jeremy made a startling sound. They all turned. The boy looked distractedly around the room; his hands twitched as though he were attempting sign language.

"Sweetie, it's okay. We're just talking," Janice said softly. She turned to Dan. "It's the hands. When he does that it means he's getting agitated."

Jeremy repeated the sound, halfway between a growl and a yawn. To Dan it sounded as if he disapproved of something, making him wonder about the boy's capacity to understand what they were saying. Just as suddenly, he turned his attention back to his drawing pad.

"Go on," Dan said. "Tell me about it."

"Eli and Elroy were at each other's throats," Janice said. "It went on for months. We were terrified. Then suddenly, a few weeks back, everything was fine between them. It was as if they were best friends again. Only they were never friends to begin with. Two days ago the calls and threats started again. Eli was afraid to go to bed at night."

"Are you saying Eli's death may not have been an accident?"

"We never trusted Elroy," Ashley said. "Eli called him a businessman. We knew what it meant. He's a dealer. Sarah's dealer."

"He already knows that," Janice said. "You might as well tell him everything. There's no sense keeping the rest of it back now."

"It was the treatment. So expensive." Her expression was one of disapproval. "But Eli was adamant. He would raise the money. Anything for Jeremy. So he made the deal with Elroy."

"Do you think Elroy killed Eli?" Dan asked.

"We don't know what to think." Janice wiped a hand across her brow. "For the past few days we've been followed by a navy blue car every time we leave the house. That's why we're getting out of here."

"If you think you're in danger, I can make arrangements for you to stay elsewhere."

She shook her head. "No. We'll be okay."

"Theda McPhail probably thought the same thing."

She shivered. "I can't think what possible connection there might be. I don't even know who she was."

Jeremy suddenly made another high-pitched sound.

"What is it, sweetie?"

She knelt and stroked his hair, turning a page of his pad. He went back to drawing. Clearly, he did know how to communicate. And his mother knew how to interpret what he was saying.

If anything redeemed her, Dan saw, it was her love for her child. Apart from that he hadn't even been able to see her as a likeable person. She knew how to charm, but she was too hard and inaccessible otherwise. Then again, people said that of him.

Her eyes were similar to Jeremy's. Dan's eyes had been like his mother's too. Grey. *Wolf eyes*, she'd called him to his delight, though hers had been more like quicksilver. After her death he'd come across a mineral kit in science class. This was in Sudbury, where mining lay at the core of everything. Alongside pyrite, and a stringy piece of asbestos before such things were deemed dangerous, was a vial of mercury. The liquid metal had fascinated him. He'd prised the cap off, spilling it across the floor in all directions. In a panic, he'd tried to rebottle it, only to discover its elusive nature. It had reminded him of his mother's eyes. But Dan's eyes had not stayed wolf-like. *Glacial* was what people said now. Distant and chilled, as if what lay inside him had somehow been turned outside.

There was a knock at the door. Janice and Ashley glanced at one another. Dan saw the fear.

"Are we expecting someone?" Ashley asked.

"No."

Ashley went down the hall.

"Be careful," Janice called out.

She turned to Dan. He could see a question forming on her lips. Speak, don't speak. Speak, don't speak.

"Is there something you want to say?" he asked.

She looked startled. "No. It's okay."

Don't speak.

Voices carried in from the hall. Footsteps came toward them. Ashley appeared first. Sarah Nealon stopped in the hallway behind her, her face half in shadow.

"Sarah!" Janice cried. "You can't come here."

"I know!"

She stepped forward into the light. Denim skirt and a baby-doll top. *No pregnancy*, Dan thought. Feet bare. Her ankle monitor was missing. Then he saw the bruises.

"My god! What happened?" Janice cried.

"He hit me!"

"Who?"

"Elroy!"

"Is he here?" Janice turned to Ashley. "Did you look?"

"He's not on the street. I didn't see him."

Janice turned back to Sarah. "Why did he hit you?"

"He didn't get his money."

"What money?"

But Sarah was staring at Dan now, her expression fearful. "What's *he* doing here?"

"Dan is trying to help us figure things out," Janice said quietly. It was the voice of a patient adult speaking to a child. "We've had some very bad news, Sarah."

Sarah put her fingers to her belly. "Is it my baby?"

"No, Sarah." Janice shook her head. "It's Eli. He's dead."

Sarah sat quickly, folding herself onto the chair. Her eyes darted around the room, as if searching for the reassuring swirls of the sun-catcher.

"Did — did Elroy — ? Oh, no!"

A high-pitched shriek filled the room. They all turned to see Jeremy flailing his arms. He threw the drawing pad against the wall. It splashed back then skidded across the floor, landing at Dan's feet.

Janice went to him. "Baby — what's wrong?"

He fought off her attempts to hold him. The shrieking continued.

"Poor Jeremy," Sarah said, her voice rising.

Janice turned to Ashley. "Can you please get her out of here?"

"We have to bring her with us," Ashley said. "She's not safe."

"She can't come with us, Ash. She's high as a kite."

"I'm sorry!" Sarah cried.

"I can't deal with this on top of everything else," Janice said. "She needs to be at CAMH."

"She'll never get a bed. It took six hours last time."

"Fine. You deal with her."

Ashley glared. "Sometimes I think you're not even human."

"Tough!"

Sarah sobbed. "It's all my fault."

Ashley turned to Sarah. "Come on. It's not your fault. Let's go for a walk." She took her by the arm, leading her out of the room.

"Fucking junkie," Janice said, watching them go.

Just then Jeremy let out another howl. Wolf-like. Feral. His eyes were ravaged, like someone witnessing desolation first-hand.

"I knew this would happen. He's having a meltdown." Janice brushed the hair from his forehead. "It's okay, baby."

Dan leaned down and picked up the drawing pad. The exposed pages showed a tangle of scrawls like oversized fingerprints. Shadowy blurs and half-human shapes hidden in the background. Lives blending in with other lives, the unfathomable skein of relationships between people and things. Things only Jeremy could understand and interpret.

"That son-of-a-bitch, hitting her like that," Janice said softly, hugging her son and rocking him as his protests continued.

"Do you think Elroy did it?" Dan asked.

She turned and stared. "Of course he did it. You saw her face!"

"She's a drug addict. I wouldn't take her word for a lot of things," Dan said. "She isn't wearing her ankle monitor. She must have cut it off."

"Lucky for us," Janice said. "That's all we need is the cops here."

"I followed Elroy to the airport two days ago," Dan said. "He was headed out of town."

"Good riddance," she said dismissively. Then it dawned on her. "Then that would mean he wasn't here when Eli died."

"Exactly," Dan said. "In fact, he's never around when things happen."

"He could have hired someone to do it," Janice insisted.

"But why wouldn't Elroy get his money if he and Eli masterminded the kidnapping?"

"How should I know? Maybe Eli decided to keep it all for himself." She continued rocking Jeremy. "This isn't how it was supposed to be," she said softly.

"How was it supposed to be? Tell me."

She glared at him. "Better. Different. Not like this."

Jeremy's whimpering slowed then finally stopped. Janice stood and went over to a drawer. She pulled it open and removed a handgun.

"Yes, I have a permit," she said, catching Dan's look. "This is coming with us when we leave."

"What about Eli? Who's making arrangements for him?"

She stared at him. "He's dead, Dan. There's nothing anyone can do for him now."

Dan sat in his car outside in the street. He had Nick on the phone.

"I'm sorry," Nick began. "I really tried to make it."

So many people had been sorry for so many things of late that it took Dan a moment to realize what he was talking about.

"Oh, the barbecue! No, it's okay."

"Meaning what? No one noticed I didn't show up?"

"No, it's …" Dan ran a hand through his hair. "I need you to do something for me. It's important. Eli Gestner died today."

"What? The father of that kid?"

"Yes. Car accident."

"Jesus."

There was a long pause.

"Are you sure it was an accident, Dan? What's going on?"

"Eli left a message for me yesterday saying Elroy was angry with him again. That was the last I heard from him. Now Janice and Ashley are leaving town. Someone in a blue car has been following them. They're worried for their safety."

"Do they want protection?"

"No."

"I guess they're entitled to leave if they want."

"Janice is taking a handgun."

"Christ. Don't let her shoot someone."

"I'll try not to. In the meantime, could you look into a few things for me?"

Nick sighed. "I'm still on nights. But I can pass them by Lydia before I start. With any luck, I'll have some answers for you tomorrow."

TWENTY-SEVEN

The Oracle

DAN BARELY SLEPT THAT NIGHT and when he did it was fitful. Nevertheless, he got up early the next morning and made a big breakfast — scrambled eggs, sausages and pancakes. It was Ked's last day. Ralph lay at Ked's feet through the entire meal, as if the suitcases at the front door had alerted him that parting was imminent. Afterward, Dan cleared the dishes while Ked loaded his bags in the car. Then they set off.

Ked talked excitedly about his upcoming courses, describing professors and other students he was looking forward to seeing again. He mentioned a favourite restaurant on Davie Street. He was upbeat despite leaving his parents and girlfriend behind.

"It's only temporary," he said, more to console himself than Dan. "I'll be back."

He declined to give his father further tips on dating, however. It was as if the subject had been exhausted.

Ked's flight left at nine-thirty. When he arrived in Vancouver it would still be morning there, Dan calculated, though it would already be afternoon here in Toronto. Another time zone, another life. And one he knew little of. Elizabeth had declined to see him off. Not wanting an emotional leave-taking, was his guess. He wasn't the only one uncomfortable with feelings.

They said a quick goodbye. Dan hugged his son and watched him disappear through the sliding glass doors, the same doors Elroy James had vanished behind three days earlier.

He got back in his car and drove north out of the city, keeping the windows rolled up and the AC blasting. Outside, the air was sweltering, fields of corn and cabbages threatening to burst. Summer at its fullest was also summer waiting to catapult into fall, another year coming to an end. *And what have I accomplished?* Dan wondered. A sense of futility pervaded things.

He tried Janice's cellphone to see if they had arrived safely, wherever they were going. He hadn't asked their destination and she hadn't volunteered it. The call went straight to voice mail. Out of range, Dan conjectured. Meaning they were likely back in the Bruce Peninsula. Wherever they were, he hoped they were safe.

After half an hour, he swung the car around in the middle of a deserted stretch of highway and headed back to the city. He hadn't set foot in his office for nearly a week. Maybe there was something there that could shake him out of his doldrums. In fact, there was, but it wasn't the kind of shaking he wanted. A notice tacked to the corkboard next to his door announced that the building was being refurbished before being put on the market. That was all he needed. Nick was losing his boss and Dan would soon be losing his home base.

He'd been calling this office home for four years, but now it was coming to an end. Developers. The profit-takers had caught the scent of a kill. They weren't in the death throws yet, but it was inherent in new ownership. You didn't just buy a building. You took it over — girders, beams, roofs — and milked it. You took away what it had been before and made it yours. And no one ever stopped to worry whether the old tenants would be able to afford the new rates. *Tant pis.* He wasn't looking forward to moving, but there was no doubt it was coming. Just as Nick would inevitably have a new boss, a changing of the guards. Like it or not.

At first change happened incrementally, so slowly you could barely see it. Then one day it came on sudden, overwhelming you as you did whatever it took to hold everything in place. He wondered if it had been like that for his father when he sensed his wife's death approaching, like a giant wave tilting everything around him or flattening it to the ground like a helicopter's blades on landing.

Sometimes you were able to withstand the change; other times you crashed and burned. He thought of Eli Gestner. One moment you were alive, the next you were gone.

At least for now, Dan was still here. He would weather the new owners till they forced him out. Nick would stand up to a new boss till one of them cracked.

Nick was there when he got home. Dan thought of telling him that Ked had said goodbye, but that would be a lie.

Instead, he said the leave-taking had been quick and painless. Ked would see them at Christmas.

"Any news about the new boss?"

Nick shrugged. "Nothing I don't already know. Sometime before the end of the year is what it looks like."

"So you'll have time to adjust."

"Should do, yes."

Ralph was lying on his cushion in the kitchen, already moping over his absent master. Nick passed Dan a cup of coffee then pulled out a sheet of paper and placed it on the table.

"Your list," he said.

Dan looked over. "Yes?"

"First off, Eli Gestner."

"Was there an insurance policy dated about a year ago?"

"Yes." Nick stared at him. "Lots of people have insurance policies. How did you know it was made out a year ago?"

"That's when they got Jeremy's official diagnosis. Eli knew it was going to cost them a lot of money."

Dan thought of Eli that first day on leaving his office: *My son is everything to me. I would do anything for Jeremy.* Had it included killing himself? It would be nice to be sure. But then that was the point. If anyone could prove it was suicide there would be no insurance. He might never have the certainty of knowing.

Nick was nodding. "There are no other benefactors. Not even Janice Bentham. Just his son."

"Something to ponder," was all Dan said.

"I also did a little follow-up on his finances. He was well off after both parents died a couple years apart about a decade ago. He lived on that for a while, but something took a chunk out of his savings a few months ago."

"The bad business deal," Dan said. "The one with Elroy James."

"Sounds like you're already there." Nick turned back to the papers. "And then there's this little nugget: Marietta Valverde's parents? The ones she sponsored to come to Canada?"

"When are they coming?"

Nick looked triumphant. "They're already here. They've been in Canada for over a month now."

Dan felt a jolt. "Why would they —?"

"Lie? You tell me," Nick said. "It's your list."

Dan sipped his coffee, pondering the unexpected information. "So where are they?"

"Still working on that. I also followed up on the mothers. Clarice Bentham is a very successful businesswoman, no unanswered questions about finances or anything like that. If there's dirt, I couldn't find it. And as I already said, Ashley's mother disappeared after she was released from the home. I couldn't find anything new on her, but I found the mother of the surrogate, Sarah Nealon. She's another one who checks out as clean as far as the law is concerned. Apparently there is very little contact between her and her daughter. And she plans to keep it that way."

"She said that?"

"That and more. She's all but disowned her daughter."

"So nothing useful then," Dan said.

"Not until we get to Janice Bentham. As a teenager, she went from being a model student to getting kicked out of one school after another for bad behaviour. Truancy, drugs."

"That would tally up with the abuse she was experiencing at home," Dan said.

Nick nodded. "It makes sense. But there's more. I found a court-ordered ban on something that happened at her last school."

Dan put his coffee cup down. "A ban? Because she was still a juvenile?"

"Not quite sixteen."

"That's around the time she said she left home. Any indication what it was?"

"There was nothing in the file."

"Can you find out?"

Nick's look was pure rebuke. "You want me to break a court order?"

"If you can."

"Sure, no problem. I'll just put my job in jeopardy for you. Again."

Dan reached across the table and took Nick's hand. "Isn't that what love is all about?"

Nick sighed.

"And Elroy James?" Dan asked.

"Elroy James is the mystery man in all of this. Never finished high school, in and out of juvie for a few years. Then suddenly, hey, presto! He's rich. Only it's not entirely clear how. Elroy Enterprises owns a couple of small bars in the Caribbean and a strip club in Kapuskasing. None of those would have made him a millionaire, though."

"What about the recent trip?"

"His flight was to North Bay. I pulled a favour and had him followed when he landed. Two hours to Killarney, in fact, where he spent the night at a cabin owned by some bikers. Great place up on some rocks overlooking the lake. It's a meth lab. I couldn't bust them, but I'm told that's coming. At least now we know what he does."

"Sure, but does that make him a killer who would run a business partner off the road?"

"Hard to say. Crooks don't care where the money comes from. If you pay your debts, then you're home free. But if you don't ..." He left it unfinished. "Now your turn. And don't tell me you still don't have any suspects, because there are enough here to sink a ship or cast a B movie. At least give me your theories."

Dan smiled. "Okay, theory number one: Eli and Elroy concocted the kidnapping together."

"So they just pretended to be enemies?"

"No — I think they really were enemies after the business deal went sour. They stayed that way until one of them came up with a plan. Because Eli still needed to pay off Elroy."

"In that case, why would Elroy kill Eli if the kidnapping was successful?"

"Good question. Which leads me to theory number two: Eli concocted the kidnapping on his own to pay off Elroy. But instead of paying him off, he decided to keep the money for his son."

Nick whistled. "So Elroy might have killed him for revenge."

"Correct." He looked at Nick. "There's a third possibility. Eli had nothing to do with the kidnapping and simply resorted to his original plan, which was to kill himself so Jeremy could cash in on the insurance policy."

"Then who has the money you left in the cottage in the Bruce?"

"That I do not know. But someone has it. And it's not Theda McPhail."

"Too bad you can't ask her," Nick said.

"No, I can't," Dan said, as a thought struck him. "But I know someone I *can* ask."

It was a beautiful afternoon. The neighbourhood was calm and serene. Theda McPhail's neighbour, Carole, answered his knock promptly.

"Oh, there you are!" she said with a smile, as though she'd just been waiting all that time for him to return.

"Good morning, Carole. How are you?"

"I'm fine. I was just trying to figure out how to get in touch to let you know about the funeral," she said. Her smile took a sudden downturn. "But then you didn't know her, did you?"

"No, I didn't know her."

"You don't look anything like her nephews. I'm not sure why I thought that."

"I'm a private investigator," Dan said.

Carole's face lit up as though it made up for her disappointment. "That must be exciting!"

"Carole — would you mind if I asked you a few questions?"

The idea seemed to appeal to her. "If you think it would help. Yes, of course."

She glanced behind her into the house as though considering whether it was safe to invite him inside. Curiosity won out. They went into the living room, nearly identical in layout to Theda's but with a mint-green carpet.

Dan waited as she made coffee.

"Did you speak to her often?" he asked, accepting the cup she offered.

"All the time!" Her eyes widened, as though she suddenly realized it would never happen again. "Hardly a day went by that I didn't see her, sometimes in the morning when she was leaving for work and again when she came home in the evening. She loved her job, you know. She was always friendly, always had time for a chat. A really good neighbour."

She cradled her cup and sat looking off, clearly thinking what a good neighbour Theda had been.

"Had anything been disturbing her lately?" Dan asked. "Anything she might have mentioned, even casually?"

"Apart from the cancer, you mean? Well, let me think." She cast back in her mind. "Now what did we talk about recently? About her retirement, certainly. That had just started. And I seem to recall she said something about having the plumbing looked at. Her basement floods when it rains and she said how she needed to find someone to do that."

"Did she have someone in to look at the plumbing?"

"No, I don't think she did. In fact, I remember she said she would do it next week, because there was something else she needed to clear up first."

"What was that?"

"Something to do with a former student," she said. "She said she'd had a shock. This was a few weeks back now. She was sitting on her porch and she was doing the puzzles.

But it wasn't the same day she discovered her name was an anagram for death." Carole stopped for a moment to glance out the window at Theda's front yard. "Imagine going your whole life and not knowing your name is an anagram for death. Seems a bit odd, doesn't it?"

"Yes. It does."

"They're funny, aren't they? Anagrams, I mean."

"Listen," Dan said. "Silent."

Silence had always worked for him. In fact, it was the only way he could hear his inner thoughts.

"Hmm?" She cupped a hand to her ear. "I can't hear anything."

He shook his head. "No, I was just ... please continue."

She nodded. "Well, it got me thinking, you know."

"Yes?"

"I started wondering what my name would be an anagram for. Carole — with an *e*. Can you guess?"

"No," Dan said.

"Oracle!" she said. "I'm the oracle!"

Dan sat tight. It was like waiting for Horace to get to the point.

"But you asked what might be disturbing her. She did say it had something to do with the death of one of her students. A young man. She said something didn't add up right."

Dan's ears pricked up. "What was that?"

She looked off for a moment then shook her head. "I'm afraid I can't remember. But I got the feeling it was some time ago."

"Can you recall anything else? Where the death took place?"

"Well, it would have been here in Toronto. Theda always taught school in Toronto."

"And did she say what she planned to do about it?"

"I don't know that she was going to do anything about it, just that she was going to look into it."

"Did she mention the young man's name?"

"Yes, I think she did. Now let me see." She put a hand to her forehead, an oracle waiting for intuition to strike. "No, it's not coming to me, but I seem to recall it was one of those ambiguous boy-girl names. Like Jesse or Robin." She gave him a bemused look. "I once knew a woman who named her daughter Michael, if you can believe it. And also a boy named Shirley."

Another five minutes produced no further revelations. Dan put down his cup and held out his card.

"Thank you for speaking with me, Carole. Please call me if you remember anything else."

"*Dan Sharp, Private Investigator.*" She read the card with a look of amazement. "I will certainly let you know if I do."

Pleasant Valley had probably never seemed so exciting.

TWENTY-EIGHT

O.D.

DAN GOT NICK ON HIS CELL. He sounded as though he'd just woken up. It struck Dan that a great deal of their relationship took place over the phone between Nick's shifts. Not unlike Ked's different time zones.

"The neighbour said Theda McPhail remembered something about the death of a former student. She said Theda told her that something didn't add up right and she was going to look into it."

Nick was silent.

"The court-ordered blackout in Janice's record. You said the incident took place at a school?"

"Correct."

"If it's still on the records it would have to have been something serious. Like aggravated assault or even manslaughter."

"Sure — it's a good likelihood." He cleared his throat.

"But it's still being suppressed?"

"Confidentiality, rules — you know how it is. I could try to find someone involved in the case. They might be able to tell me something. Unless there was money involved."

"Like a payoff for certain privileges?"

"It's possible."

"Janice said Theda McPhail showed up at her front door twice, but left without saying why she'd come. She came back a third time, but fled when Janice took a photo of her. Obviously she had something on her mind."

"And you think Janice was a former student of McPhail's?"

We met in a stupid posh school for rich kids, Janice had said when he asked where she'd met Eli.

"That's what I'm thinking. Her mother's rich. She could have paid to have the file suppressed. Not necessarily out of love, but to protect her own reputation."

"I could look into it," Nick said, "but what would it prove? What do you think is really going on here?"

"I think no one is telling me the truth and it's been like that from the beginning."

A beeping interrupted his reply.

"Hang on a second," Dan said. "I've got a call coming through."

He put Nick on hold. "Sharp."

"Hi, my name is Elaine. From Café Frederic?" The voice was hesitant. "I work with Ted."

"Hello, Elaine. How can I help?"

"He said if — if I was ever worried about him to call you. He said you'd know what I meant."

"Yes?" Dan's mind was instantly on the alert.

"He hasn't shown up for his shift. He's never done that before. I've been calling his number, but there's no answer. I went over to his place on my break, but he didn't answer when I knocked. I heard his cat meowing inside."

"Is there any reason he might not be answering?"

"His grandmother died yesterday. They were very close. Still, it's just not like him to not return my calls. I'm just — worried."

"What's his address?"

She gave him the address and unit number.

"I'll head over now," Dan said.

He got Nick back on the line.

"I'll meet you there," Nick said.

It turned out to be a small walk-up with four floors and a shabby lobby. The front door was unlatched. Nick got there first. Together, they headed up the stairs.

Nick pounded on the door. "Ted? Are you in there?"

There was no answer. Nick looked to Dan and shook his head. "We don't have time to wait."

He pressed his shoulder to the door and pushed once, twice. The third time it flew inward with a snapping of wood and frame.

A neighbour's head stuck out of the door at the end of the hall.

Hey!" he called out.

"Police business," Nick called back. "Have you seen your neighbour lately?"

"No."

Nick held out his badge. "Please go inside."

The neighbour hesitated then seemed to decide that Nick was the real deal. He closed his door softly behind him.

Dan was glad to have Nick with him; he'd hate to break into Ted's apartment then have the police arrive. They stepped past the broken frame. The place was shrouded in a soft gloom. A cat hissed and cowered behind an armchair. The only window, on the far side of the room, emitted a faint afternoon light. There was a smell of sickness in the air.

"Ted?"

They headed down the hall. Ted lay on the floor inside a darkened bedroom.

Nick was on his knees, shaking his unresponsive figure. "Ted! Ted, can you hear me?"

Dan turned on the light and looked around. A dusting of grey-white powder streaked the bedside table. Several small see-through envelopes lay beside it.

Nick pulled Ted's eyelids down. The white was shot through with red. A tremor shook his hands.

"He's breathing. Call 911," Nick commanded.

Dan reached emergency services, giving the address and explaining the situation.

"Come on, Teddy!" Nick slapped Ted's face lightly. "Come back. Ted! Ted!"

As he watched them, Dan felt a buzz. He pulled out his phone. The incoming number wasn't familiar, but he answered anyway, thinking it might be Elaine again.

"Sharp."

"Hello, Mr. Sharp?"

It was a woman's voice, but not one he recognized right away.

"Yes."

"It's Carole Dawson. Theda McPhail's neighbour. You said to call —"

"I'm sorry, Carole. It's not a good time." Dan cast an eye outside on the street. There was no ambulance yet. No sound of a siren in the distance.

"It's just that I remembered what she said. She said the wrong person got blamed. In the death, I mean. She also said there was a girl involved. That was what she wanted to look into. Theda said the girl's name was Kathy."

Kathy.

Janice's real name. The name Theda had called her. It was exactly the sort of thing a school teacher would know and remember. And what had Eli said that night driving up to the Bruce? *I used to take the blame for her.*

Dan looked over to where Nick was cradling Ted's head.

"Can you get him to the hospital?"

"What?" Nick demanded without looking up.

"I have to go," Dan said.

"Go where?"

"To the Bruce Peninsula."

"What? Wait for me. I can help you, whatever it is."

Ted moaned. Nick turned to the unconscious young man. "Come on, Teddy! Come back."

"This can't wait," Dan said.

"All right, go. I'll take Ted to the hospital."

Dan headed for the door. A siren sounded in the distance.

Nick's voice called after him. "And don't turn your goddamn phone off this time!"

"I won't," Dan yelled back.

"Don't do anything dangerous. I'm not done with you yet."

That I can't promise, Dan thought.

TWENTY-NINE

The Human Code

A TEACHER HAD WITNESSED the death of a student. Years later she still dwelt on it, believing a second student had been involved and that the blame had fallen on the wrong shoulders. Somehow she had been alerted to the existence of that former student, now grown up. And the pieces tumbled together. For whatever reason, Theda McPhail had decided it was time to do something about it.

Dan was halfway up the parkway when his phone buzzed.

"We're at the hospital. We got him here in time," Nick said. He sounded both exhilarated and exhausted.

"How is he?"

"Hard to say. He's alive. I gather he's got a ways to go before anyone will say he's out of danger." He paused. "What's going on?"

"I'm on my way up to the Bruce."

"I know that. Why?"

It was his interrogator's voice.

"I think Janice is there with Ashley and Jeremy. And possibly Sarah. That call I took was from Theda McPhail's neighbour. She remembered the name of a student who was involved in the death of a fellow classmate. It's Kathy. That's Janice Bentham's real first name. I think whatever happened was what got blacked out of Janice's record because she was underage."

"And what does that have to do with the kidnapping?"

"I don't know yet. But it sure makes Janice look good for Theda's murder. And I think they might be trying to leave the country. When I was at Janice's yesterday, Sarah Nealon showed up. She said she'd been beaten up by Elroy James. That was when Janice tried to convince me that Eli and Elroy took the money."

"But now you don't believe it?"

"What if *Janice* arranged the kidnapping to pay for Jeremy's treatment? If she's capable of murder, she's capable of this. And she certainly felt entitled to her mother's money. Eli told me she let him take the blame for things she did. I think she's doing it again."

"Are you saying she killed him?"

Dan paused. "I don't think so. But clearly she didn't know he'd kill himself. She said, 'This isn't how it was supposed to be.' I didn't know what she meant then. Now I do. I'm going to try to stop anything else from happening."

"Call the local police. It's their jurisdiction."

"They'll never find them."

"Wait! We can have Sarah's ankle bracelet tracked if she's with them."

"She wasn't wearing it last night. She must have cut it off."

"Shit! You can't do this on your own! You said she has a gun."

"I'm already on my way. Just do me one favour. Find out what's blocked by the court order."

"Dan — wait for me! I'll come up there with you."

"Ted needs you. He has no one else, remember? You have to be there for him."

"Damn it!"

"What's that? I can't hear you. Hello?"

He ended the call.

He headed north, his AC blasting all the way as four lanes dwindled to two, one highway connecting to others all the way across the lonely continent, like the unfathomable skein of relationships in Jeremy Bentham's drawings, the invisible ties connecting one person to another.

Ahead the sky was a curious washed-out colour, like an over-exposed photograph, as though the heat had singed the air. Dan thought of Jeremy Bentham's ravaged eyes while he was having his meltdown. It had been like seeing through his skull to all the terrifying things that trapped him in there.

But if Janice had faked the whole kidnapping, how had she kept him hidden all that time? Then it hit him: the face without eyes Jeremy had drawn in his book. *Marietta's father is blind,* Janice had said. He'd felt all along that Marietta and Ramón were involved. Her parents must have looked after him until, with a little help from PI Dan Sharp, Janice convinced her mother to give her the ransom money. She'd used him very skilfully. And she very nearly got away with it.

Because if everything had gone according to plan, the money would have just conveniently disappeared. Because there were no kidnappers. And because no one was supposed to die. Not Eli Gestner or Theda McPhail. But somehow, somewhere, a retired schoolteacher had seen her former pupil and remembered something from the past. A terrible secret.

He recalled Janice's story about chasing away the bear. She would do anything to help her child, including pretending to kidnap him to raise money or killing a woman who might speak out and separate them.

He headed for the cottage first, but he already knew they wouldn't be there. Someone had notified the local OPP. A cruiser sat outside the door. *Nick*, Dan thought.

He turned around and drove off before he was seen. A quick check on Cemetery Road showed no trace of Janice and Ashley's vehicle. He was halfway to Horace's farm when he thought of the old trail to Gun Point.

He found their car parked at the foot of the trail. They would have to go up first to reach the campsite on the far side. If they were really intending to take a boat out of the country, that is. In his worst-case scenario, he saw three bodies lying at the bottom of a cliff. No — only two. She would never kill Jeremy. But Ashley and Sarah, yes, if she was desperate.

As he climbed, the trees became taller and denser, the shadows darker where the sky was blotted out. Despite the shade the heat was oppressive, the air sticky. He passed a good-looking man in hiking gear coming back down the trail, nylon rope coiled over his shoulder. *Rock climber*, Dan thought.

A blue blaze indicated a right-hand turnoff to some spectacular view. He hadn't time for views. Ferns edged the path alongside clusters of tiny pink orchids. Bluegreen lichen scarred and puckered the rocks. He trudged along, gripping the face of a boulder as he slid through a narrow cleft where a wall of limestone had fractured along intricate horizontal lines. It appeared man-made, as though only human hands could have achieved such precision.

He'd gone back to talk to Clarice Bentham briefly the day after he and Janice left with the boy. It had felt like unfinished business. He was thinking there was something he needed to tell her, when, in fact, it was something she needed to tell him. *Should have figured it out*, he realized, berating himself for his blindness as he kept up the climb.

Clarice had greeted him with an icy gaze. She'd opened the door herself. Maid's day off. He apologized for intruding. She invited him in, but didn't offer him a drink. Not a cordial visit, just a perfunctory wrapping up of business. He'd helped her daughter walk away with a cool million and her newfound grandchild, after all. Though all he'd ever promised to do was return Janice and Jeremy safely, as far as he was able.

"Sometimes I would look at that beautiful face and wonder if she was capable of feeling," Clarice told him. "I said to her once, 'Sometimes I think you're not even human.'"

They were Ashley's exact words to Janice when they were arguing over whether to take Sarah with them to keep her safe.

"You must have noticed her strange ways," Clarice said as they walked down the hallway. "How she was never comfortable with people. Like they might figure out she wasn't one of them. There was something different about her."

"How do you mean?"

"When someone displeased her, it was like she thought they deserved to die. You could see the anger seething, all that resentment beneath the skin. But she found the code and buried all that."

"The code?"

"The human code. It was a remarkable study of a human being. Whenever she wanted something she was all smiles, until she thought you couldn't see her. Then the mask came off." She shook her head. "What'd she do?"

"Do?"

"I always knew she'd do something. Step out of line. Break the mould and get found out."

No, he wanted to say. *I'm not here for that. I came here to apologize for how things ended between you and your daughter*. But he hadn't read between the lines. *Please fight for your grandson. Only you can help him now.*

"Despite everything," she said, "I still love my daughter beyond reason. Just as I'm sure she loves that boy. You may not understand it."

"Why is that?" he asked, thinking of Kedrick.

"Being a man, I mean."

"Ah. Because men don't feel as much, you mean."

"Not having given birth, how could you? It's only natural."

"I see." He let it pass.

"Did Janice tell you I introduced her to Ashley?"

Dan shook his head, another surprising piece of the puzzle.

"I thought you would have recognized her in the posters." She nodded to the gallery of framed photographs. He remembered how he'd felt there was something familiar about the face. He recognized her now.

"Ashley was my poster girl for a while. Of course she looks wildly different without make-up. I hired her as a stenographer, but I saw her potential and sent her off to a modelling studio. I thought she'd be grateful, but she wasn't."

"Is that why you stopped speaking to Janice?"

"One of several reasons."

"The other being Jeremy?"

"Yes. If I hadn't introduced them none of this would have happened."

He was nearing the top now. His thighs strained as he leapt over a log and nearly slipped. Somewhere near here was where Janice had fallen, stumbling through the woods till she came to Horace McLean's farm. Had it not been for that, it would have been relatively easy for her to get back to the car and drive within cellphone range to report a missing four-year-old. Setting the gears in motion.

Nevertheless, she'd fooled them all. Though Dan had suspected something was going on, he hadn't fully understood it. Not until now. *All of this is about revenge*, he should have said, should have realized. *It's not really about your son and it's only secondarily about the money. This is about you getting back at the people who hurt or disappointed you.*

"I grew up poor," Clarice told him as she saw him to the door. "I used to think money was the most beautiful thing until I learned the value of love. Too late, it seems. *La belleza cuesta*."

Beauty costs.

Almost without warning, he reached the promontory, stepping out between the trees to a sudden expanse of sky. His vision blurred. It was alarmingly hot. The view was like something in a dream: the blue bay with a single sail in the distance, the silence like a vacuum. Horace was right. From here it would be easy to board a boat and slip across to the States by night when no one was watching.

He saw the rope knotted to a stump and stepped closer to the edge. The orange nylon fell straight down, disappearing where it was swallowed up from view. He felt dizzy. His heart pounded from the climb. *Getting out of shape*, he told himself.

His cell beeped with an incoming message. Way out in the middle of nowhere, it had picked up a signal. Below, surrounded by forest, there had been no way for anyone to get through. Up here, everything was open and uninhibited.

He dialed his voice mail, waiting impatiently as it asked for his password then finally picked up somewhere, wherever messages were stored.

"For fuck's sake, Dan!" Nick breathed hard. He was angry. "I looked up the records. You've got it wrong! There were two kids. A girl named Kathy and a brother who died. His name was —"

He didn't hear the rest of Nick's message. The phone went flying from his hand, clattering across the rocks and over the edge of the cliff. There was an unexpected red mist as he fell to his knees. Only it wasn't mist. It was a fine spray of blood. His own.

He tried to turn. The exhilarated expression, hair flying in the wind.

"It's a rough climb."

The branch struck him across the side of his face. Too late, he raised his hands as he fell against the rock. A foot kicked out, once, twice. A third kick and he was over the edge. He had barely time to grab the rope. It burned through his hands. The pain was excruciating, though the fear was worse. His howl echoed over the valley. But if there was no one to hear, what good would it do?

Her face leered down at him. "Are you a bird? Can you fly?"

She stamped at his fingers, bringing her boots down again and again while his hands danced and flew from side to side to avoid being struck. She caught him on the next blow. His left hand went numb; he couldn't feel to grip.

He let himself slip farther down where her feet couldn't reach, but she made up for it by wielding the branch, smashing at his fingers and head. He wouldn't be able to hold out long. The best thing was to let himself slide all the way down. Then again, that might just be making it easier for her. All she had to do was untie the knot and let him fall. The unending flight. Only it would end, in a crunch of bone and sinew hitting rock and bleeding out.

He looked down and saw with a start that the rope extended just a dozen feet below. There was no escape. He clung to it, feeling strangely disembodied. Part of him watched himself clinging from above, while another part wondered how long he could manage to hold on.

She struck again with the branch, her face an enraged snarl. "I think you're trouble. I see through everyone."

"You think you can see through me?"

"I see it all. The insecurities, the hurts and aches. The old wounds. Family troubles. It always comes back to families, doesn't it?"

She was smooth and cool on the outside, but wired within. Something coiled and waiting to strike out.

"What about you?"

"I'm invisible. No one ever sees me for what I am."

Clarice Bentham was right. She was alien in some way, though she was good at hiding it. She'd learned how to behave like a human, but it didn't make her one. Her eyes searched him, as though he might reveal something she needed to know. A key. A code.

"Where are the others?"

She cocked her head.

"Not far." She seemed to be listening to something just beyond the edge of the cliff. "Can't you hear the screaming?"

"No."

Her look was pitying, as though he were missing out. "That doesn't mean it's not real. It's just on another level of existence."

The sun was behind her. It blinded him when he tried to look up.

"What are they screaming about?"

"They're saying someone is going to die."

She was right. There was a crackling in the air. He heard it in the cries of the gulls: *Death! Death!* She stood there looking outward as though seeing something that wasn't there.

He recalled Horace's words: *You've got the lions on your side.*

"Theda McPhail was your teacher," he gasped out. "She kept coming around the house because she wanted to talk to you."

"Yes," she sneered. "She was the same Mrs. McPhail I remembered from school. 'How are things at home? How are your studies going? If you ever need to talk, just let me know.' She was tedious."

"And so you killed her too."

"Stupid. She invited me in. I strangled her. I had to. She figured it out. I'm Kathy."

"She knew you killed your brother."

"You're smarter than I thought. That's too bad."

"How will you explain killing me?"

"It was an accident. You tried to rescue me. You fell." She turned and looked off as though seeing something in the distance.

"It's happening," she said.

When he looked up again, she had moved off. For a second, he thought she was going to leave him there. Not so.

When she returned, she held a good-size rock in her hands, hefting it over him. He steeled his grip, determined to hang on. Everything blurred in the heat waves sizzling around them, the monotonous whine of cicadas buzzing through his brain.

As she raised her arms a voice rang out. Biblical, retributive. An Old Testament voice. Both prophet and warrior.

"Put it down, Leah," Dan heard. "Leah — put it down!"

Then a crack followed by a scream as Horace shot the woman Dan knew as Ashley Lake.

†

They'd been standing in the hallway. Dan was listening to Clarice speak, waiting for the right moment to leave.

"She was like a butterfly given new wings. I knew she'd come from a broken family, a disaster of a family. Suddenly she was adored. She was wanted by everyone. For five years she was our poster girl. I gave her every opportunity. But she wasn't grateful. 'You owe me,' she said when I told her we had to find someone new. 'I am the reason your products sell.' As if a face could make a success of anything without hard work and effort behind it."

Clarice turned away from the poster Dan had only just recognized as Ashley Lake. She was luminescent. A creature of light, insubstantial. Horace's angel.

"Five years is a long time for a model. I kept saying it wasn't the end for her. She'd made a bit of money and could do whatever she wanted with the rest of her life. But she hated me for letting her go. After that I never had a moment's peace with Janice. Ashley took every opportunity she could to cause trouble between us. We were no longer mother and daughter, but bitter enemies. I knew Ashley was only after the money, so I kept it from Janice."

"She manipulated Janice to get back at you."

"Manipulated doesn't cover it. She was a monster. She destroyed relationships. First with me, then with Dennis. When I let her go from Clarice Magna, she went straight after Janice. Pretending to care. Helping look after Jeremy while driving us apart. Ashley doesn't even like children. I doubt she ever loved anyone but herself for one moment. It was all for the money. I could see that, but Janice couldn't."

"She didn't succeed."

"But she will. One day it will all go to Janice and Ashley will be there waiting, pretending to be a part of that family."

Dan looked now to where Ashley lay stretched out on the rock. No longer waiting.

She gazed up at him. "You," she said accusingly.

Dan heard the bitterness in her voice. All the colour had drained from her face. Horace was pressing down on her leg, stanching the wound for all he was worth.

"Everything for that damn child," she said, with a strange air of disappointment. "I didn't sign up for that."

Dan clutched his bloodied hands to his sides, trying to quell the pain. "No, I guess you didn't."

He turned to look over the bay and was momentarily blinded by the light. When his eyes adjusted, he could see the town in the distance. Neither he nor Horace would make it down in time.

"Did I fail her?" Clarice had asked as they stood at the door, both of them wishing the meeting was over, neither of them quite willing to end it. "Janice, I mean."

"Do you think you failed her?" Dan had replied.

"People will see it that way. Because it's always the mother's fault, isn't it? Janice always said I knew. I look back and I think, no, I didn't know. Maybe I saw the signs, but I don't think so. Fathers destroy and mothers get the blame. That's just how it goes. I think of Ashley's mother sometimes and I wonder what she was really like. Maybe not as bad as they say."

THIRTY

Exit Wounds

Despite his pain, Dan was surprised by how much he enjoyed the ball game. Even more so having Nick there to explain the intricacies of the plays.

"Why doesn't the guy on first run to second?" Dan asked after a batter hit a pop fly.

"He's waiting to see if the ball is caught."

The ball skyrocketed briefly then fell neatly into the outfielder's waiting glove. The play ceased.

"But what if the guy had fumbled it? The runner could have been halfway to second base."

Nick shrugged. "Too risky. That's just the way it is."

Five minutes later everything came to a halt again after a runner stole second base. The umpire declared him out, but the runner stayed in position.

"If he's out, why doesn't he leave the base?"

Nick laughed. "Because he doesn't agree with the decision. He's waiting for a review of the play."

They watched as the action was replayed in slow motion overhead on giant screens. The stadium erupted as the umpire's call was overruled and the runner remained on base.

"I can't keep track of what's going on. There are too many rules," Dan grumbled. "Just like this damn city we live in."

"You could always move," Nick said.

"Never. This is my home."

Dan turned back to the playing field. *Other people's rules*, he reminded himself. But he knew he shouldn't be surprised by how easily Nick took to rules. After all, he was a cop.

The game ended with a Jays' win. Home team victory. Dan cringed when Nick grabbed his arm in his excitement.

"Sorry!" Nick's face was creased with concern. "I forgot. Are you okay?"

"I'm okay. Just a bit — bruised."

"Did you enjoy the game at least?"

"Surprisingly, yes. Thanks for suggesting it."

"How is it you grew up without learning to play baseball?"

"I'm a northern boy," Dan said. "We played lacrosse and basketball. Good Canadian games. Why don't these guys play basketball instead?"

Nick laughed. "Not tall enough, for one thing. And for another, most of them aren't Canadian. They probably wouldn't even know basketball was invented by a Canadian."

"What? It should be compulsory training for professional athletes."

The night was fine. The edge had been taken off the hyper-inflated temperatures, the humidity escaping like a slowly decompressing balloon as they walked along.

They stopped on the Queen Street Viaduct and stood gazing down at the water, pink and somnolent in the afterglow of evening. Overhead, sketched in iron across the bridge, read the inscription *This river I step in is not the river I stand in.*

Nick looked over at Dan. "So you found them in the same cave?"

"Yep, the one where I found the rosary. It was Eli who initially took the boy and brought him to Ramón for Marietta to deliver to her parents. I guess Ashley thought no one would think of looking there this time around."

"Had she intended to kill them?"

They'd been drugged. He'd had to help them crawl to the surface on their hands and knees — Janice, Sarah, and Jeremy.

"I don't know. Maybe she miscalculated the dose or maybe she only wanted to drug them till she got away. She had the money in a knapsack. She was going to ditch them and head across the water to the U.S. From there she could have gone anywhere."

"How did she do it?"

"The night we stayed at the cottage, Janice and Ashley switched most of the bills for newspaper. I thought the box felt different in the morning, but I didn't have a chance to check. Elroy's men picked it up in the boat, but they were under strict orders not to open it. They had no idea what was inside. Probably thought it was dope."

"So they double-crossed Elroy?"

"Yes. As far as Janice was concerned, it was her money. She wasn't about to give it to away again. So they told Eli —"

"That Elroy kept all the money. He probably thought Elroy was lying about not getting his share. Did Eli kill himself?"

"That's my guess. Although he planned the kidnapping with Janice and Ashley, he didn't know about the switch. Afterward, he would have thought that there was nothing for Jeremy's treatment."

"Didn't Janice realize it was stupid to double-cross a biker?"

"Was it any stupider for her to kidnap her own child?"

Nick shrugged and looked off.

"So this teacher, Theda McPhail — Janice assumed she was calling her Kathy when she came to her home, but it was actually Ashley standing behind her. McPhail knew who she was."

"Yes. As you somewhat belatedly discovered —"

"'Belatedly'? At least I figured it out. The report said 'twins.' We thought they were both girls."

"I'm not criticizing. Just stating a fact. Theda McPhail knew her as Kathy, but she took her brother's name after he died. She'd moved away by then, so maybe she thought it was safe to become Ashley. That was the boy-girl name her neighbour couldn't remember at the time."

"And Sarah Nealon was a witness?"

"Apparently," Dan said. "They were friends together at school. But whatever she saw she kept to herself. It was only later, with her addiction, that she became obsessed with the boy's death. That's probably why Ashley kept in touch with her. To keep tabs on what she remembered."

"And Sarah's bruises the night she showed up at the house?"

"She gave them to herself. She figured out somehow the women were leaving and wanted an excuse for them to take her with them. That worked in nicely with Ashley's plans."

"So Ashley — was she nuts?"

Dan shrugged. "You tell me. It's pretty hard to categorize who's nuts and who's just sociopathic and desperate these days."

Nick laid a hand on Dan's shoulder as they stood staring out over the water. Reassuring, not possessive.

"One thing's for sure," Dan said. "Horace didn't intend to kill her. He tried as hard as he could to save her, but the bullet severed an artery and went right through her leg. If it had stayed inside, she might have survived till they got her off the mountain."

"Luck of the draw."

"He's pretty cut up about it. He doesn't believe in killing. Said it was Old Testament judgment that took her off. He's strictly a New Testament kind of guy. Forgiveness and sacrifice and all that."

"Well, he saved you at least. Tell him I'm grateful for that."

They crossed to the far side of the bridge. Dan's neighbourhood. Leslieville had changed considerably over the past few years, gentrification setting in, rents going up. Nothing ever stayed the same. *This river I step in …*

"And the older Filipinos were looking after the boy! Who would have thought?"

"They fooled me. I thought they were religious fanatics from the way they spoke about Janice and Ashley. They had planned it well enough in advance that Janice could fire Marietta and make it look as though there was no connection between them. Of course, they made sure their alibi was well in place. Apart from the rosary, that is. And when the time came, Ramón got himself fired to be free to participate in the plans. He was the go-between with the parents. She couldn't risk it. If it had been me, I would just have taken my vacation then."

"If it had been *you* —!"

"Yeah, I guess you're right. It would have looked just as suspicious. I would have been much sneakier." Dan winked. "But I was right about one thing — Marietta loved that boy enough to lie for him."

"The parents never knew they were hiding a kidnapped child?"

"The father's blind. The mother had her hands full looking after him and the boy. They don't speak English, so they wouldn't have been watching the daily news."

"And the ex-husband had nothing to do with it?"

"That's the really devious part," Dan said. "I think Dennis Braithwaite was set up to look like the bad guy. Janice texted him to ask about the cottage, realizing he'd go up there to look for her. Boom — no alibi." Dan looked sidelong at Nick. "Should I be telling you this? I mean, as an officer of the law and all that?"

Nick thumped his shoulder. "*And all that?* You make it sound like some sort of inconvenient afterthought."

"I'm talking about the divide between us."

"What divide is that?"

"The one Donny thinks is insurmountable. The one that says I might turn a blind eye to someone who breaks a law I don't agree with and you'd have to come down on my head for it."

Nick smirked. "Who says I wouldn't do the same?"

"Are you saying you would?"

"I'm not all status quo. You should know that by now. Some days there's nothing more I want than to contribute to the crisis in human identity, to push it over the edge so we have to start again. Maybe we'd get it right next time."

Dan laughed. "A radical in conservative's clothing."

"Something like that."

They turned down Dan's street. Dan looked up at the lofty boughs arching overhead like a cathedral's dome.

"We're nearly home," he said.

"Home? We? Are you sure?"

"Definitely. We — are — home."

"I like the sound of that."

"Then get used to it. Do you think you can do that?"

"If I have to. I'm a cop, remember? I do what I'm told. You're the one who has trouble taking orders."

Dan opened the door and reached for the light switch.

"No, leave it," Nick said.

He took Dan's hand and led him down the hall. Dan followed awkwardly, trying not to bump into walls. Ralph got up from his cushion and scrambled after them. Dan shut him out when they reached the bedroom.

"Sorry, Ralphie," he said. "It's big-boy time."

"I like the sound of that too," Nick said, breathing into Dan's neck. "You're saying all the right things. Keep talking."

He reached out, lightly running his fingers over the bruises on Dan's face, before bringing his battered hands to his lips, kissing them.

"Don't tell me it turns you on," Dan said. "That's like necrophilia."

"You're not dead."

"Not today. But yesterday I was."

Nick rubbed his chin stubble against the back of Dan's hand. Dan clenched his teeth.

"No S&M, please."

"Why would I hurt you? I already know how to make you do everything I want."

In the mirror, Dan saw two people — two men — trying to bridge the gap between them. *How long can this go on?* he wondered as Nick circled him with his arms. He felt removed, one part of him enjoying the sensation of being held and the other watching from a distance. For a moment he was back on the cliff at Gun Point, seeing rather than feeling it all. *Why the divide?* Why were emotions so much easier for some people? Nick cared for him. He had integrity and a generosity of spirit. In fact, Dan would never want to be with anyone who didn't. So why was everything so much harder when he looked in the mirror? *I want certainty*, he told himself. *But if I always hold back, how much certainty can there be?*

Maybe that was why closeted gay men married women while knowing they weren't attracted to them. Because it was safe. When Dan had asked him, Nick said, "It's what men did in the world I grew up in. I don't excuse it. I just didn't understand that I could choose." More rules.

But Dan was a loner and a rebel. When he looked over a fence he saw choices. He'd known instinctively he was in charge of making those choices, one of which was to marry or not. Another had been to leave home at the age of seventeen, before finishing high school, knowing he could no longer live in his father's world. Against all odds, he'd landed on his feet.

He turned from the mirror.

Nick knelt and unbuckled his belt, pulling his khaki shorts down. He leaned in and inhaled. "I love your smell," he said. "This is the smell of a man."

Nick buried his face there, rubbing him with his nose and chin before taking him in his mouth. Dan gasped.

"What do you want me to do?" he whispered, cradling Nick's head and running his fingertips through his hair.

Nick lifted his feet for him one at a time, freeing them from the tangle of cloth, and peeled his socks off.

"I want you to wake up," he said. "I want you to see who you are."

Before she died, Theda McPhail wrote a letter to the police. It was discovered later, with some bills on her kitchen table. Had it been opened earlier, Dan thought, things might have turned out differently.

To Whom It May Concern:

My name is Theda McPhail. In 1996, I was a teacher at Sir John A. Macdonald Elementary School in Toronto. Ashley Lake, a boy in one of my classes, died in a tragic playground incident. Although the death was blamed on his mother, I have always believed Ashley was killed by his twin sister, Kathy.

I was new to the school then. For months I watched as Kathy lashed out at her brother. I saw hatred in her eyes every time he overshadowed her accomplishments. I knew there was trouble at home. The mother, Miriam Lake, was a single parent struggling with psychological issues. It was obvious to me that the boy was wanted, but the girl was not.

I surmised this after asking Kathy about her home life, which she was only too willing to reveal. All those childish feelings of jealousy and anger were bottled up inside her until they reached a boiling point. One day she went too far.

When I try to piece together what happened that day, I recall that Ashley and Kathy were playing on the monkey bars after school. Mrs. Lake had just arrived and was trying to talk them both down. Ashley was taunting his sister while avoiding his mother's attempts to grab his legs. I was inside my classroom, looking out the window and wondering whether to have a word with the mother about Kathy, when Ashley slipped and got his head wedged between the bars.

I heard him scream. To my horror, I saw Kathy kick at him. I ran outside to help before anyone got seriously hurt. When I got there, however, Ashley was hanging limply from the bars. His sister was nowhere to be seen.

Together, Mrs. Lake and I got the boy down. He was dead. The coroner later determined that Ashley's neck was broken in two places. I attended the inquest and told what I had seen. Mrs. Lake, however, claimed that Kathy had run off and that Ashley died when she, Mrs. Lake, struck him in a fit of anger for disobeying her. Because of her psychological issues, she was deemed not criminally responsible and the death ruled an accident.

Dan remembered Janice telling him about the death of Ashley's twin. *It was devastating for Ash*, she'd said. Only Janice had believed it was a twin sister. And Ashley was only too happy to keep her in the dark, lest someone question her story and, ultimately, her borrowed name.

Ashley and I have these dark things in common, she had said. *Things we never discuss*. Like the truth about the death of a twin or the blacked-out portion of a police report where it stated Janice had been molested by a boy at school. What it didn't say was that she had beaten him to a pulp. Or that her friend Eli had covered for her, claiming he had done it to protect her, and got himself expelled in the process. And the boy, ashamed at having been beaten by a girl, didn't correct him. But, unlike Ashley, Janice had never killed anyone.

It's hard to say how you know these things, Theda's letter concluded, *but teachers develop a sense early on about which kids will grow up to be okay and which ones are destined for a life of social or even criminal abnormality. When Kathy returned to school the following week, I watched her carefully. During class, an announcement was made over the PA system to say that her brother had died. I looked for signs of grief, or something to say that she was sorry. But instead, what I saw was a look of triumph. I knew that day, looking in the face of that twelve-year-old girl, that she had, in fact, killed her brother. And I knew she hated me for knowing it.*

Kathy did not stay much longer at the school. Arrangements were made for her to live with family, and so I thought I had seen the last of her. It was a surprise then, when I saw her recently at a local mall. Some instinct made me follow her. When she arrived at what I took to be her home, I saw another woman with a small child. I was worried for the boy, but I hesitated to say anything. Still, I am fearful for him, which is why I am writing to you now in the hope that you can advise me on what to do.

Yours truly,

Theda McPhail

†

Nick stood before him. He lifted Dan's T-shirt over his head then turned and draped it across the eyes of a wooden rocking horse, one of the few mementos of Dan's childhood.

"I can't have any witnesses to what I'm about to do to you," he said, turning him around gently.

His beard scraped the back of Dan's neck. Arms outstretched and fingers entwined, they were like high flyers, twinned. Trapeze artists. Emotional acrobats.

"Is it your body or is it your mind?"

"Pardon?"

"Which is it? Which one is holding you back?"

"I don't know. Both."

"Then let go of both."

Dan snorted. "Is this some sort of New Age exercise?"

"No." Nick pushed him face-forward onto the bed. "It's me trying to turn you on to the point where you will let me in without fear."

"As if that will ever happen," Dan mumbled into the mattress.

He heard a cap snapped open, felt a quick glisten of oil squirted along his back. Nick's hands ran slowly up and down his spine then reached under to pull him onto his hands and knees.

"Do you remember all your lovers?" Nick asked.

"All of them?" They weren't coming to mind as Nick took over his body. "Some. A few. Why?"

"I want you to forget them. There's just us now."

Dan turned his head. In the mirror, he looked like a dog being mounted.

When Sandy disappeared that final day at the cottage, Dan had run up and down the shore looking for him while his parents packed, yelling as loud as he could to get his pet's attention. But Sandy never came back. As they drove away, a piece of Dan's heart had stayed behind on those lost shores. *Let us find him on the road going out*, Dan pleaded silently. But they didn't. Then his mother said the thing about the movie where the dogs and cat found their way home after months in the wilderness. *Let him find his way back*, Dan had said to himself, *and I will be good forever.*

He felt Nick's fingers pressing inside him one at a time. The feeling was curious, but not objectionable.

When his mother died, Dan knew it was because he hadn't been good. He hadn't done all he could to save her. *Let her come back and I will be good forever*, he'd thought. *For real this time. I promise.*

Nick rolled him onto his back and hoisted his legs in the air.

"Still flexible, that's good." He leaned forward, never taking his eyes off Dan's face.

"I don't … know how to do this."

"It's easy," Nick said. "Just let me in."

Dan gasped. Nick reached out and touched his face.

"Did I hurt you?"

"No." Dan shook his head. "No. Just — keep going."

He reached up and grasped Nick around the neck. He felt like a boy again, no longer in control. He wanted to say, *I give in, I give up. I give myself over to you.* But the words wouldn't come.

"*Daniel, Daniel, Daniel*," Nick crooned, repeating his name over and over.

It was the most erotic thing he'd ever heard. The plaintiveness, the need, the longing. As though this moment might not happen again and they both had to believe in it and remember it in case it never returned.

Dan cried out.

"Take a breath," Nick commanded. "It's called trust. If you want me here, you have to get used to it."

"I'm trying," Dan said.

Dan thought how people believed that things could change them: getting tattoos, having children, marrying. Only to find that life went on just as it had before. *Everywhere I go, there I am*. Take a job, lose a job; take a lover, lose a lover. Whatever came next was anybody's guess. Then one day your number was up and all change ceased. No more struggling. Maybe you moved to a farm like Horace McLean. Or maybe you died, like Dan's father. No more ups and downs on the elevator of life.

Done. Gone. Game over. Thanks for coming out.

Was there ever any better time than now?

Dan thought he had convinced himself he could do without love. It was a risk. Like a bullet to the heart, leaving exit wounds. Yet it had happened in the unlikeliest time and fashion. With a cop, of all people. Another recovering alcoholic. What other curve balls did life have to throw at him? *There's only one way to find out*, he thought, as Nick surged into him, filling empty space. Stealing home.

It struck him then how he still thought of that damn dog, the memories coming so unexpectedly that even now they brought tears to his eyes.

THIRTY-ONE

The Key

Café Frederic was particularly festive that evening. It had taken some doing, but Dan finally convinced Donny and Prabin to join him and Nick for supper.

"Do it for me," he told Donny over the phone. "Because I nearly died."

"Way to guilt-trip a guy," Donny grumbled. "But okay. We will show."

Even so, Dan could see that his friend was shocked when he saw the bandages.

"I take it this is not a fashion statement," Donny said. "Because if it is, I'm giving failing grades across the board."

"Just practising for Halloween."

"Okay. But the dried blood is a bit over the top."

Once they were seated, Dan looked at his friends seated around the table.

"I want everyone to know that it's official. I gave Nick my house key yesterday," he said.

"What about the other key?" Prabin asked.

"To my ... chastity belt?"

"No — to your heart." Prabin winked.

"He already has that," Dan said.

Nick beamed. And Donny actually laughed.

They all looked up as Ted arrived bearing an armload of menus. His hair had been cut short with a severe part on the left and his cheeks were freshly shaved. He looked none the worse for his recent ordeal. He seemed not to notice that Donny and Prabin were staring at him openly as he placed a basket of bread on the table. Then he stood back and put a hand on Nick's shoulder.

"Welcome to Café Frederic, gentlemen. We've got a few tasty specials to tempt you with."

He recited the dishes then headed back to the kitchen. Donny exchanged glances with Dan.

"Who's the sexy boy all hotted up for Nick?"

"That's Ted," Dan said. "Our favourite waiter. Straight, by the way. And not looking for polyamorous connections at present."

Prabin mugged a frown. "Tragic!"

Drinks arrived. Dan's recovery was toasted. Donny busied himself with buttering a piece of rye bread, recounting work affairs of officious managers and bumbling staff.

"But I will survive," he declared, brandishing his knife.

He was polite, Dan noticed, but so far he had barely spoken to Nick.

A trumpet glissando cascaded in the background. Nick cocked his head.

"Is that Clifford Brown?" he asked of no one in particular.

Donny stared. “You know Clifford Brown?”

“Sure. I’m a fan.”

Donny looked over at Dan. “Did you know about this?”

Dan shook his head. “No. And although you’ll think I’m crass, I don’t think I recall who Clifford Brown is.”

His friend gave a shiver of distaste.

“After all the teaching I’ve done, you don’t know Clifford Brown? One of the most influential jazz trumpeters of all time? I feel like a failure.” He turned to Nick. “If you’re a true-blue fan, you’ll know how he died.”

“Car crash,” Nick said without blinking. “Twenty-five years old.”

Donny’s lips formed a silent *Whoa!* “Next you’ll be telling me you can tell whether a cat is black or white by the sound of his horn.”

“I always thought I could, though I’ve never tried to prove it.”

“The next time the two of you are over at our place I will give you the test.”

“Which you failed once, I seem to recall,” Dan told Donny.

Donny held up a warning finger. “I did not fail. You cheated!”

Ted returned with a platter piled with seafood — lobster tails, scallops, shrimp. He set it on the table and stood back. “I’d just like to say this meal is on me.”

There was a burst of protest, but Ted nodded. “I’m serious.” He stood between Nick and Dan, this time with one hand on each of their shoulders. “These guys saved my life. And I am very, very grateful.”

He turned and walked back to the kitchen. Donny and Prabin looked around in stupefaction.

"Is this for real?"

Dan nodded. "Overdose. We found him in his apartment. But it was mostly Nick's doing. He broke the door down and got him to the hospital. I was already on my way to the Bruce Peninsula."

Prabin nodded sagely. "Where you nearly got thrown off a cliff?"

"Yes." He shrugged. "I keep all the fun stuff to myself."

The platter made its way around the table. Donny bit into a scallop.

"Such tender little morsels," he said, looking over at Dan. "Did you just blush?"

More food arrived. Music swelled as the restaurant filled up around them. Donny stood, pushing his plate to one side.

"I am going for one of my famous cigarette breaks." He put a hand on Nick's shoulder as he moved from the table. "Excuse me — do not wait for me when the next course arrives."

Dan watched him exit then turned to Nick. "Looks like you've made a new friend."

Prabin grinned. "Yeah — Donny's particular about his jazz. But I think the superhero stuff definitely pushed it over the edge." He nodded to Dan. "So you solved the kidnapping?"

"If you can call it that. It wasn't a real kidnapping. It was faked by the kid's mothers. Both of them. One of them attacked me on the Bruce Peninsula."

"Rough stuff," Prabin said.

"It's not like you haven't seen that side of things," Dan reminded him.

"Me? I'm just a mild-mannered stockbroker."

"Stay that way. It's safer." He turned to Nick. "What's the word from Lydia?"

"Janice Bentham might get off fairly easy, all things considered. There'll be a plea bargain. I think the judge will be lenient because of her special-needs son and her history of sexual abuse. Also, the money was actually hers when you think about it. She just took a very roundabout way of asking for it. Her mother showed up at the hearing."

"Did that help or hurt?"

"It helped. She said she gave it to her daughter willingly. Sarah Nealon has agreed to enrol in a rehab program." He shrugged. "With the drugs these days, though, who knows if she stands a chance?"

"Worth a try," Dan said. "And Marietta and Ramón?"

Nick made a zipping motion with his fingers over his lips. "I didn't say a word. Janice Bentham says it was all her and Ashley's doing."

The evening progressed. Music played on, the candles burned down. Dan glanced up at his friends then over at the other customers enjoying themselves. It was … *pleasant*. Was this life, this thing he and Nick were cobbling together? Or was it just a rehearsal? It didn't feel like a rehearsal. It felt like the real thing at last. As if it had come to him and he had damn well better grab it before it disappeared. Who knew how long any of it might last? Would he one day look back when it was gone and think that that had been it? And that it had passed him by? He hoped not.

He turned back to his meal.

When he looked around again, the restaurant was empty except for staff. They had outlasted everyone else.

"Sorry for keeping you so late," Dan said, as Ted returned to check on them.

"Not at all, guys. You're welcome to stay as long as you want."

"That could be all night." Dan took Nick's hand, with a look at Donny and Prabin. "But I know when it's time to say goodbye."

ACKNOWLEDGEMENTS

THANKS TO THE GANG AT DUNDURN — Kirk, Beth, Margaret, Carrie, Synora, Karen, Carmen, Kathryn, Laura, Jesse, Jenny, Jaclyn, Kyle, and Michelle — and everyone else for helping me bring Dan Sharp to life over the course of seven books. It's been great working with all of you. In particular, I want to thank editors Michael Carroll, Allister Thompson, Shannon Whibbs, Allison Hirst, and Jess Shulman for their hands-on contributions. Thanks also to David Tronetti for letting me read the books aloud to him, to Geordie Johnson for his keen insight and for taking me to a Blue Jays Pride game, and to Gail Price for sharing her insights on childhood psychopathy, as well as her friendship. I would also like to acknowledge my debt to Allen Barnett (1955–1991) and his groundbreaking *The Body and Its Dangers*. Throughout this series I have tried to maintain his level of unsparing honesty when writing about sex and sexuality. As well, his personal connection to poet-suicide Thomas James, whom I learned of through the same book, has stayed with me. I cherish these ephemeral through lines that give us something back of all that has been lost. A shout-out goes to Bob Dylan, Jean Sibelius, Kate Bush, and Arvo Pärt for the musical accompaniment to this volume. If you listen, you will hear them between the lines. And although I borrowed the surname of my childhood friend John Sharp for my hero, no connection is intended between my Sharps and the Sharp family as I knew them growing up in Sudbury, other than as a fond reflection on our shared past. And, finally, thanks always to you for reading.